Thomas Edward Kebbel

Life of Lord Beaconsfield

Thomas Edward Kebbel

Life of Lord Beaconsfield

ISBN/EAN: 9783337415679

Printed in Europe, USA, Canada, Australia, Japan

Cover: Foto ©Raphael Reischuk / pixelio.de

More available books at **www.hansebooks.com**

OF

LORD BEACONSFIELD.

BY
T. E. KEBBEL.

PHILADELPHIA:
J. B. LIPPINCOTT COMPANY.
1888.

PREFACE TO THE SERIES.

THE intention of the Statesmen Series is, as its title implies, to comprise a collection of brief biographical studies of the great men who have influenced the political history of the world. Its scope is, therefore, extremely catholic, embracing the ancients and the moderns, continental as well as English statesmen, and including not only those who have shaped our foreign policy and domestic institutions, but also the creators of our Indian and Colonial Empires. And the list of subjects will not be confined to those who have been statesmen in the narrower sense of the term, that is, to ministers of State and members of legislative assemblies. A statesman, according to Dr. Johnson, is "one who is versed in political affairs," and statesmanship is exercised not only by Czars and Popes who act as their own Prime Ministers, but also by constitutional sovereigns who, though in theory they reign but do not govern, have frequently, as Sir Theodore Martin's *Life of the Prince Consort* shows, brought into action a very appreciable amount of personal authority. Even to modern republics, Thucydides' description of the Athenian constitution in the time of Pericles is invariably applicable — they are ostensibly democracies, but are, as a matter of fact, ruled by their first man. Presidents, therefore, and sovereigns—*rois fainéants* always excepted—will find places in the Statesmen Series.

Though the Series will be comprehensive, it does not pretend to be exhaustive. Completeness of treatment is no doubt desirable in books of reference, the primary object of which is to supply information on points that general reading fails to illuminate, but would be unattainable in a collection of volumes which, though deriving a certain amount of strength from unity, must ultimately stand or fall by the merits of each individual work. Nor is the arrangement in which the volumes are to appear affected at all by any considerations of chronology. Their publication in historical order would, perhaps, have some advantages, but gaps would inevitably occur in the ranks, and the groups would fail to form a picture. The provinces of history and biography are, after all, widely different, and the old view of history which regarded it as a string of lives of great men has long since been consigned to the limbo of rejected fallacies.

Political biography has, however, a distinct value and interest of its own ; for if the statesman is the child of his epoch, none the less is his epoch moulded by the statesman ; nor can the relative importance of great social movements be properly understood without an adequate knowledge of the human forces by which they are impelled or controlled. It is the aim of the Statesmen Series to supply that knowledge, in a compact form, and without prejudice to the larger works which, for those who have leisure to consult them, must always contain the most authoritative, because the most detailed, accounts of great political careers. And of incident and interest the lives of great statesmen, as a rule, possess a far greater measure than those of literary men, though less, perhaps, than those of men of action. For if much of a statesman's time is passed in the solitude of the study, much also is passed in the passionate precincts of the Senate and in the hardly less dramatic debates round the council-table.

Within the limits of a well-defined subject,

the selection, then, will be purely arbitrary; and what the Series will lose in continuity of interest it will perhaps be thought to gain in variety. It so happens that the volumes in preparation, as well as that now published, deal with the present century, and may, therefore, be considered to derive a certain amount of additional interest from that quality which it is the fashion to call actuality. They are as follow: *The Prince Consort,* by Miss Charlotte Yonge; *O'Connell,* by J. A. Hamilton; *Prince Gortschakoff,* by Charles Marvin; *Gambetta,* by F. T. Marzials; *Earl Russell,* by Edward Walford; *Lord Palmerston,* by the Editor. Other volumes have been arranged.

L. C. S.

PREFATORY NOTE.

"I DISAPPROVE of contemporary biography," Lord Beaconsfield once said to the present writer, "and I dislike being the subject of it." We may reasonably conclude, therefore, that none of the biographies which appeared during his lifetime owe much to his own communications. They are all in fact founded on materials accessible to the whole world; nor, down to the present time, has his death set free any information not previously known to all who had studied his career, beyond that contained in the highly interesting *Correspondence with his Sister* brought out by Mr. Ralph Disraeli. The time will come when a complete and particular account of the life and times of Lord Beaconsfield will be one of the most interesting as well as one of the most valuable works which can stand upon a statesman's shelves. Till then we must content ourselves with such provisional and preliminary biographies as, in the case of almost all our great men, precede the one final and authentic narrative which disposes of the subject and clears the field of all competitors. Of intermediate works of this description there are, in the case of Lord

Beaconsfield, only three with which I am acquainted, pretending to the character of regular biographies, one by Mr. Thomas Macknight, published in 1854, one by Mr. T. P. O'Connor, published in 1878, and one, by much the best, by Mr. A. C. Ewald, published in 1883. Beside these, a very clever and appreciative study of Mr. Disraeli, by Mr. George Henry Francis, was republished in 1852 from *Fraser's Magazine*, while the public life of Lord Beaconsfield has been brought out more recently by Mr. Hitchman. A German study of Lord Beaconsfield by G. Brandes, of which a translation was published by Mr. Bentley in 1880, is, I believe, worth reading, and I am sorry that my attention was not called to it till it was too late to consult it for the purpose of the present volume. Of course, of the various pamphlets, memoirs, and quasi-biographical notices of Lord Beaconsfield which have appeared during the last forty years the name is legion, and to give anything like a complete list of them on the present occasion would be impossible. The obituary notices of him which appeared in the principal daily papers contain much interesting matter, and the *Standard* notice was republished by Messrs. Macmillan in a small octavo volume. From the numerous volumes of political memoirs, diaries, and correspondence, of which the last few years have been so fertile, abundant particulars relating to both the public and private life of Lord Beaconsfield are to be collected, especially from the *Greville Journals*, the *Memoirs of an Ex-Minister*, by Lord Malmesbury, *St. Petersburg and London*, by Count Vitzthum, the *Croker Papers*, and the Lives of Lord Palmerston, Lord Melbourne,

Lord Lyndhurst, Bishop Wilberforce, and Mr. Herries, which have all appeared within the last twenty years.

The first complete edition of Lord Beaconsfield's works down to that date, was published in 1853. Another, in ten volumes, appeared in 1857 ; and a second impression of it in 1870. The Hughenden edition of his tales and novels was published in 1881. A very useful and well-executed edition of the *Letters of Runnymede*, the *Vindic ition of the British Constitution*, and the *Spirit of Whiggism*, has also been published by Mr. Hitchman. And two volumes of speeches, edited by myself, with explanatory prefaces attached, were issued by Messrs. Longmans in 1881.

T. E. K.

CONTENTS.

LIFE OF
LORD BEACONSFIELD.

CHAPTER I.

PRÆ-PARLIAMENTARY PERIOD.

1804–1837.

Birth and boyhood—First appearance in print—*Vivian Grey*—Travels on the Continent—Letters to Sarah Disraeli—Entrance into Society—Literary and political activity—Attempts to get into Parliament—Popular Toryism—The *Crisis Examined*—Quarrel with O'Connell—Disraeli's vindication of his public conduct—Relations with Hume—Disraeli and Lyndhurst—Elected for Maidstone

BENJAMIN DISRAELI was born in London on the 21st of December, either in the year 1804 or 1803, the son of Isaac Disraeli, author of the *Curiosities of Literature*, and Maria Basevi, sister of the well-known architect; but whether he first saw the light in Bloomsbury Square, in the Adelphi, or in King's Road, Gray's Inn, is still uncertain. It is proved by the Parish Rate Book that at the date of his eldest son's birth Isaac Disraeli was tenant of a house in the last-mentioned street. But against this is to be set the direct statement made by

1

Lord Beaconsfield himself to Lord Barrington, that he was born "in a set of chambers in the Adelphi"; and likewise the testimony of Mr. Jones, son of the medical man who attended Mrs. Disraeli at the time. In favour of Bloomsbury Square, besides the local tradition, we have merely the statement that when Lord Beaconsfield was asked if he was born there, he said that he had been told so. The best extant account of his own family is contained in his Preface to an edition of the *Curiosities* published in 1849, from which we learn that his ancestors, who belonged to the Sephardim, or purest branch of the Jewish race, which never left the shores of the Mediterranean, were driven out of Spain by the Inquisition, and settled in Venice at the end of the fifteenth century. His grandfather came to England in 1748, at the age of eighteen, where he acquired a moderate fortune, and died at Enfield in 1817 at the age of ninety. Isaac was born in 1766, and died in 1848 at Bradenham in Buckinghamshire, where he had resided for more than twenty years. The future statesman was one of four children, three sons and a daughter, one of whom alone, Mr. Ralph Disraeli, is now living. Of the other brother, I am not aware that anything is known, beyond the circle of his own family; but the sister, Sarah Disraeli, has lately been introduced to us in a series of very interesting letters, to which reference will frequently be made in this narrative. Benjamin, who was baptized at St. Andrew's, Holborn, July 31, 1817, was educated at a school kept by the Rev. John Potticarey at Blackheath, where he was popular with his schoolfellows, who usually called him "Jack." His favourite game was "playing at horses," which is so far curious that in after life he took no interest whatever in horses or anything relating to them. At the age of seventeen he was articled to Messrs. Swain and Stevenson, solicitors in the Old Jewry, where he gave such promise of excellence, that his master recommended his father to send him to the bar. Of this period of his life no anecdotes have been preserved; but, born in a library, as he used to say of himself, he was not long in putting his literary powers to the test.

It is commonly said that his first appearance in print was in the *Representative* newspaper, brought out by Mr. Murray in January 1826; but Mr. Disraeli himself denied that he had any connection with it. A share in the *Star Chamber*, a paper which appeared every Wednesday, between the 19th of April and the 7th of June in the same year, has also been attributed to Mr. Disraeli, who is said to have written in it a poem, called the "Modern Dunciad," in imitation of Pope. But as the poem is extremely poor, and as *Vivian Grey*, which was published only two days before the appearance of the *Star Chamber*, is described in it as the work of one who "is not a very young man," his connection with this short-lived periodical must still remain a doubtful point. *Vivian Grey* was published on the 17th or 18th of April 1826, and established his reputation at a single stroke. But whether the ignorance of its author professed by the writer in the *Star Chamber* was real or assumed, we have no means of ascertaining.

Satisfied for the time with the sensation which he had created, Mr. Disraeli seems to have spent the next two years in rambling through Italy, Switzerland, and parts of Greece. But the *Young Duke* was written before the passage of the Roman Catholic Emancipation Bill in 1829, and in July 1830 we find Disraeli, who was then at Malta, writing to his sister to send a copy of the book to Lady Don, the wife of the Governor of Gibraltar, which place Disraeli had just quitted.

He had started from England a second time on the 1st of June 1830, and it was now that he began the correspondence with his sister which has just been mentioned, extending to May 1831, within which space of time he visited the south of Spain, Greece, Albania, Constantinople, the Holy Land, and Egypt. The companions of his journey were James Clay and William Meredith, of whom the former lived to be Liberal Member for Hull, and a well-known personage both in Parliament and society; the latter, a young man of the highest promise, and engaged to Mr. Disraeli's sister, died at Cairo, on his way back to England, in 1831. The friends, however, did not always keep together, and during the greater part of the time Disraeli seems to have been alone. His letters are always piquant, full of that sprightly and playful egotism, half real and half affected, which was peculiar to himself. He occasionally appears as the hero of rollicking adventures, and indulging in a strain of jocularity difficult to reconcile with the calm and somewhat scornful repose which was the habitual expression of his features in more advanced years. But we prefer to quote his account of peaceful life and society at Granada :—

After dinner you take your siesta. I generally sleep for two hours. I think this practice conducive to health. Old people, however, are apt to carry it to excess. By the time I have risen and arranged my toilette it is time to steal out, and call upon any agreeable family whose Tertullia you may choose to honour, which you do, after the first time, uninvited, and with them you take your tea or chocolate. This is often *al-fresco*, under the piazza or colonnade of the patio. Here you while away the time until it is cool enough for the alameda or public walk. At Cadiz, and even at Seville up the Guadalquivir, you are sure of a delightful breeze from the water. The sea-breeze comes like a spirit The effect is quite magical. As you are lolling in listless languor in the hot and perfumed air, an invisible guest comes dancing into the party and touches them all with an enchanted wand. All start, all smile. It has come; it is the sea-breeze. There is much discussion whether it is as strong, or whether weaker than the night before. The ladies furl their fans and seize their mantillas, the cavaliers stretch their legs and give signs of life. All rise. I offer my arm to Dolores or Florentina (is not this familiarity strange?), and in ten minutes you are in the alameda. What a change! All is now life and liveliness. Such bowing, such kissing, such fluttering of fans, such gentle criticism of gentle friends! but the fan is the most wonderful part of the whole scene. A Spanish lady with her fan might shame the tactics of a troop of horse. Now she unfurls it with the slow pomp and conscious elegance of a peacock. Now she flutters it with all the languor of a listless beauty, now with all the liveliness of a vivacious one. Now, in the midst of a very tornado, she closes it with a whir which makes you start, pop! In the midst of your confusion Dolores taps you on the elbow. You turn round to listen, and Florentina pokes you in your side. Magical instrument! You know that it speaks a particular language, and gallantry requires no other mode to express its most subtle conceits or its most unreasonable demands than this slight, delicate organ. But remember, while you read, that here, as in England, it is not confined alone to your delightful sex. I also have my fan, which makes my cane extremely jealous. If you think I have grown extraordinarily effeminate, learn that in this scorching clime the soldier will not mount guard without one. Night wears on, we sit, we take a panal, which is as quick work as snapdragon, and far more elegant; again we stroll. Midnight clears the public walks, and but few Spanish families retire till two. A solitary bachelor like myself still wanders, or still lounges on a bench in the warm moonlight. The last guitar dies away, the cathedral clock wakes up your reverie, you too seek your couch, and amid a gentle, sweet flow of loveliness, and light, and music, and fresh air, thus dies a day in Spain.

Disraeli as well as Pope could make the same ideas serve his purpose twice, as the above description figures again in *Contarini Fleming.*

The last letter of this series is dated from Cairo, May 28th, 1831, giving an account of a voyage up the Nile as far as Nubia, and the next we hear of him is from his lodgings in Duke Street, St. James', February 18th, 1832.

Disraeli was now about to make his entry into
London society, and there is no reason to distrust his
own account of the reception which he met with. The
second series of letters to his sister, extending from
1832 to 1852, is our chief authority on this point, and
they clearly show that he mingled with people of the
highest rank at as early an age as most men who are
not born in the purple. His father's reputation and
his own, combined with the fact that he had travelled
in countries then but little known to Englishmen, were
sufficient at once to secure him an introduction to that
border land in which literature and fashion meet; and
having secured his footing so far, he did the rest for
himself. In 1833 he dines with Lord and Lady St.
Maur. In the following year Lady Tankerville, who
shared with Lady Jersey the leadership of the fashionable world, admits him to Almack's. He is intimate
with Lady Chesterfield and Lady Londonderry. In
1836, before he was a Member of Parliament, he was
elected at the Carlton, and, in fact, there is over-
whelming evidence to show that the critics who sneered
at his portraits of lords and ladies in *Coningsby* and
Sybil, as being drawn exclusively from his own imagination, only showed their own ignorance of that great
world which had long before thrown open its doors to
him.

Disraeli, however, makes no secret of his position.
So far from disguising the fact that he has won his own
way into the charmed circle, instead of having taken his
place in it from the first as his natural and proper
sphere, the language in which he writes of his social
successes proclaim it with almost boyish exultation.
He writes like a youthful conqueror, marching from
victory to victory, and every fresh card of invitation is

a fresh certificate of his prowess. Of the style in which he boasts of the attention that was paid to him by the great, had it been intended for any other eyes than those of the little circle at Bradenham, the good taste might perhaps be called in question. But the letters were written to a sister; and much that might otherwise be set down to intoxicated vanity, may fairly be attributed to the desire to amuse, and possibly to divert her mind from brooding over recent troubles.

It was soon after his plunge into the world of fashion that he first met, at Lytton Bulwer's, in April 1832, his future wife, Mrs. Wyndham Lewis, whom he describes as " a pretty little woman, a flirt, and a rattle ; indeed, gifted with a volubility I should think unequalled, and of which I can convey no idea. She told me she liked ' silent, melancholy men.' I observed that I had no doubt of it." It was about this time, also, that he met Lord Melbourne at Mrs. Norton's, and when Melbourne enquired how he could serve him, replied that he desired to be Prime Minister. It is quite clear that he had already made his mark in society, and was a familiar figure in some of the best London drawing-rooms several years before he entered Parliament.

The five years which lie between 1832, when Disraeli returned to England, and 1837, when he became member of the House of Commons, present a tangled skein to the biographer. They are the five years of his greatest literary industry, and they are also five years of incessant political activity, during which it must often have seemed doubtful to himself whether politics or letters were to be his ultimate passport to immortality. Novels, essays and poems, speeches, addresses, and personal controversies pour upon us in such quick succession, and so frequently solicit our attention at the same moment, that it is perhaps better to keep the two threads distinct, and reserve all notice of the purely literary works which he published during this period till we come to consider his literary position by itself. Our space will thus be left clear for the continuous treatment of his public life during its most complicated and ambiguous stage, of which, however, it is absolutely necessary that we should form some clear idea, if we would either comprehend or do justice to the principles by which his subsequent career was regulated.

On the 22nd of February 1832, Disraeli writes to his sister : " I think peers will be created, and Charles Gore has promised to let me have timely notice if Baring be one." Mr. Thomas Baring was then the member for High Wycombe, the seat on which Disraeli had his eye, and when, a few months afterwards, the expected peerage was conferred upon him, the young aspirant issued his address. His opponent was Colonel Grey, the son of the Prime Minister; and Disraeli, whose home was now at Bradenham, only a few miles from Wycombe, came forward as the local candidate. Disraeli, who, at this time, declared his sole principle of action to be opposition to the Whigs, considered himself justified in accepting assistance from all who agreed with him on this point, whatever their opinion on other matters. Lytton Bulwer, at that time his great friend, and a strong Radical, applied to Daniel O'Connell and Mr. Hume to know whether they had any interest in the constituency. They replied that they had none, but in terms sufficiently complimentary to induce Mr. Disraeli's committee to print their letters. But Mr. Disraeli was neither a Radical nor a Home Ruler. He had told O'Connell that he could not listen to the Repeal of the Union; and on this question there could

be no doubt. Whether he had been equally explicit with
Joseph Hume remains uncertain. Hume himself may
naturally have supposed that the advocate of the Ballot
and Triennial Parliaments was a Radical all round.
But Disraeli said nothing to confirm this opinion in his
speeches or addresses. He declared himself even then
a staunch supporter of the Established Church, the
House of Lords, and our territorial constitution; and,
as we shall see, he did not get the Radical vote a second
time.

He had, in fact, fashioned out a creed for himself,
which he never appears to have renounced. He tried
to fit the Toryism of 1730 to the circumstances of 1832;
but notwithstanding some points of resemblance which
are more than superficial, there are fundamental points of
difference between the two periods which rob all his analogies, however interesting and original, of that element
of actuality which is necessary to give them any *locus
standi* in the domain of practical politics. In each case
a revolution had been effected by the Whigs, of which
the real and the ostensible motives were not the same.
In each case it seemed that a great party triumph had
been won from which the people were to gain but little,[*]
and on each occasion there may have appeared to be
some real danger lest the balance of power should
be destroyed. But the change of dynasty in 1688 was
a patrician revolution. The Reform Bill of 1832 was a
popular revolution. The Whigs may have turned it to
their own account. But the impulse came from below.
And when Mr. Disraeli raised the banner of popular
Toryism, recent events were too fresh in men's minds to
make it seem otherwise than fantastic. Down to the

---

[*] Mr. Gladstone's *Gleanings of Past Years*, vol. i. p. 148.

end of the war the Tories undoubtedly *had* been the popular party as well as the monarchical party. Even after that time their administration has been much misrepresented. But their resistance to the Reform Bill was a fact which nobody could get over. Appeals to Bolingbroke and Wyndham fell flat· on men's ears who saw the Duke of Wellington and Lord Lyndhurst, and Sir Robert Peel and Mr. Croker walking about the streets of London, and even then perhaps engaged in some plot against " the people's rights." The revival was premature. A few years later, when the air began to clear, and the passions of 1832 to lose their bitterness, the elements of truth which Mr. Disraeli's theory contained had a better chance of being appreciated; and Young England ideas made a place for themselves in our political system. But when the author of them first stood for High Wycombe they were totally unintelligible.

It may be doubted, however, whether they did not serve Mr. Disraeli's purpose just as well as if they had been more generally comprehended. He could not have carried the seat whatever he had said; and his political opinions had the great merit of originality. If they did not win him the suffrages of Wycombe, they secured for him the friendship of Lord Lyndhurst, and enlisted the admiration of even Sir Robert Peel, who, on reading the *Vindication of the British Constitution*, in December 1836, said that he was gratified and surprised to find that a familiar and apparently exhausted topic could be treated with so much of original force of argument and novelty of illustration.

It was at the general election in November 1832, when Mr. Disraeli again stood for Wycombe, that he explained more clearly what he meant by popular Toryism, and denied its affinity to Radicalism. But he had lost the confidence of the Radicals, and was of course defeated. In 1833 he consented to stand for Marylebone, but, the expected vacancy not occurring, he was delivered from the embarrassing position in which the contest certainly would have placed him. A story was current at the time, that being asked by a Marylebone elector on what he intended to stand, he replied, "upon his head." But he himself seems to have treated it as an invention of the newspapers. With 1834 came the famous crisis which he has depicted with such vivacity in *Coningsby*, and which, oddly enough, from a letter to his sister of June 4th, he himself seems to have foreseen. "My own opinion is that in the recess the King will make an effort to try and form a Conservative Government with Peel and Stanley." This is exactly what occurred when the death of Lord Spencer raised Lord Althorp to the Lords, and deprived the House of Commons of its leader : and when it became obvious that a dissolution must take place, he for a third time issued an address to the electors of the little Buckinghamshire borough. He had no better success than before, but his speech of December 16th was republished under the title of the *Crisis Examined*, and is worth reading, if only for the very characteristic observations to be found in it on the duties and position of a statesman.

The people [he says] were content to accept the Reform Bill as a great remedial measure which they had often demanded, and which had been often denied, and they did not choose to scan too severely the previous conduct of those who conceded it to them. They did not go about saying, "We must have reform, but we will not have it from Lord Palmerston, because he is the child of corruption, born of Downing Street, and engendered in the Treasury, a second-rate official for twenty years under a succession of Tory Governments, but a Secretary of State under the Whigs." Not they, indeed ! The people returned Lord Palmerston in triumph for Hampshire, and pennies were subscribed to present him with testimonials of popular applause. The people then took reform as some other people take stolen goods, " and no questions asked." The Cabinet of Lord Grey was not ungenerously twitted with the abandonment of principles which the country had given up, and to which no man could adhere who entertained the slightest hope of rendering himself an effective public servant. The truth is, gentlemen, a statesman is the creature of his age, the child of circumstances, the creation of his times. A statesman is essentially a practical character; and when he is called upon to take office, he is not to inquire what his opinions might or might not have been upon this or that subject; he is only to ascertain the needful and the beneficial, and the most feasible measures are to be carried on. The fact is, the conduct and the opinions of public men at different periods of their career must not be too curiously contrasted in a free and aspiring country. The people have their passions, and it is even the duty of public men occasionally to adopt sentiments with which they do not sympathise, because the people must have leaders. Then the opinions and prejudices of the Crown must necessarily influence a rising statesman. I say nothing of the weight which great establishments and corporations, and the necessity of their support and patronage, must also possess with an ambitious politician. All this, however, produces ultimate benefit; all these influences tend to form that eminently practical character for which our countrymen are celebrated. I laugh, therefore, at the objection against a man, that at a former period of his career he advocated a policy different to his present one. All I seek to ascertain is whether his present policy be just, necessary, expedient; whether at the present moment he is prepared to serve the country according to its present necessities.

The dissolution of Parliament in January 1835 did not give Sir Robert Peel an absolute majority, and in the following April he resigned office, and made way for the return of Lord Melbourne. Mr. Labouchere, the new Master of the Mint, on seeking re-election at Taunton, was opposed by Mr. Disraeli, who in the course of his canvass, gave that provocation to O'Connell which the agitator never forgave. In a speech, of which no report has been preserved, Mr. Disraeli said that the Whigs had " grasped the bloody

hand of O'Connell." The meaning of this was that the
Whigs, who had themselves accused O'Connell of
treasonable and rebellious practices, had now stooped to
solicit his assistance. The attack was upon the Whigs,
not upon O'Connell; but when the words found their
way into a London paper, the latter chose to accept it
as a personal offence, and, in a speech made soon afterwards at Dublin, stigmatised Disraeli as the descendant
of the impenitent thief. Mr. O'Connell having killed
a man in a duel,* had declared that nothing henceforth should induce him to fight another. But Mr.
Morgan O'Connell, who, in the previous May, had
acted as his father's representative in a duel with Lord
Alvanley, whom O'Connell had called a "bloated
buffoon," was at once challenged by Mr. Disraeli in a
letter dated from Park Street, Grosvenor Square, May
6th, 1835. The son declined to fight in the father's
quarrel a second time, and so far Disraeli came out
of the affair with flying colours. But in the newspaper controversy which followed he does not show
to equal advantage. The whole story of his connection with Hume and O'Connell in 1832 was, of
course, raked up against him, combined with taunts and
insinuations which evidently stung him to the quick;
and in his retorts upon the editor of the *Globe*, who
was the chief offender, he loses his temper, and in-
dulges in a species of vituperation, of which we may at
least say what he said of one of his own assailants many
years afterwards, that "it wants finish."

All Disraeli's letters on this subject appeared in the
Times, and though the personal abuse contained in them

---

* Mr. Esterre, a member of the Dublin Corporation, who challenged
O'Connell for calling the corporation "beggarly."

borders upon Billingsgate, still, in one letter, of the 31st of December 1835, is to be read the best vindication of the writer's public conduct down to that date, which is anywhere to be found. My readers will, perhaps, thank me for the following brilliant specimen of it, in which he anticipates *Coningsby.*

I was absent from England during the discussions on the Reform Bill. The Bill was virtually, though not formally, passed when I returned to my country in the spring of 1832. Far from that scene of discord and dissension, unconnected with its parties, and untouched by its passions, viewing as a whole what all had witnessed only in the fiery passage of its intense and alarming details, events have proved, with all humility be it spoken, that the opinion I formed of that measure on my arrival was more correct than the one commonly adopted. I found the nation in terror of a rampant democracy. I saw only an impending oligarchy. I found the House of Commons packed, and the independence of the House of Lords announced as terminated. I recognised a repetition of the same oligarchical *coup d'état* from which we had escaped by a miracle little more than a century before; therefore I determined to the utmost of my power to oppose the Whigs. Why then, it may be asked, did I not join the Tories? Because I found the Tories in a state of ignorant stupefaction. The Whigs had assured them that they were annihilated, and they believed them. They had not a single definite or intelligible idea as to their position or their duties or the character of their party. They were haunted with a nervous apprehension of that great bugbear "the people," that bewildering title under which a miserable minority contrives to coerce and plunder a nation. They were ignorant that the millions of that nation required to be guided and encouraged, and that they were that nation's natural leaders, bound to marshal and to enlighten them. The Tories trembled at a coming anarchy: what they had to apprehend was a rigid tyranny. They fancied themselves on the eve of a reign of terror, when they were about to sink under the sovereignty of a Council of Ten. Even that illustrious man, who, after conquering the Peninsula, ought to deem nothing impossible, announced that the King's Government could not be carried on. The Tories in 1832 were avowedly no longer a practical party; they had no system and no object; they were passive and forlorn. They took their seats in the House of Commons after the Reform Act as the Senate in the Forum when the city was entered by the Gauls, only to die.

He then goes on to say :—

I challenge anyone to quote any speech I have ever made, or one line I have ever written, hostile to the institutions of the country. On the contrary, I have never omitted any opportunity of showing that on the maintenance of those institutions the liberties of the nation depended; that if the Crown, the Church, the House of Lords, the Corporations, the Magistracy, the Poor Laws, were successfully attacked, we should fall, as once before we nearly fell, under a grinding oligarchy, and inevitably be governed by a metropolis. It is true that I avowed myself the supporter of triennial Parliaments, and for the same reasons as Sir William Wyndham, the leader of the Tories against Walpole, because the House of Commons had just been reconstructed for factious purposes by the Reform Act, as in the days of the Septennial Bill: I thought with Sir William Wyndham, whose speech I quoted to the electors, that the Whig power could only be shaken by frequent elections. Well, has the result proved the shallowness of my views? What has shaken the power of the Whigs to the centre? The general election of this year. What will destroy the power of the Whigs? The general election of the next. It is true that I avowed myself a supporter of the principle of the ballot. Sir William Wyndham did not do this, because in his time the idea was not in existence, but he would, I warrant it, have been as hearty a supporter of the ballot as myself, if with his principles he had been standing on the hustings in the year of our Lord 1832, with the third estate of the realm reconstructed for factious purposes by the Whigs, the gentlemen of England excluded from their own chamber, a number of paltry little towns enfranchised with the privilege of returning as many members to Parliament as the shires of this day, and the nomination of these members placed in a small knot of hardhearted sectarian rulers, opposed to everything noble and rational, and exercising an usurious influence over the petty tradesmen who are their slaves and their victims.

" More than three years after this," he continues—

came my contest at Taunton against the Master of the Mint, to which the editor of the *Globe* has alluded. I came forward on that occasion on precisely the same principles on which I had offered myself at Wycombe; but my situation was different. I was no longer an independent and isolated member of the political world. I had felt it my duty to become an earnest partisan. The Tory party had in this interval roused itself from its lethargy; it had profited by adversity; it had regained not a little of its original character and primary spirit; it had begun to remember, or to discover, that it was the national party of the country; it recognised its duty to place itself at the head of the nation; it professed the patriotic principles of Sir William Wyndham and Lord Bolingbroke, in whose writings I have ever recognised the most pure and the profoundest sources of political and constitutional wisdom; under the guidance of an eloquent and able leader, the principles of primitive Toryism had again developed themselves and the obsolete associations which form no essential portion of that great patriotic scheme had been ably and effectively discarded. In the great struggle I joined the party with whom I sympathised, and continued to oppose the faction to which had ever been adverse. But I did not avow my intention of no longer supporting the questions of short Parliaments and the Ballot, merely because the party to which I had attached myself was unfavourable to those measures, though that, in my opinion as to the discipline of political questions, would have been a sufficient reason. I ceased to advocate them because they had ceased to be necessary. The purposes for which they had been proposed were obtained. The power of the Whigs was reduced to a wholesome measure; the balance of parties in the State was restored; the independence of the House of Lords preserved. Perpetual change in the political arrangements of countries of such a complicated civilization as England is so great an evil, that nothing but a clear necessity can justify a recourse to it.

In the second of these extracts peeps out Disraeli's favourite theory, that one object of the Reform Bill was to destroy the legitimate influence of the country gentlemen.* But before concluding this passage of his life, it remains to notice what passed between himself and his critics on the subject of his relations with Mr. Hume. It amounts to no more than this—that Mr. Hume very naturally did not understand the new Toryism which Mr. Disraeli had adopted, and supposed that everyone who supported the changes which he advocated himself, did so with the same object. He could make no approach to the point of view from which the Ballot and Triennial Parliaments

* Vide *Vindication of British Constitution* and *Spirit of Whiggism,* passim.

seemed favourable to Toryism, and, excusably, therefore, when Mr. Disraeli announced himself a Tory,
thought he had been deceived. Mr. Hume's memory
played him false in some particulars, as, for instance,
in supposing that he had an interview with Mr. Disraeli in Bryanston Square in 1833, when the latter
made a personal declaration of his principles. Mr.
Disraeli called during his canvass for Marylebone,
but only saw Mr. Hume's private secretary, that gentleman himself being confined to his bed. But these
details are of little consequence. The general conclu-
clusion is that Mr. Disraeli was mistaken by the Radicals for one of themselves, because they did not know
that what was a Radical measure in 1832 had been a
Tory one in 1734, and that it was possible to be in
favour of the ballot without being an enemy to the
Constitution. That Mr. Disraeli took advantage of
their ignorance is, perhaps, the worst that can be said
of him. But we gladly turn from what is, after all,
but an ambiguous phase in his career, to the days, now
rapidly approaching, when he should appear in his
true colours, as the preacher of a new creed and
the founder of a new party.

His correspondence at this time is full of Lord
Lyndhurst, whom he regarded as his political chief,
and who seems to have been the only man of any note
who really tried to understand what he meant. Lyndhurst occasionally went down to Bradenham, and seems
to have enjoyed a ramble among the Chilterns with
his eccentric young *protégé*, who probably told the
older man a good deal that he did not know before.
The two had much in common. Both were daring to
the verge of recklessness, cool, and self-reliant—
"pleased with the danger when the waves ran high."

2

Both came to the consideration of English politics with comparatively open minds, and both had arrived at conclusions eminently unfavourable to the Whigs.

The year 1836 passed away. *Henrietta Temple* had been out some time, and *Venetia* was just finished, when it was announced that William IV. was suffering one of his customary attacks of hay fever. Those who were behind the scenes knew better, and began to prepare for a Dissolution. After lingering, the centre of hopes and fears, for some weeks, William IV. expired early in the morning of the 20th of June 1837. Parliament was dissolved on the 18th of July, and Mr. Disraeli was returned for Maidstone in company with Mr. Wyndham Lewis, on the 27th. Mr. Lewis polled 707 votes, Disraeli 616, and Colonel Thompson, the Liberal candidate, 412. Disraeli had now got his foot in the stirrup, and his boast of 1833 was to be put to the test, " Heard Macaulay's best speech, Shiel, and Charles Grant. Macaulay admirable ; but, between ourselves, I could floor them all. This *entre nous*. I never was more certain of anything than that I could carry everything before me in that House."* His chance had now come to him ; as, according to himself, it comes to every man, if he can only wait. He was to take his seat among the men whom the country looked up to as its leaders, and measure himself against them ; and it cannot be denied that his wonderful self-confidence was justified. In writing of Addison, Thackeray says, ' You could hardly show him an essay, a sermon, or a poem, but he felt he could do it better." And, sitting in judgment on Disraeli's overweening self-esteem, we must make allowance for that consciousness of genius

---

* Letter to his sister, Feb. 7, 1833.

which told him of his own superiority, and "prophesied of his glory," even through the mists of failure. Seeing what he really was, we must feel that these bubbles of egotism welled up from intellectual depths which the world had not yet fathomed; and though it took a rather exceptionable form, in substance it was far from unwarrantable.

2 *

CHAPTER II.

THE GREAT CONSERVATIVE PARTY.

1837–1843.

State of Parties in 1837—Disraeli's maiden speech—Evidence as to
its merits—Position in the House—The Bedchamber plot—The
Chartist Petition—Disraeli's marriage—Change in his circumstances—Dissolution of 1841—Disraeli returned for Shrewsbury
—Exposition of his views on Protection.

DISRAELI took his seat in the House of Commons on
the 15th of November 1837, on the second bench just
behind Sir Robert Peel.   The state of parties at this
time has been so accurately described by himself in his
political novels that the reader who is curious about it
will do well to consult them for himself.   Within two
years of the meeting of the first Reformed Parliament
the Whigs had run through nearly all the popularity
which that measure had acquired for them ; and after
the General Election of 1835 the Tory party, which had
apparently been annihilated, rose from its ashes in numbers far from contemptible, in ability, experience, and
debating powers greatly superior to its opponents.   It
was calculated by the whips and wire-pullers that after
another registration Peel would have a clear majority.
These hopes were nipped in the bud by the accession of

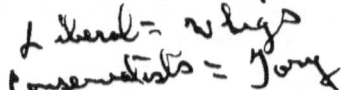

the young Queen while the Whigs were still in office, which gave them the chance of appealing to the country as *her* ministers, an advantage which gained them so many seats that they were able to retain their hold on office through another Parliament.

But the reaction, temporarily arrested, soon set in again more strongly and steadily than ever. By their Irish policy, their ecclesiastical policy, and their financial policy, the Whigs disgusted and alarmed thousands of independent men, and alienated, at the same time, many of their old friends, who found it necessary to become Conservatives to ensure being ruled by men of business. But it will be seen, as Mr. Disraeli saw, that the tide of opinion which set in against the Liberals from 1837 to 1841 was only very partially and superficially a Conservative or Tory movement. The middle classes began to turn to Sir Robert Peel as the safest and most experienced statesman to whom their fortunes could be entrusted. But they went no farther. Of Tory principles as they were then understood, the Toryism of Eldon and Wetherell, they were certainly not enamoured, and they knew of no other. If a peaceful, economical and constitutional Government, including the ablest administrators of the day, and prepared to give the country such measures as the times required, chose to call itself Conservative, then the nation was Conservative, but not in any other sense. But a party of this kind could never restore that "faith" which the Reform Bill had destroyed, and which, even if devoted to an obsolete system, is still the fountain light of all political creeds. This truth did not dawn on Mr. Disraeli all at once any more than it did on Mr. Gladstone. Both imagined they saw something in the apparent revival of Toryism between

1835 and 1841 which was not there. Mr. Gladstone
says, in his *Chapter of Autobiography*, that no sooner
were his friends in office than he found there was not a
single man prepared to act on these principles. And
Mr. Disraeli, who made a similar discovery about the
same time, expressed his sentiments in *Coningsby* and
Sybil. But in 1837 all this was to come. Mr. Disraeli
had as yet unbounded faith in Sir Robert Peel, and
looked to him to play the part which he afterwards
assigned to Young England.

Full of these ideas he passed within the portals of
those "proud and passionate halls," of which he was
destined one day to be the ruler, confident in his
destinies, and little dreaming, perhaps, of the trials that
awaited him, and which were not to be the least severe
when he had apparently distanced all competitors. His
maiden speech was delivered on the 7th of December
1837, when he experienced a foretaste of the malignity,
the injustice, and the persistent misrepresentation which
pursued him through his whole career. The subject of
debate was a motion made by Mr. Smith O'Brien,
relating to an alleged subscription fund in Ireland for
promoting petitions against the return of members who
belonged to Mr. O'Connell's party. Disraeli followed
O'Connell, and his voice was immediately drowned in
the clamour raised by a host of members below the bar,
consisting of the agitator's "tail," and a few English
Radicals who combined with them. Of the speech itself
it is enough to say that it was in his early style, while
his rhetoric was still green, and when he had not yet
learned the due proportion in which epigram should be
mixed with solid argument. But it does not appear that
his reception by the House at large was altogether
unfavourable. We read in his own account of it that

Sir Robert Peel cheered him repeatedly; that Sir John Campbell, the Attorney-General, assured him that the front bench had been very anxious to listen to him, and had no control over the clique below; and that Sheil, who heard the speech, said to some friends at the Athenæum: "If ever the spirit of oratory was in a man, it is in that man." There is no difficulty in believing that competent judges saw the promise of future excellence under all these disadvantageous conditions, and notwithstanding the eccentric exterior of the ambitious neophyte. Bulwer asked Sheil to meet him at dinner, and in the course of the evening the experienced orator gave him the following good advice :—

If you had been listened to, what would have been the result? You would have made the best speech that you ever would have made. It would have been received frigidly, and you would have despaired of yourself. I did. As it is, you have shown to the house that you have a fine organ, that you have an unlimited command of language, that you have courage, temper, and readiness. Now get rid of your genius for a session. Speak often, for you must not show yourself cowed, but speak shortly. Be very quiet, try to be dull, only argue, and reason imperfectly; for if you reason with precision, they will think you are trying to be witty. Astonish them by speaking on subjects of detail. Quote figures, dates, calculations, and in a short time the House will sigh for the wit and eloquence which they all know are in you; they will encourage you to pour them forth, and then you will have the ear of the House and be a favourite.

But we have still among us a living witness of the scene, whose testimony to the real merits of the speech must be held to be conclusive. "My lords," said Lord Granville, on May 9th, 1881, "I myself, assisted by some of those social advantages which Mr. Disraeli was without, came into the House six months before Mr. Disraeli took his seat in that assembly. I had thus the opportunity of hearing that speech famous for its failure, and I am convinced that if that speech had been made in a House of Commons which knew him better it would have been received with cheers and sympathetic, not derisive, laughter." Mr. Disraeli never spoke again without being listened to with attention. Ten days after his first appearance, he presented himself to the House again on Talfourd's Copyright Bill, detaining his audience a very little while, making a practical suggestion to influence Talfourd, and winding up with a point which told very well. "As for myself, I trust that the age of literary patronage has passed, and it will be honourable to the present Government if, under its auspices, it be succeeded by that of legislative protection."

His course was now clear. It was soon understood that whatever the general character of his speeches, they were pretty sure to contain something that was original, and probably something that was witty; and though more than this is necessary to make a man a power in the House of Commons, it is enough, at all events to secure him a fair field, and prevent him from being " howled down."

The two principal events affecting Mr. Disraeli's political career during the existence of his first Parliament were the Chartist insurrection and the Bedchamber Plot, such being the name given to a so-called Palace intrigue, whereby the Whigs, it is said, endeavoured to secure their own return to power after resigning on the Jamaica Bill in 1839. Sir Robert Peel, on being sent for, found that Her Majesty desired to retain about her person the ladies of the Bedchamber. It turned out that there were only two whose dismissal Sir Robert thought essential. But the Queen continuing firm, he declined to form a ministry, and

the Melbourne Government was reinstated.   Opinion
was much divided at the time on the conduct of the
different parties concerned.   Disraeli thought Sir
Robert wrong.   He thought it was both ungraceful
and impolitic on the part of the leader of the Tories
to thwart a young sovereign, "and that sovereign a
woman," in the first exercise of her prerogative.
With his head full of a monarchical revival, it was
natural that he should think so; as natural, perhaps, as that Sir Robert Peel, who remembered the
effects of female influence in a previous reign, should
think the reverse.   However, the Whigs took little
by the manœuvre.   They only gained time to re-
double their own unpopularity, so that if the advice
which Lord Melbourne gave the Queen was really
unconstitutional, he paid the penalty.

It would have been wiser, however, in Sir Robert
Peel, to have waived the point and trusted to the
Queen's good sense to save him from the difficulties
which he apprehended; and he too, perhaps, would
have had his reward, for had he taken office in 1839,
instead of 1841, he would not have come into power
so irrevocably committed to the Corn Laws, and his
repeal of them would have looked less like the betrayal
of confidence than it did under the actual circumstances.   It is rather curious that in Disraeli's letters
to his sister we find no reference to this affair, and
only a very brief mention of the Chartist disturbances, in which he took so lively an interest, and of
which he has left us so animated an account in *Sybil.*

It was on the 12th of July 1839 that he made his
speech on the Chartist Petition, presented to Parliament by Mr. Attwood, member for Birmingham, and
demanding what were called the five points—manhood

suffrage, vote by ballot, electoral districts, annual
parliaments, and payment of members. He writes
about this speech to his sister in his usual style: "I
made a capital speech last night," he says. But at
all events it was a very remarkable speech, and the
one which, it is said, first gained him the ear of the
House. Six years afterwards he described it again in
the novel we have just named. Sybil, the heroine, the
beautiful, refined, and highly-educated daughter of a
Chartist leader, and enthusiastically devoted to the
cause, is sitting in St. James's Park on a fine summer
morning reading the report of the debate.

> Yes, there was one voice that had sounded in that proud Parliament,
> that, free from the slang of faction, had dared to express immortal
> truths: the voice of a noble who, without being a demagogue, had
> upheld the popular cause; had pronounced his conviction that the
> rights of labour were as sacred as those of property; that if a diffe-
> rence were to be established, the interests of the living wealth ought
> to be preferred; who had declared that the social happiness of the
> millions should be the first object of a statesman, and that, if this
> were not achieved, thrones and dominions, the pomp and power
> of courts and empires were alike worthless.

The speech itself is chiefly remarkable for a passage
in which Mr. Disraeli expresses his distrust of the
middle classes as a foundation for any system of government. But his sympathy with the Chartists of that
day was quite sincere, though he did not agree with them
practically; and his kindly reception of Cooper the
Chartist, five years after the speech was delivered, was
referred to in terms of high approval by Mr. Gladstone
in his great funeral oration over his rival's tomb.

Throughout the correspondence for the years
1838–39, the name of Mrs. Wyndham Lewis occurs
frequently. Sometimes Disraeli accompanies her to the
theatre. When he got his Coronation medal he pre-

sented it to "Mrs. W. L.," and after her husband's
death, which took place on the 14th of March 1838,
nobody was surprised at hearing who was to be his
successor. They were married in London on the 28th
of August 1839, and went to Tunbridge Wells for the
first days of their honeymoon. They stayed at the
"Kentish," then one of the principal hotels in that
charming little watering place, and visited Bayham
Abbey and Penshurst, where Disraeli found, of course,
that his friend De Lisle was out shooting. They only
stayed about ten days in England, and then set out for
Germany, arriving at Baden-Baden on the 16th of September. "The most picturesque, agreeable, lounging
sort of place you can imagine," he writes; "a bright
little river winding about green hills, with a white
sparkling town of some dozen palaces, called hotels, and
some lodging-houses like the side scenes of a melo-
drama, and an old ruined castle or two on woody
heights." Mrs. Disraeli, however, pronounced it "not
much better than Cheltenham," so they left it in about
a week, and went on to Munich. At Munich they
passed about three weeks, and early in November they
were at Paris. The end of the month found them in
England and settled at Grosvenor Gate. Lord Malmesbury met them at dinner in the following season, and
describes Mrs. Disraeli as a very remarkable woman
both in mind and manner.

Disraeli's marriage made a great change in his circumstances. He was now for the first time beyond the
pressure of pecuniary cares, and rich enough to take
upon himself the style and fashion of an English
country gentleman. He did not, however, become the
owner of Hughenden immediately; and as late as September 1843 made Bradenham his country home. It

was here, "in his old writing-room," next to his sister's room, that, in the autumn of 1843, he finished *Coningsby*, which he had sketched out at Deepdene early in September. He was master of Hughenden before 1847, and that is all that I can ascertain.

Parliament met in the month of January,. and the Whigs struggled desperately on through this session and the next. But at this time, in the days of the old ten-pound franchise, and before the growth of that singular product of our own day, the High Church Radical, the three great interests in the country, the moneyed interest, the agricultural interest, and the Church interest, could, when united, carry all before them, and Sir Robert Peel had united them. This was " the great Conservative Party." The motley combination of Repealers, Free Traders, and Dissenters, which was all the Whigs had to oppose to him, was no match for this solid phalanx. They were gradually deserted by their own followers in the House of Commons, and, finally staking their all on the popularity of a fixed duty on corn, they were defeated, in the session of 1841, by a majority of thirty-six, and Sir Robert Peel, who would "rather be the leader of the country gentlemen of England than possess the confidence of sovereigns," and who opposed the fixed duty avowedly on the ground that it must lead in the end to Free Trade, gave notice shortly afterwards of his intention to move a vote of want of confidence. This was carried against Government by a majority of one, and on the 23rd of June Parliament was dissolved.

The Conservative cause was everywhere triumphant. Mr. Disraeli was returned for Shrewsbury. And Sir Robert Peel became Prime Minister with a majority of seventy at his back. Guizot prophesied that he would

be the Walpole of the nineteenth century, and had he
adhered to the principles which brought him into
power, it is difficult to see what could have turned him
out of it. He might have stayed in for two Parliaments
at all events, and probably for a third also. But scarcely
was he seated in power, ere doubts began to creep into
his mind concerning the truth of the commercial theories which, for six years, he had been so diligently in-
culcating on his followers. What was he to do? The
rank and file of the party began to complain of his cold-
ness, his reserve, his pride, his arrogance, his impe-
riousness. This is just the behaviour we should expect
from one who, being at the head of a great party,
and trusted by them implicitly as the champion of a
political creed, becomes suddenly infected with scepticism, and knows not where to look for sympathy. We
may pity a man placed in such a position as this, but
we cannot acquit him of a serious error if he takes
advantage of the power he has gained by advocating
one set of principles to effect the triumph of another;
and, without taking his followers into his confidence or
making a single effort to convert them, suddenly, and
almost contemptuously, abandons the cause which they
had entrusted to him, espouses the system which he had
taught them to abhor, and requires of them at a
moment's notice, and on his own *sic volo sic jubeo*, to
adopt it entirely, on pain of destroying the position
which it had been the work of their leader to build up.

It was not, however, till Peel had been in office two
years that any signs of insubordination began to show
themselves. Disraeli defended his earlier financial measures in speeches of marked ability, both in the House
of Commons and in an address to his constituents at
Shrewsbury. On the 25th of April 1843, when Mr.

Ricardo, the Member for Stoke, moved "That the remission of duties should not be postponed to the execution of commercial treaties," Mr. Disraeli delivered a speech which, "to this day," says Mr. Morley,* "is remarkable for its large and comprehensive survey of the whole field of our commerce, and for its discernment of the channels in which it would expand." But it is remarkable for more than this. For it distinctly predicts the position in which England would find herself if, while she adopted Free Trade, the rest of Europe clung to Protection; and he endeavoured to impress upon his audience the very important truth that the great Powers of the Continent place political considerations first and political economy second.

This was his own practice as well. If he was a Protectionist, he was a Protectionist on political not upon commercial principles, and in his speech at Shrewsbury, May 9th, 1843, he expounded his ideas at some length. After showing that Sir Robert Peel was only treading in the footsteps of Mr. Pitt and Lord Liverpool, he continued as follows :—

I never will commit myself upon this great question to petty economical details. I will not pledge myself to miserable questions of 6d. in 7s. 6d. or 8s. of duties about corn. I do not care whether your corn sells for this sum or that, or whether it is under a sliding scale or a fixed duty; but what I want and what I wish to secure, and what, as far as my energies go, I will secure, is the preponderance of the landed interest. Gentlemen, when I talk of the preponderance of the landed interest, do not for a moment suppose that I mean merely the preponderance of " squires of high degree," that, in fact, I am thinking only of justices of the peace. My thought wanders farther than a lordly tower or a manorial hall. I am looking, in using that very phrase, to what I consider the vast majority of the English nation. I do not undervalue the mere superiority of the landed classes; on the contrary, I think it a most

* *Life of Cobden,* vol. ii. p 336.

necessary element of political power, and national civilisation; but I am looking to the population of our innumerable villages, to the crowds in our rural towns; aye, and I mean even something more than that by the landed interest. I mean that estate of the poor which, in my opinion, has been already tampered with, dangerously tampered with; which I have also said, let me remind you, in other places besides Shrewsbury. I mean by the estate of the poor, the great estate of the Church, which has, before this time, secured our liberty, and may, for aught I know, still secure our civilisation.

Gentlemen, we hear a great deal in the present day upon the subject of the feudal system. I have heard from the lips of Mr. Cobden— no, I have not heard him say it, as I was not present to hear the celebrated speech he made in Drury Lane Theatre—but we have all heard how Mr. Cobden, who is a very eminent person, has said, in a very memorable speech, that England was the victim of the feudal system, and we have all heard how he has spoken of the barbarism of the feudal system and of the barbarous relics of the feudal system. Now, if we have any relics of the feudal system, I regret that not more of it is remaining. Think one moment —and it is well you should be reminded of what this is, because there is no phrase more glibly used in the present day than the barbarism of the feudal system. Now, what is the fundamental principle of the feudal system, gentlemen? It is that the tenure of all property shall be the performance of its duties. Why, when the Conqueror carved out parts of the land and introduced the feudal system, he said to the recipient, "You shall have that estate, but you shall do something for it; you shall feed the poor; you shall endow the Church; you shall defend the land in case of war; and you shall execute justice and maintain truth to the poor for nothing." It is all very well to talk of the barbarities of the feudal system, and to tell us that in those days when it flourished a great variety of gross and grotesque circumstances and great miseries occurred; but these were not the result of the feudal system; they were the result of the barbarism of the age. They existed not from the feudal system, but in spite of the feudal system. The principle of the feudal system, the principle which was practically operated upon, was the noblest principle, the grandest, the most magnificent and benevolent that was ever conceived by sage, or ever practised by patriot. Why, when we hear a political economist, or an Anti-Corn-Law Leaguer, or some conceited Liberal reviewer, come forward and tell us a grand discovery of modern science, twitting and taunting, perhaps, some unhappy squire who cannot respond to the alleged discovery—when I hear them say, as the great discovery of modern science, that "Property has its duties as well as its rights," my answer is that that is but a feeble plagiarism of the very principle of that feudal system which you are always reviling. Let me next tell those gentlemen who are so fond of telling us that property has its duties as well as its rights, that labour also has its rights as well as its duties. And when I see masses of property raised in this country which do not recognise that principle; when I find men making fortunes by a method which permits them (very often in a very few years) to purchase the lands of the old territorial aristocracy of the country, I cannot help remembering that those millions are accumulated by a mode which does not recognise it as a duty " to endow the Church, to feed the poor, to guard the land, and to execute justice for nothing." And I cannot help asking myself, when I hear of all this misery, and of all this suffering ; when I know that evidence exists in our Parliament of a state of demoralisation in the once happy population of this land, which is not equalled in the most barbarous countries, which we suppose the more rude and uncivilised in Asia are—I cannot help suspecting that this has arisen because property has been permitted to be created and held without the performance of its duties.

If we recur to the continental system of parcelling out landed estates, I want to know how long you can maintain the political system of the country? That estate of the Church which I mentioned; that estate of the poor to which I referred ; that great fabric of judicial rights to which I made allusion; those traditionary manners and associations which spring out of the land, which form the national character, which form part of the possession of the poor not to be despised, and which is one of the most important elements of political power—they will tell you " Let it go." My answer to that is, " If it goes, it is revolution, a great, a destructive revolution. For these reasons, gentlemen, I believe, in that respect faithfully representing your sentiments, that I have always upheld that law which I think will uphold and maintain the preponderance of the agricultural interests of the country. I do not wish to conceal the ground upon which I wish to uphold it. I never attempted to uphold it by talking of the peculiar burthen which, however, I believe, may be legitimately proved, or indulging in many of those arguments in favour of the Corn Laws which may or may not be sound, but which are always brought forward with a sort of hesitating consciousness which may be assumed to be connected with futility. I take the only broad, and only safe line, namely, that what we ought to uphold is that the preponderance of the landed interest has made England ; that it is an immense element of political power and stability ; that we should never have been able to undertake the great war in which we embarked in the memory of many present ; that we could never have been able to conquer the greatest military genius the world ever saw with the greatest means at his disposal, and to hurl him from the throne, if we had not had a territorial aristocracy to give stability to our constitution.

This whole argument for Protection, which takes it out of the region of arithmetic and transfers it to the higher ground of political philosophy, was alien from the mind of Peel, who was by nature a political economist, and whose creed, as has well been said, was the conservatism of the bank and the counting-house, not of the cloister and the manor-house ; and if we would have the key to Young England in a few words, it was a revolt against *bourgeois* politics, against the hard and uninteresting aspect which Conservatism in the hands of Sir Robert Peel was beginning to assume. There was food for the imagination both in Toryism and Radicalism ; but not in that sober, prudent, middle-class compromise, which was rightly described by Mr. Tadpole, in *Coningsby,* as composed of Tory men and Whig measures.

CHAPTER III.

YOUNG ENGLAND.

1843.

Young England Toryism and Conservatism—Disraeli's position —
Breach with Peel—*Coningsby*—The Young England creed—
Didactic elements in *Coningsby*—Its portraits and types—Tour in
the manufacturing districts—*Sybil*—Theme of the novel—Disraeli's political ideal—Young England and the Anglican revival.

THE whole of the speech from which the extracts in
the above chapter have been taken, and which was
delivered by Mr. Disraeli at Shrewsbury on the
9th of May 1843, three months before the first breach
with Sir Robert Peel, is a foreshadowing of the position
which Young England was presently to assume, and of
the forthcoming indictment against the great Conservative party, which made the hair of Tadpole and Taper
stand on end. That party had not been true to the principles therein sketched out. Its support of the Poor Law,
and its issue of the Ecclesiastical Commission, were
blows struck at the territorial position of the Church,
and the authority of the landed gentry, which were,
in Mr. Disraeli's eyes, among the most sacred de-

posits of Toryism. Sir Robert Peel was willing to establish the supremacy of the House of Commons over the two other estates of the realm, and the Crown as well. Conservatism, after all, was only Whiggism under another name. Why Mr. Disraeli did not discover this before is one of the innumerable questions in the history of his political opinions to which no satisfactory answer will ever probably be returned. In 1835, when he looked to Sir Robert Peel as the saviour of the State, the Tamworth Manifesto and the Ecclesiastical Commission, the objects of his bitterest scorn and keenest invective in 1843, had both been issued. Nor could it have been only Sir Robert Peel's change of opinion on Protection which made the difference between Young England Toryism and Conservatism, for, in the first place, Young England was born before Peel's change of front became apparent, while, what is much more important, not only had the political infidelity which it was the object of Young England to expose nothing whatever to do with such questions as the Corn Laws, but the great statesmen to whom the new party looked for inspiration—Bolingbroke, Shelburne, and Pitt—had themselves been free-traders. Perhaps he waited to see what a Conservative Government would bring forth before declaring himself more openly. Perhaps he felt some natural reluctance to break with the only party to which he could look for political advancement till he felt more sure of the ground under his own feet, and of his own ability to create a party for himself. At one time it was unblushingly asserted, and therefore not unfrequently believed, that he had applied to Sir Robert Peel for some appointment in the Government, and that the Prime Minister's refusal was the cause of his declaration of hostilities. This calumny, however, has been exploded long ago, and we can only explain his attitude between 1835 and 1843 by falling back on the simple expedient of believing that he spoke the truth; that he really meant what he said in his letter to the *Times*,* which we have already quoted, and in another, which will be found below; and that, the Tamworth Manifesto notwithstanding, it was the pristine Toryism of the time of Anne and George the First that Sir Robert Peel, emerging from the darkness of 1832, was expected to restore. That he continued in this faith for the space of eight years is not, of course, to be believed. Scepticism must have been germinating in his mind for some years before it broke out into open mutiny. But at what moment his disbelief in Peelite Conservatism became absolute and final it is, of course, impossible to say.

It was in August 1843 that the storm burst. On the 9th of that month Sir Robert Peel's Irish Arms Bill was read a third time, and Mr. Disraeli, Lord J. Manners and others commented on it with some severity. In this they were severely taken to task by the Treasury Bench, and warmly defended by the *Morning Chronicle* and the *Times*. This was the first open breach, and it was never healed. *Apropos* of this affair Mr. Disraeli, writing to the *Times*, on the 11th of August 1843, expresses himself to the following effect :—

I voted for " the industrial measures of Sir Robert Peel last year, and defended them during the present, because I believed, and still believe, that they were founded on sound principles of commercial policy; principles which were advocated by that great Tory statesman, Lord Bolingbroke, in 1713; principles which, in abeyance during

* December 31, 1835.

the Whig Government of seventy years, were revived by that great Tory statesman Mr. Pitt; and, though their progress was disturbed by war and revolution, which were faithful to the traditional policy of the Tory Party, sanctioned and developed, on the return of peace and order, by Lord Liverpool. It is not merely with reference to commercial policy that I believe that a recurrence to old Tory principles would be of great advantage to this country. It is a specific, in my opinion, and the only one, for many of those disquietudes which now perplex our society. I see no other remedy for that war of classes and creeds which now agitates and menaces us but in an earnest return to a system which may be described generally as one of loyalty and reverence, of popular rights and social sympathies.

The young men round about him who shared in those ideas were Lord John Manners, the Hon. George Smythe, Mr. Bailie Cochrane, and some others; and out of Parliament they seem to have found a ready sympathiser in Mr. Henry Hope, of Deepdene, where Disraeli now spent a good deal of his time. Here he and his wife spent the Christmas of 1840, with many "merry gambols, charades, and ghosts"; such a Christmas, perhaps, as he afterwards describes at Eustace Lyle's, when Buckhurst was Lord of Misrule. And it was amid these glades and alleys and in close communion with these gifted friends that those ideas were ripened, which were now to find expression in the most remarkable political fictions which our literature has produced. He writes to his sister from Deepdene, in September 1843, that he is coming to Bradenham, and wants a workroom. If it does not inconvenience anybody, he would like to have his old writing-room next to hers. It may easily be supposed that his request was granted, and here, amid the beautiful beech-woods of his favourite Buckinghamshire, he composed *Coningsby*.

The main object of *Coningsby* was to protest against the elimination of the royal prerogative from our Constitutional system, which had been effected by

the revolution of 1688, and to recall to the public mind
the writings of Bolingbroke as representing the true
principles of the Monarchy.   The downfall of the oli-
garchic system in 1832 might, he thought, pave the way
for the revival of them. But Young England went farther than this. It embraced that emancipation of the
Church from Parliamentary dictation in matters purely
spiritual, which is now universally desired by all sober
and moderate High Churchmen : that maintenance of
ancient local jurisdictions, and, if necessary, the creation of new ones, which somehow or other the Liberal
Party, with its unrivalled powers of mystification, has
contrived to represent as its own invention ; and that
improvement in the condition of the labouring classes,
both urban and rural, of which Mr. Disraeli lived to
accomplish much, and which his successor is now
occupied in completing.

But it was not so much the particular measures to be
adopted by the Tory party in order to re-establish its
title to be " the popular political confederacy " of this
country, as the spirit in which the work was to be
undertaken, that distinguished the teaching of Young
England.   Coningsby told his grandfather that he
wished to see the restoration of political faith, which,
to Lord Monmouth, was foolishness.   But that these
words, in the year 1844, had a real meaning in the
eyes of sober politicians may be gathered from an
article in the *Edinburgh Review*, vol. lxxx., in which
the writer says of the old *régime* : " This was a system
on which one's moral nature could repose, a solid
temple in which one could sincerely worship."   With
these words may be compared Mr. Gladstone's :—

One of my objects in this brief retrospect is to suggest what
party prejudice appears to forget, that the true character of our

working Parliamentary system is not determined exclusively by the condition of the franchise and what is termed the distribution of seats. Another is to make an apology for those who felt that, in surrendering the former system as a whole, to substitute for it the scheme of 1832, they were committing themselves to a series of changes, and not to one alone. The convictions of men like Mr. Burke, Lord Grenville, Mr. Canning, Mr. Hallam, in its favour represent something much higher, much more historical, than has since been, or could be, arrayed in defence of schemes essentially intermediate and provisional, against further modification.*

Voilà tout. Here is the whole foundation and justification of that "unparalled betrayal" in which so many good Conservatives were only too willing to believe.

It is true that Mr. Disraeli himself was no admirer of the old *régime,* which fell in 1832. Both the Edinburgh Reviewer and Mr. Gladstone would have admitted that it was worn out. But in at least half the nation it did still inspire real faith. With all its corruptions, with all its exclusiveness and intolerance, were combined great elements of strength, and ancient and glorious associations. It had on its side all the weight of antiquity, experience, and prescription. Men had sat under its shadow for many generations, in peace, happiness, and prosperity. It represented distinct principles which were not mere names; a monarchy which, however limited, still possessed real power; an aristocracy which really governed, and a Church which was still the one recognised religion of the nation, and possessed a legal claim on the support of the entire people. These were principles, erroneous or otherwise, for which men felt that they could fight; and the hope of establishing something in its place, which should inspire the like degree of reverence, and rest on the same solid founda-

---

* *Gleanings,* vol. i. p. 137.

tions, was the mainspring of the Young England creed. Mr. Gladstone seems to have come to the conclusion that this was not possible, and that it was the wisest course to throw over the past altogether, and go forward to meet the democracy with open hands. Mr. Disraeli and his party thought otherwise. They hoped that it was not yet too late to obliterate the traces of mis-government which had prejudiced the working classes against all established institutions, and to rekindle that attachment to the Throne, the Church, and the landed proprietors of the kingdom, "the natural leaders of the people," which, though the flame burned low, was yet far from being extinct.

In *Coningsby,* the dramatic and didactic elements are not so closely interwoven with each other as not to admit of being separated, and it is perfectly possible to convey to the reader a clear idea of the chief positions which are maintained in it, without trenching on the province of the literary critic, or anticipating the re-marks we have to make on the plot, the characters, and the language.

Harry Coningsby is the grandson and only lineal de-scendant of the Marquis of Monmouth, a great noble of colossal fortune, the incarnation of common sense, cyni-cism, and selfishness, though disposed to act kindly to those who do not thwart him ; a worshipper of Pitt, but practically a supporter of the later school of Toryism, which was developed by the French Revolution. We are introduced to the boy and the man, the representa-tives of the old generation and the new, in May 1832, just as the old constitution was making its expiring effort. And on the character of the Parliamentary Re-form which the Whigs succeeded in establishing, Mr. Disraeli has the following very interesting remarks, of which much of Mr. Gladstone's, essay on the County Franchise is only a repetition :—

When the crowned Northman consulted on the welfare of his kingdom, he assembled the estates of his realm. Now an estate is a class of the nation invested with political rights. There appeared the estate of the clergy, of the barons, of other classes. In the Scandinavian kingdoms to this day, the estate of the peasants sends its representatives to the Diet In England. under the Normans, the Church and the Baronage were convoked together with the estate of the community, a term which then probably described the inferior holders of land, whose tenure was not immediate of the Crown. This third estate was so numerous that convenience suggested its appearance by representation; while the others, more limited, appeared, and still appear, personally. The third estate was reconstructed as circumstances developed themselves. It was a reform of Parliament when the towns were summoned. In treating the House of the third estate as the House of the People, and not as the House of a privileged class, the Ministry and Parliament of 1831 virtually conceded the principle of universal suffrage. In this point of view, the ten-pound franchise was an arbitrary, irrational, and impolitic qualification. It had, indeed, the merit of simplicity, and so had the constitutions of Abbé Sièyes. But its immediate and inevitable result was Chartism. But if the Ministry and Parliament of 1831 had announced that the time had arrived when the third estate should be enlarged and reconstructed, they would have occupied an intelligible position; and if, instead of simplicity of elements in its reconstruction, they had sought, on the contrary, various, and varying, materials, which would have neutralized the painful predominance of any particular interest in the new scheme, and prevented those banded jealousies which have been its consequences, the nation would have found itself in a secure condition. Another class, not less numerous than the existing one, and invested with privileges not less important, would have been added to the public estates of the realm; and the bewildering phrase " the People " would have remained what it really is, a term of natural philosophy and not of political science.

Passing over the intermediate years which are taken up with the boyhood of Coningsby, we come to the political crisis of 1834–5, which introduces us to a fine dissertation on the Duke of Wellington and Sir Robert Peel, with an account of the Liverpool Administration in its earlier and later.stages. In the former it was the " Cabinet of Mediocrities," which has now become a household word. In the latter, " it had come to be generally esteemed as a body of men who for Parliamentary eloquence, official practice, political information, sagacity in council, and a due understanding of their epoch, were inferior to none that had directed the policy of the Empire since the Revolution."

At this point Mr. Disraeli enters at once upon the historical and constitutional theory for the sake of which the book was written, and of which the following passage presents, perhaps, an adequate epitome :—

If we survey the tenor of the policy of the Liverpool Cabinet during the latter moiety of its continuance, we shall find its characteristic to be a partial recurrence to those frank principles of government which Mr. Pitt had revived, during the latter part of the last century, from precedents that had been set us either in practice or in dogma during its earlier period, by statesmen who then not only bore the title but professed the opinions of Tories. Exclusive principles in the Constitution and restrictive principles in commerce have grown up together, and have really nothing in common with the ancient character of our political settlement or the manners and customs of the English people. Confidence in the loyalty of the nation, testified by munificent grants of rights and franchises, and favour to an expansive system of traffic, were distinctive qualities of the English sovereignty, until the House of Commons usurped the better portion of its prerogatives. A widening of our electoral scheme, great facilities to commerce, and the rescue of our Roman Catholic fellow-subjects from the Puritanic yoke, from fetters which have been fastened on them by English parliaments, in spite of the protests and exertions of English sovereigns ; these were the three great elements and fundamental truths of the real Pitt system—a system founded on the traditions of our monarchy, and caught from the writings, the speeches, the councils, of those who, for the sake of these and analogous benefits, had ever been anxious that the 'Sovereign of England should never be degraded into the position of a Venetian Doge. It is in the plunder of the Church that we must seek for the primary cause of our political exclusion and our commercial restraint. That unhallowed booty created a factitious aristocracy, ever fearful that they might be called upon to re-gorge their sacrilegious spoil. To prevent this, they took refuge in political religionism, and paltering with the disturbed consciences or the pious fantasies of a portion of the people, they organized themselves into religious sects. These became the unconscious Prætorians of their ill-gotten domains. At the head of these religionists, they have continued ever since to govern, or powerfully to influence, this country. They have in that time pulled down thrones and churches, changed dynastics, abrogated and remodelled parliaments; they have disfranchised Scotland and confiscated Ireland. One may admire the vigour and consistency of the Whig Party, and recognise in their career that unity of purpose that can only spring from a great principle ; but the Whigs introduced sectarian religion, sectarian religion led to political exclusion, and political exclusion was soon accompanied by commercial restraint.

But even the Government, which was led in one House by Mr. Canning and Sir Robert Peel, and supported in the other by the splendid reputation, ripe sagacity, and disinterested patriotism of the Duke of Wellington, was not equal to the occasion :—

This Ministry, strong in the confidence of the Sovereign, the Parliament, and the people, might, by the courageous promulgation of great historical truths, have gradually formed a public opinion that would have permitted them to organize the Tory Party on a broad, a permanent, and national basis. They might have nobly effected a complete settlement of Ireland, which a shattered section of this very Cabinet was forced a few years after to do partially, and in an equivocating and equivocal manner. They might have concluded a satisfactory reconstruction of the third estate, without producing that convulsion with which, from its violent fabrication, our social system still vibrates. Lastly, they might have adjusted the rights and properties of our national industries in a manner which would have prevented that fierce and fatal rivalry that is now disturbing every hearth of the United Kingdom. We may, therefore, visit on the *lâches* of this Ministry the introduction of that new principle and power into our constitution which ultimately may absorb all—agitation. This Cabinet, then, with so much brilliancy on its surface, is the real parent of the Roman Catholic Association, the political unions, and the Anti-Corn Law League.

Next comes the Tamworth Manifesto, the account of which is made the vehicle for a description of Conservatism which, as has been already pointed out, contrasts strangely with his opinion of it in 1835, just after that document had been published.

> Conservatism assumes in theory that everything established should be maintained; but adopts in practice that everything that is established is indefensible. To reconcile this theory and this practice, they produce what they call "the best bargain"; some arrangement which has no principle and no purpose, except to obtain a temporary lull of agitation, until the mind of the Conservatives, without a guide and without an aim, distracted, tempted, and bewildered, is prepared for another arrangement, equally statesman-like with the preceding one. Conservatism was an attempt to carry on affairs by substituting the fulfilment of the duties of office for the performance of the functions of government; and to maintain this negative system by the mere influence of property, reputable private conduct, and what are called good connections. Conservatism discards Prescription, shrinks from Principle, disavows Progress; having rejected all respect for Antiquity, it offers no redress for the Present, and makes no preparation for the Future.

Two years afterwards Coningsby leaves school, and during an excursion in the long vacation through the Midland counties, falls in with Sidonia. He meets him at an inn in a forest, where both take refuge from a thunderstorm—all the elements of romance combining to lend an interest to the interview—and that day is a turning point in Coningsby's career. The stranger—a Jew of the purest race, and a complete citizen of the world—knows everything, has been everywhere, and has seen everybody; a colossal capitalist, and the resource of half the statesmen in Europe in their pecuniary difficulties, he is acquainted with the inner life of all the Continental Governments, looks on all institutions with a calm, unprejudiced eye, and notes their merits and defects in the tone of an unconcerned spectator. The first thing which Coningsby learns from him is the "influence of the individual," and then that "the history of Heroes is the history of Youth."

They meet again soon afterwards at Coningsby Castle, the seat of Lord Monmouth in the North, where Sidonia gives his pupil some further lessons in history, politics, and ethnology, and teaches him that theory of the Jewish race, which took the world as much by surprise as the theory of the British Constitution.

Coningsby goes up to Cambridge bent upon " conquering knowledge," and with the foundation to build upon with which Sidonia had supplied him, he was soon equal to the task of opening the minds of his companions. The following is his first letter to Buckhurst, Lord Vere, and Lord Henry Sydney :—

I repeat it [said Coningsby], the great object of the Whig leaders in England, from the first movement under Hampden to the last more successful one in 1688, was to establish in England a high aristocratic republic, on the model of the Venetian, then the study and admiration of all speculative politicians. Read Harrington, turn over Algernon Sydney, and you will see how the minds of the English leaders in the seventeenth century were saturated with the Venetian type. And they at length succeeded ; William III. found them out. He told the Whig leaders, " I will not be a Doge." He balanced parties. He baffled them as the Puritans baffled them fifty years before. The reign of Anne was a struggle between the Venetian and the English systems. Two great Whig nobles, Argyle and Somerset, worthy of seats in the Council of Ten, forced their sovereign on her death-bed to change the Ministry. They accomplished their object ; they brought in a new family on their own terms. George I. was a Doge, George II. was a Doge ; they were what William III., a great man, would not be. George III. tried not to be a Doge, but it was impossible materially to resist the deeply-laid combination. He might get rid of the Whig magnificoes, but he could not rid himself of the Venetian constitution. And a Venetian constitution did govern England, from the accession of the House of Hanover till 1832. Now, I do not ask you here to relinquish the political tenets which in ordinary times would have been your inheritance. All I say is, the constitution introduced by your ancestors having been subverted by their descendants your contemporaries, beware of still holding Venetian principles of government when you have not a Venetian constitution to govern with.

Coningsby goes to see his friend Milbank at Oxford, and his theme is still the same, the degradation of the Monarchy and the Church, the transitory character of the settlement of 1832, and the possibility of finding in the Crown a cure for "the moral and material disorganization" which society presents. For this purpose, says Coningsby—

I would accustom the public mind to the contemplation of an existing though torpid power in the constitution, capable of removing our social grievances were we to transfer to it those prerogatives which the Parliament has gradually usurped and used in a manner which has produced the present material and moral disorganization. The House of Commons is the house of a few; the Sovereign is the sovereign of all. The proper leader of the people is the individual who sits upon the throne.

Representation is not necessarily, or even in a principal sense, parliamentary. Parliament is not sitting at this moment, and yet the nation is represented in its highest as well as in its most minute interests. Not a grievance escapes notice and redress. I see in the newspaper this morning that a pedagogue has brutally chastised his pupil. It is a fact known over all England. We must not forget that a principle of government is reserved for our days, that we shall not find in our Aristotle, or even in the forests of Tacitus, nor in our Saxon Wittenagemotes nor in our Plantagenet parliaments. Opinion now is supreme, and Opinion speaks in print. The representation of the Press is far more complete than the representation of Parliament. Parliamentary representation was the happy device of a ruder age, to which it was admirably adapted—an age of semi-civilization, when there was a leading class in the community—but it exhibits many symptoms of desuetude. It is controlled by a system of representation more vigorous and comprehensive, which absorbs its duties and fulfils them more efficiently, and in which discussion is pursued on fairer terms, and often with more depth and information.

If we are forced to revolutionise, let us propose to our consideration the idea of a free monarchy established on fundamental laws, itself the apex of a vast pile of municipal and local government ruling an educated people, represented by a free and intellectual press. Before such a royal authority, supported by such a national opinion, the sectional anomalies of our country would disappear.

The future fortunes of Coningsby himself we shall

refer to at a later stage. But from the above extracts the reader will be able to discern for himself the nature of the political system which was recommended in the pages of *Coningsby,* as a cure for the social chaos and disintegration which had followed the Reform Bill of 1832. That subsequent events have justified a good deal of the language which fifty years ago was thought fantastic, and even puerile, will hardly be denied. The House of Commons has certainly not risen in public opinion since *Coningsby* first saw the light. Many of the problems therein referred to have only increased in intensity within the last half century. *Coningsby,* therefore, has quite lived down the charges originally brought against it of having been written exclusively for effect without any regard to sober reality, or probability. What was then despised, ridiculed, and made a butt for the sarcasms of every fifth-rate political hack who trod the pavement of Pall Mall has actually come to pass. Toryism has appealed to the people, and appealed with success; the degeneracy of the House of Commons is admitted and lamented by all parties; the restoration to local jurisdictions of many of the powers which Parliament has absorbed into itself is the acknowledged remedy. And if the progress of events has not strengthened the prerogative of the Crown, it has made the " individual" more powerful, for a modern Prime Minister with a party majority at his back is much more absolute now than he was before the Reform Bill.

Coningsby was published in the spring of 1844, and for a time nothing else was talked about. Many years afterwards Mr. Croker pretended that he had never heard of *Coningsby.* Let those believe it who will. The book contained several striking portraits,

but the most striking of all was Rigby. John Wilson
Croker was Rigby, Lord Henry Sydney was Lord John
Manners, Buckhurst was Bailie Cochrane, Eustace
Lyle, Ambrose Philips. Coningsby was George Smythe.
Beaumanoir, of course, was Belvoir. But of all the portraits in the gallery Rigby was *facile princeps*. The
likeness was recognised at once. Whatever might
be thought of the charges of meanness and base-
ness brought against him, there were some qualities
assigned to him about which there could be no mistake.
His love of contradiction and dictation, his determination
to be always in the right, and to allow no one to be right
except himself, were too well known for anyone acquainted with the original to doubt for a moment who
Rigby was. The Duke of Wellington, whose intimacy
with Croker never cooled, said that he once tried to
prove to him that he did not know the difference between
a scarp and a counterscarp. This story by itself is
sufficient to prove that Rigby was no exaggeration.

The clubs rang with the inimitable satire. In every
house in the country which pretended to any interest
in either politics, literature, or fashion, the book lay
upon the table. Have you read *Coningsby*? was the
stock question which people asked each other at dinner
parties. And then for Mr. Croker to pretend some
years afterwards that he had never heard of *Coningsby*
is too heavy a tax on our credulity.

But, as types distinct from individuals, the palm is
borne off by the two brothers-in-arms, Tadpole and
Taper; the two political underlings, half hacks, half
adventurers, employed to do the dirty work of the
party, and trusted to some extent in consequence;
members of the Carlton, received in society, and rather
courted than otherwise by noble and wealthy outsiders,

but the incarnation of all that is lowest and meanest in public life, mistaking dodges for statesmanship, and party slang for the vocabulary of political wisdom.

But only half of what Disraeli had in his mind when he undertook the exposure of Peelite Conservatism was completed by the publication of *Coningsby*. In *Coningsby* we have laid before us the history of English Parties, and its effect upon the Monarchy and the Church. We are now to advance a step farther and observe its effect upon the people. He had only touched the fringe of the labour question in *Coningsby*. Henry Sydney and his Maypoles, Eustace Lyle and his doles, were only little prettinesses, which did not pretend to go to the root of the matter. In *Sybil* he struck a deeper note.

On the 30th of August 1844, he writes to his sister that Manchester has invited him to take the chair at its literary meeting. He accepted the invitation, and took the opportunity thus afforded him of making a tour through the manufacturing districts, and inspecting the working of the factory system with his own eyes. He was accompanied by Lord John Manners and the Hon. George Smythe, and the speeches which they delivered at Manchester and at Bingley, in Yorkshire, were republished in 1885, under the title of *Young England*. On the title page we read—"As attempts are being made to persuade the new electors that small farms, allotments, and opportunities for physical and mental recreation are new inventions of the new Birmingham school of Socialistic politicians, it has been thought well to republish this little volume exactly as it appeared 40 years ago." No editor's name appears on the title page. But we can scarcely be wrong in assigning that office to Lord John Manners himself.

Near the town of Bingley, Mrs. Ferrand had recently established some allotments for the benefit of operatives, and it was in reference to these that Lord John Manners spoke some forty-three years ago, in support of those views which the Radicals have since stolen from the Tories, and in which many of the Tories themselves do not recognise their ancient inheritance. But it is chiefly in connection with Mr. Disraeli's observations on the state of factory labour that this visit will be remembered, although his description of " war to the cottage," in the pages of his second great political novel, is inferior only to the vivid picture which he has drawn of the cellars and garrets, the " butties" and the " Tommy shops," of our great mining and manufacturing capitals.

The " degradation of the people," then, is the theme of *Sybil*, and in it Mr. Disraeli discovers that palliation of Chartism which he had glanced at in his speech of 1839. Sybil Gerard is the daughter of an operative, but both father and daughter are exceptional members of the class. Gerard is the descendant of an ancient family, which has gradually sunk into the ranks of labour, but still retains its traditions, and the hope of regaining its estates. He is a manly, generous, good-hearted Radical of the Cobbett type, and leader of the physical force section of the Chartists. He earns excellent wages at a mill which is conducted on exceptionally humane and kindly principles, and he and his daughter live in a cottage outside the town, quite above the reach of poverty. They are Roman Catholics, and Sybil, young, beautiful, and highly educated by the Abbess of a neighbouring convent, is destined for the veil, as it is totally impossible she could marry in her own station of life. When Sybil, we suppose, is about eighteen, she accidentally makes the acquaintance of Charles

Egremont, the brother of Lord Marney, the owner of large estates in the neighbourhood, and one of the worst specimens of the worst class of English aristocracy, a cynical and selfish utilitarian, whose character is Disraeli's masterpiece. Charles Egremont, however, is of a very different mould. He is so struck with the conversation of Gerard, who tells him at their first meeting that the Queen reigns over " two nations, the Rich and the Poor," that he resolves to see more of the people ; assumes the character of a journalist unattached, and takes lodgings near the town of Mowbray. The rest may easily be imagined. Egremont falls in love with Sybil, and Sybil and Gerard between them almost convert Egremont. The reader now knows enough to understand the following extracts. Sybil and Egremont meet upon an errand of charity, the latter accompanied by the clergyman of the parish, Mr. St. Lys :—

" You feel deeply for the people," said Egremont, looking at her earnestly.

"And do you not? Your presence here assures me of it," said Sybil. " When I remember what the English people once was ; the truest, the freest, and the bravest, the best natured and the best looking, the happiest and most religious race upon the surface of this globe, and think of them now, with all their crimes and all their slavish sufferings, their soured spirits and their stunted forms, their lives without enjoyment and their deaths without hope, I may well feel for them, even if I were not the daughter of their blood."

After Egremont has become intimate with the Gerards, their conversation generally turns on these subjects. Gerard tells his friend that England is still divided between the conquerors and the conquered :—

" But do not you think," said Egremont, "that such a distinction has long ceased to exist ? "

"In what degree?" asked Gerard. " Many circumstances of oppression have doubtless gradually disappeared ; but that has arisen from the change of manners, not from any political recognition of

4 *

their injustice. The same course of time which has removed many *enormities*, more shocking, however, to our feelings than to those who devised and endured them, has simultaneously removed many alleviating circumstances. If the mere baron's grasp be not so ruthless, the champion we found in the Church is no longer so ready. The spirit of conquest has adapted itself to the changing circumstances of ages ; and however its results vary in form, in degree they are much the same."

" But how do they show themselves ? "

" In many circumstances, which concern many classes ; but I speak of those which touch my own order, and therefore I say at once, in the degradation of the people."

" But are the people so degraded ? "

" There is more serfdom in England now than at any time since the Conquest. I speak of what passes under my daily eyes when I say that those who labour can as little choose or change their masters now, as when they were born thralls. There are great bodies of the working classes of this country nearer to the condition of brutes than they have been at any time since the Conquest. Indeed, I see nothing to distinguish them from brutes except that their morals are inferior. Incest and infanticide are as common among them as among the lower animals. The domestic principle wanes weaker and weaker every year in England ; nor can we wonder at it when there is no comfort to cheer and no sentiment to hallow the home."

" I was reading a work the other day," said Egremont, " that statistically proved that the general condition of the people was much better at this moment than it had been at any known period of history."

" Ah ! yes. I know that style of speculation," said Gerard. " Your gentleman who reminds you that a working man has now a pair of cotton stockings, and that Harry the Eighth himself was not as well off. At any rate, the condition of classes must be judged of by the age, and by their relation with each other. One need not dwell on that. I deny the premises. I deny that the condition of the main body is better now than at any other period of our history ; that it is as good as it has been at several. I say, for instance, the people were better clothed, better lodged, and better fed just before the War of the Roses than they are at this moment. We know how an English peasant lived in those times ; he ate flesh every day, he never drank water, was well housed, and clothed in stout woollens. Nor are the chronicles necessary to tell us this. The Acts of Parliament, from the Plantagenets to the Tudors, teach us alike the price of provisions and the rate of wages ; and we see in a moment that the wages of those days brought as much sustenance and comfort as a reasonable man could desire."

"I know how deeply you feel upon this subject," said Egremont, turning to Sybil.

"Indeed it is the only subject that ever engages my thought," she replied, "except one."

"And that one?"

"Is to see the people once more kneel before our Blessed Lady," replied Sybil.

As the views expressed in this passage were much ridiculed when they first appeared, we would refer the reader to an authority that will be allowed to be unimpeachable : the Report, namely, of the Commission for Enquiry into the Employment of Women and Children in Agriculture, in which the connection of the peasantry with the land and their physical condition is traced from the earliest times down to the present date. The Blue-book of 1868 fully corroborates the novel of 1845, and shows that in this as in many other particulars, both in *Coningsby* and *Sybil*, which have been called in question, Mr. Disraeli's statements were founded on accurate knowledge.

We must now suppose the Chartist movement to have reached its height. The petition has been presented and rejected, and the people are represented as feeling that they have nothing more to hope for from either Party. "Once," says the author, "it was otherwise"—

once the people recognised a Party in the State whose principles identified them with the rights and privileges of the multitude; but when they found the parochial constitution of the country sacrificed without a struggle, and a rude assault made on all local influences in order to establish a severely-organized centralisation, a blow was given to the influence of the priest and of the gentleman, the ancient champions of the people against arbitrary courts and rapacious parliaments, from which they will find that it requires no ordinary courage and wisdom to recover.

In *Sybil* the political views of *Coningsby* are repeated and enforced by fresh arguments; and in the concluding pages the aims of both are thus expressed :—

And thus I conclude the last page of a work which, though its form be light and unpretending, would yet aspire to suggest to its readers some considerations of a very opposite character. A year ago I presumed to offer to the public some volumes that aimed at calling their attention to the state of our political parties, their origin, their history, their present position. In an age of political infidelity, of mean passions, and faulty thoughts, I would have impressed upon the rising race not to despair, but to seek in a right understanding of the history of their country, and in the energies of heroic youth, the elements of national welfare. The present work advances another step in the same emprise. From the state of parties, it now would draw public thought to the state of the people whom those parties for two centuries have governed. The comprehension and the cure of this greater evil depend upon the same agencies as the first; it is the past alone that can explain the present, and it is youth that alone can mould the remedial future. The written history of our country for the last ten reigns has been a mere phantasm, giving to the origin and consequence of public transactions a character and colour in every respect dissimilar to their natural form and hue. In this mighty mystery all thoughts and things have assumed an aspect and title contrary to their real quality and style; Oligarchy has been called Liberty; an exclusive Priesthood has been christened a National Church; Sovereignty has been the title of something that has had no dominion, while absolute power has been wielded by those who profess themselves the servants of the People. In the selfish strife of factions two great existences have been blotted out of the history of England, the Monarch and the Multitude; as the power of the Crown has diminished the privileges of the People have disappeared, till at length the sceptre has become a pageant, and its subject has degenerated again into a serf. It is nearly fourteen years ago, in the popular frenzy of a mean and selfish revolution, which emancipated neither the Crown nor the People, that I first took the occasion to intimate, and then to develop, to the first assembly of my countrymen that I ever had the honour to address, these convictions. They have been misunderstood, as is ever for a season the fate of Truth, and they have obtained for their promulgator much misrepresentation, as must ever be the lot of those who will not follow the beaten track of a fallacious custom. But Time, that brings all things, has brought also to the mind of England some suspicion that the idols they have so long worshipped, and the oracles that have so long deluded them, are not the true ones. There is a whisper rising in this country that Loyalty is not a phrase, Faith not a delusion, and Popular Liberty something more diffusive and substantial than the profane exercise of the sacred rights of Sovereignty by political classes. That we may live to see England once more possess a free monarchy and a privileged and prosperous people is my prayer; that these great consequences can only be brought about by the energy and devotion of our youth is my persuasion. We live in an age when to be young and to be indifferent can be no longer synonymous. We must prepare for the coming hour. The claims of the Future are represented by suffering millions; and the youth of a nation are the trustees of Posterity.

I have given copious extracts from these two novels because I desired that the author should speak for himself. What he intended to convey is clear enough; how far he thought it practical is a separate question.

Sybil was published—appropriately—on May Day 1845, and was dedicated to "a perfect wife." It attracted little less attention than *Coningsby*, and was welcomed by the High Church party as an important contribution to their literature. Lord Ashley, too, and the promoters of the Factory Acts recognised a powerful auxiliary in the hand that drew Hell House Yard, Diggs's Tommy Shop, Devil's Dust, and the lodgings of Warner, the hand-loom weaver. Henceforth Mr. Disraeli was everywhere recognised as the leader of a political and social revival which did not allow that the laws of political economy were necessarily, at all times and all places and under all circumstances, of paramount and absolute authority.

In what form, or under what conditions, he contemplated the realisation of the political ideal sketched out at this period it is impossible to say. But it is quite certain that in *Coningsby* and *Sybil*, where he pushes these views to the farthest point to which he ever carried them, he was not contemplating democracy. He was fond of using the word democracy to denote a class—not a form of government; and he generally seems to have meant by it the people in their political capacity; the people invested with political rights; and regarded as a political force. But that they should be supreme—*ut plurimum plurimi valeant*—was never his intention for a moment. We can only approach his meaning by generalising from a large number of statements published in various shapes and uttered at various times. We were to have a monarchy with real powers and prerogatives for daily use. The Sovereign was not only to reign, but to govern. Nor did his speculations point in the direction of a democratic despotism, for equally important, in his eyes, with the revival of the Monarchy and the Church, was the maintenance of our "territorial constitution," and the authority and jurisdiction of the gentry, a system incompatible with despotism in any form. In his later years he seems to have seen that one-half of this scheme, the revival of prerogative, was for the present, at all events, unattainable; and this conviction must have modified his views upon the other parts of the system which constituted the Young England creed. The extension of popular functions was to be balanced by the extension of monarchical authority. Unless the two could be combined he would, perhaps, have recommended neither. But if the first should become inevitable, as it did after Lord John Russell re-opened the Reform Question, then, in the absence of the second, we must do the best we could with our existing materials, and not disdain even the help of the oligarchy to preserve the balance of the constitution. At the cost of anticipating events we may be allowed, perhaps, at this point, to quote his speech of 1873, as showing more clearly than any other passage to which we can refer, the degree in which, at the age of sixty-eight, he still clung to his original convictions, and the form which they had taken in his mind, after thirty years' experience of progress.

I believe that the Tory Party at the present time occupies the most satisfactory position which it has held since the days of its greatest statesmen, Mr. Pitt and Lord Grenville. It has divested itself of those excrescences which are not indigenous to its native growth, but which in a time of long prosperity were the consequence partly of negligence, and partly, perhaps, in a certain degree, of ignorance of its traditions. We are now emerging from the fiscal period in which almost all the public men of this generation have been brought up. All the questions of Trade and Navigation, of the Incidence of Taxation, and of Public Economy, are settled. But there are other questions not less important, and of deeper and higher reach and range, which must soon engage the attention of the country: the attributes of a constitutional monarchy—whether the aristocratic principle should be recognised in our Constitution, and, if so, in what form? Whether the Commons of England shall remain an estate of the realm, numerous but privileged, and qualified; or whether they should degenerate into an indiscriminate multitude? Whether a National Church shall be maintained; and if so, what shall be its rights and duties? The functions of corporations, the sacredness of endowments, the tenure of landed property, the free disposal, and even the existence of any kind of property, all those institutions, and all those principles which have made this country free and famous, and conspicuous for its union of order with liberty, are now impugned, and in due time will become great and burning questions.

These may fitly be called the last words of Young England; and they breathe a spirit of Conservatism which thirty years' experience had shown to be a necessary element even of the most popular Toryism.

In spite of Mr. Disraeli's attack upon Ritualism at a later period of his life, there was much in common between the Anglican revival and Young England; *Antiquam exquirite matrem* was the motto of each. Both originated in the same source, the political and religious latitudinarianism which followed the revolution consummated in 1832, as they follow all revolutions. Each aimed at a revival of faith, by setting up before the people a better system than the one which had collapsed, and recalling to their minds what had been the essential principles of the Church of England in the seventeenth, and of the Tory party in the eighteenth, century; and the work in which Newman explains his own conception of the attempt in which he was engaged, might serve, *mutatis mutandis*, for an epitome of Mr. Disraeli's. "It remains to be tried," wrote Newman, in 1837, "whether, what is called Anglo-Catholicism—the religion of Andrews, Laud, Hammond, Butler and Wilson—is capable of being professed, acted on, and maintained on a large sphere of action; or whether it be a mere modification of a transition state of either Romanism or popular Protestantism." So, in 1843, it remained to be tried—so, at least, thought Young England—whether the Toryism of the patriot King was capable of being professed, acted on, and maintained on a large sphere of action; or whether it was a mere modification of either Absolutism or Venetianism. That the experiment has left a real and lasting impression on English politics, will be allowed, though its influence has been much more indirect and imperceptible than that of the Anglican movement; and that it sprang from some want of which modern society was only half conscious, may fairly be inferred from the fact that between Disraeli and Carlyle there is a fundamental agreement in principle. The "individual" of the one is only "the hero" of the other.

CHAPTER IV.

SIR ROBERT PEEL AND FREE TRADE.

1845-52.

First direct attack on Peel—The Post Office scandal—Debate on
agricultural distress—Tour on the Continent—Disraeli's economical policy—Fall of Peel's administration—Visit to Belvoir
Castle—Disraeli leader of the Opposition—Reconstruction of the
Conservative party—Speech on the Burdens upon Land—Success
of Disraeli's tactics—Social incidents—The *Life of Lord George
Bentinck*—The first Derby ministry—Bitterness of the Opposition
—Successes of the Government—The London Press—Result of
the general election—The Budget—Defeat of the Government.

I HAVE referred to Mr. Disraeli's speech on the Irish
Arms Bill in 1843, when he wondered why the descendants of the Cavaliers should persist in governing Ireland on the principles of the Puritans. In February
1844, he spoke on Ireland again, when he uttered the
memorable words, " An absentee aristocracy, an alien
church, and a starving population—that is the Irish
question." But it was in June 1844 that he made his
first direct attack upon Sir Robert Peel, and began the

battle, the wounds inflicted in which have scarcely healed yet.

The speech of the 17th of June was on the Sugar Duties. In the same session Ministers had been beaten on a motion of Lord Ashley's, and Sir Robert had compelled the House to rescind its vote. They were beaten a second time on the Sugar Duties by Mr. Mills, when the House was again condemned to a similar act of self-abasement. Disraeli now reminded Sir Robert of what he had said in 1841, namely, that he had never joined in the anti-slavery cry, and would not then join in the cheap sugar cry. He had now, said the speaker, joined in both, but there was one place where his ancient predilections were still allowed full play, and that was on the benches just behind him. "There the gang is still assembled, and there the thong of the whip still sounds."

The next session, 1845, was an eventful one. It began with the famous "Post Office Scandal," and included a great debate on agricultural distress, and another on the Maynooth Grant. Mr. Disraeli spoke on all three, but it was rather to the conduct of Sir Robert Peel than to the merits of the question that he addressed himself in each case. In the previous year a complaint had been made to Parliament that the letters of Mazzini and others had been opened at the General Post Office by order of the Home Secretary. A committee of inquiry was appointed, but their report was considered so unsatisfactory, that in 1845 Mr. T. Duncombe, who had moved for the first committee, moved for another. The motion was defeated by a large majority, and he then returned to the charge by demanding the production of the Post Office books. He was again beaten. But Mr. Disraeli supported him on both occasions, and reproached the Prime Minister with making a party question of what had nothing to do with party. Some ministers, he said, might be excused for acting in this manner. One who had a very small majority, or none at all, might think it necessary to exact strict obedience. But Sir Robert Peel might be more indulgent. He occupied an impregnable position. He had no need of a coalition. He had got his own majority behind him, and he had appropriated the principles of the Opposition. "The Right Honourable gentleman had caught the Whigs bathing and walked away with their clothes." He had nothing to fear from either side. He had the votes of one and the principles of the other. The sarcasm has always seemed to me to have been rather dragged in by the head and shoulders; but at the time it was irresistible.

About a fortnight afterwards, on the 17th of March, followed the debate on Agricultural Distress. It was moved by Mr. Mills " that in the application of surplus revenue towards relieving the burdens of the country, due regard should be had to the necessity of affording relief to the agricultural interest." In his speech on this occasion, Mr. Disraeli was delivered of one of the most finished and pointed satires which ever fell from his lips. Referring to Sir Robert's change of tone towards the agricultural interest, he said :—

There is no doubt a difference in the right honourable gentleman's demeanour as Leader of the Opposition and as Minister of the Crown. But that's the old story; you must not contrast too strongly the hours of courtship with the years of possession. 'Tis very true that the right honourable gentleman's conduct is different. I remember him making his protection speeches. They were the best speeches I ever heard. It was a great thing to hear the right honourable say, " I would rather be the leader of the gentlemen of

England than possess the confidence of sovereigns." That was a grand thing. We don't hear much of the "gentlemen of England" now. But what of that? They have the pleasures of memory, the charm of reminiscences. They were his first love, and though he may not kneel to them now as in the hour of passion, still they can recall the past; and nothing is more useless or unwise than these scenes of crimination and reproach, for we know that in all these cases, when the beloved object has ceased to charm, it is in vain to appeal to the feelings. You know that this is true. Every man, almost, has gone through it. My honourable friends reproach the right honourable gentleman. The right honourable gentleman does what he can to keep them quiet; he sometimes takes refuge in arrogant silence, and sometimes he treats them with haughty frigidity; and if they knew anything of human nature, they would take the hint and shut their mouths. But they won't. And what then happens? What happens under all such circumstances? The right honourable gentleman being compelled to interfere, sends down his valet, who says in the genteelest manner, "We can have no whining here!" And that, Sir, is exactly the case of the great agricultural interest—that beauty which everybody wooed, and one deluded. There is a fatality in such charms, and we now seem to approach the catastrophe of her career. Protection appears to be in about the same condition that Protestantism was in 1828. The country will draw its moral. For my part, if we are to have Free Trade, I, who honour genius, prefer that such measures should be proposed by the honourable member for Stockport (Mr. Cobden) than by one who, through skilful parliamentary manœuvres, has tampered with the generous confidence of a great people, and of a great party. For myself, I care not what may be the result. Dissolve, if you please, the Parliament you have betrayed, and appeal to the people, who, I believe, mistrust you. For me there remains this, at least, the opportunity of expressing thus publicly my belief that a Conservative Government is an organized hypocrisy.

The valet was Mr. Sidney Herbert, and the sting was never either forgotten or forgiven.

Disraeli's opposition to the Maynooth Grant, according to his own statement, broke up the Young England party, but his speech on the second reading is remarkable rather for an excursus on Party government than for any views which it contains on the question of Roman Catholic endowment. He warns Sir Robert

Peel that he is breaking up the system of Party, and that the destruction of Party means the destruction of Parliamentary government. There was plenty to be said, he added, against the Party system, only he cautioned the House not to undermine it with their eyes shut, and without seeing what they were about. The breach between the minister and the able and audacious mutineer who was rapidly forming a party of his own was now complete, and when, in the following year Sir Robert abandoned Protection altogether, even those who had condemned Mr. Disraeli's personalities were compelled to acknowledge his foresight.

In the autumn of 1845, Mr. Disraeli went abroad again, and took a house for a month or two at Cassel, where he found bad accommodation but a fine country and excellent cookery. "Our cook," he wrote to his sister, " stews pigeons in the most delicious way ; eggs, cloves, and onions in a red brown sauce, a dish of the time of the Duke of Alva." He returned by Paris in December, when he had an audience of the King and Queen, and met Washington Irving, whom he thought vulgar and stupid. It was while he was at Paris that he heard of the Ministerial crisis in England, and as the letters to his sister break off at this point, we presume he lost no time in returning to the scene of action.

There is here a gap in the correspondence, which, with one exception, extends to the beginning of 1848, and we must now turn to the *Life of Lord George Bentinck* for Mr. Disraeli's own version of the great Free Trade struggle. This book was not published till 1852. But we must avail ourselves of its contents in tracing the career of Mr. Disraeli, through the two momentous years which intervene between the autumn of 1846 and the autumn of 1848. Not that we need linger on them very long. Disraeli took up the position from the first, not that Free Trade was in the abstract indefensible, for his great heroes, Bolingbroke, Shelburne, and Pitt had been Free Traders, but that Sir Robert Peel had first of all betrayed his party and afterwards insulted it; had violated the understanding on which he had been placed in power, and then reproached and derided his followers for adhering to the lessons which he himself had taught them. It is true that Disraeli was opposed then, and was opposed to the last, to the unconditional system of Free Trade which was preached by the Anti-Corn Law League, and which had for its avowed object the transfer of political power from the territorial to the commercial aristocracy. But the purely economic aspects of the question he always thought of secondary importance. To understand his views fully we must go back to his earlier speeches. Even in 1843 he told his constituents at Shrewsbury: "Your corn laws are only the outwork of a great system, fixed and established upon your territorial property; and the only object the Leaguers have, in making themselves masters of the outwork, is that they may easily overcome the citadel." On the 20th February 1846, on the proposal to go into Committee of the whole House to consider the question of the Corn Laws, he said :—

I know that we have been told, and by one who, on this subject, should be the highest authority, that we shall derive from this great struggle not merely the repeal of the Corn Laws, but the transfer of power from one class to another—to one distinguished for its intelligence and wealth—the manufacturers of England.

And it was against this transfer that he always took up his parable.

I repeat what I have repeated before, that in this country there are special reasons why we should not only maintain the balance between the two branches of our national industry, but why we should give a preponderance—I do not say a predominance, which was the word ascribed by the honourable member for Manchester to the noble lord the member for London, but which he never used—why we should give a preponderance, for that is the proper and constitutional word, to the agricultural branch And the reason is, because in England we have a territorial constitution. We have thrown upon the land the revenues of the Church, the administration of justice, and the estate of the poor; and this has been done not to gratify the pride, or pamper the luxury, of the proprietors of the land, but because in a territorial constitution you, and those whom you have succeeded, have found the only security for self-government, the only barrier against that centralising system which has taken root in other countries.

The importance of our "territorial constitution" is the key-note of his economical policy. His speeches are full of it. And when Sir Robert Peel said that he would rather be the leader of the country gentlemen of England than possess the confidence of princes, he must have entertained the same high opinion of it as Mr. Disraeli did. Mr. Gladstone has also given us his own version of the uses of a landed aristocracy, and here it is:—

We think that we ought to look forward to bringing about a state of things in which the landlords of Ireland may assume, or may more generally assume, the position which is happily held as a class by landlords in this country—a position marked by residence, by personal familiarity, and by sympathy among the people with whom they live, by long traditional connection handed on from generation to generation, and marked by a constant discharge of duty in every form that can be suggested—be it as to the administration of justice, be it as to the defence of the country, be it as to the supply of social, or or spiritual, or moral, or educational wants; be it for any purpose whatever that is recognised as good or beneficial in a civilised society.*

Whether Protective Duties were necessary to the support of the class whose existence is so beneficial to

* House of Commons, February 17th, 1870. Speech on Irish Land Act.

society is another question, and Mr. Disraeli would
certainly not have insisted on the affirmative. All he
said was that if the Corn Law of 1815 were repealed,
the land must be relieved of those peculiar burdens for
which Protection was supposed to compensate. And
the justice of this view seems now to be admitted by all
parties.

Disraeli's speeches on Free Trade and the Agricultural
interest, extending from January 1846 to February 1851,
are remarkable for their breadth and foresight. He,
from the first, scouted Cobden's idea that the rest of the
world would follow the example of England, pointing
out very pertinently that the rest of the world did not
subordinate every other national consideration to political
economy, and he also uttered a prophecy which thirty
years afterwards he had the gloomy satisfaction of seeing
fulfilled :—

> It may be vain now, in the midnight of their intoxication, to tell
> them that there will be an awakening of bitterness; it may be idle
> now, in the springtide of their economic frenzy, to warn them that
> there may be an ebb of trouble. But the dark and inevitable hour
> will arrive. Then, when their spirit is softened by misfortune, they
> will recur to those principles that made England great, and which,
> in our belief, can alone keep England great. Then, too, perchance,
> they may remember, not with unkindness, those who, betrayed and
> deserted, were neither ashamed nor afraid to struggle for the " good
> old cause "—the cause with which are associated principles the most
> popular, sentiments the most entirely national, the cause of labour,
> the cause of the people—the cause of England.

Mr. Bright said of this speech it was the finest he
had ever heard. It was delivered on the 15th of May
1846, on the third reading of the Corn Importation
Bill, and in the spring of 1879, exactly one generation
afterwards, Lord Beaconsfield was called upon to answer a motion in the House of Lords praying for a

Royal Commission to enquire into the distressed state of agriculture. "The dark and inevitable hour" had at last arrived. But, as he then told his complainants, it was too late. We could not retrace our steps. The country had decided after due deliberation, and by that decision we were bound.

It was at half-past one o'clock on the morning of Friday, June 26, 1846, that the division was taken on the Irish Coercion Bill which put an end to Sir Robert Peel's Administration, and of which so vivid a picture has been left us in the *Life of Lord George Bentinck.*

But it was not merely their numbers that attracted the anxious observation of the Treasury Bench as the Protectionists passed in defile before the Minister to the hostile lobby. It was impossible that he could have marked them without emotion, the flower of that great party which had been so proud to follow one who had been so proud to lead them. They were men to gain whose hearts, and the hearts of their fathers, had been the aim and exultation of his life. They had extended to him an unlimited confidence, and an admiration without stint. They had stood by him in the darkest hour, and had borne him from the depths of political despair to the proudest of living positions. Right or wrong, they were men of honour, breeding, and refinement, high and generous character, great weight and station in the country, which they had ever placed at his disposal. They had been not only his followers but his friends, had joined in the same pastimes, drunk from the same cup, and in the pleasantness of private life had often forgotten together the cares and strife of politics. He must have felt something of this while the Manners, the Somersets, the Bentincks, the Lowthers, and the Lennoxes passed before him. And those country gentlemen, those gentlemen of England, of whom but five years ago the very same building was ringing with his pride of being the leader—if his heart were hardened to Sir Charles Burrell, Sir William Jolliffe, Sir Charles Knightly, Sir John Trollope, Sir Edward Kerrison, Sir John Tyrrell, he surely must have had a pang when his eye rested on Sir John Yarde Buller, his choice and pattern country gentleman, whom he had himself selected and invited but six years back to move a vote of want of confidence in the Whig Government, in order, against the feeling of the Court to install Sir

5 *

Robert Peel in their stead. They trooped on: all the men of metal and large-acred squires whose spirit he had so often quickened, and whose counsel he had so often solicited in his fine Conservative speeches in Whitehall Gardens: Mr. Bankes, with a parliamentary name of two centuries; and Mr. Christopher from that broad Lincolnshire which Protection had created; and the Mileses and the Henleys were there; and the Duncombes, the Liddells, and the Yorkes; and Devon had sent there the stout heart of Mr. Buck, and Wiltshire the pleasant presence of Walter Long. Mr. Newdegate was there, whom Sir Robert had himself recommended to the confidence of the electors of Warwickshire, as one of whom he had the highest hopes; and Mr. Alderman Thompson was there, who, also through Sir Robert's selection, had seconded the assault upon the Whigs, led on by Sir John Buller. But the list is too long, or good names remain behind.

The Government were beaten by a majority of seventy-three. When Sir Robert was told, as he sat upon the Treasury Bench before the numbers were announced, " he did not reply, or even turn his head. He looked very grave and extended his chin, as was his habit when he was annoyed, and cared not to speak. He began to comprehend his position, and that the Emperor was without his army."

During the recess Disraeli paid a visit to the Duke of Rutland at Belvoir Castle, which he seems then to have seen for the first time. On the 10th of August he writes to his sister :—

I thought you would like to have a line from Beaumanoir, though it is not in the least like Beaumanoir, but Coningsby Castle to the very life; gorgeous Gothic of a quarter of a century past, and slopes and shrubberies like Windsor; the general view, however, notwithstanding the absence of the Thames, much finer. Granby and myself arrived here in a fly on Thursday, and were received by two rows of servants, bowing as we passed, which very much reminded me of the arrival of Coningsby himself. Nothing can be more amiable than the family here, agreeable and accomplished besides. George Bentinck went off this morning at dawn, the Duke of Richmond on Saturday. On that day we rode over to Harlaxton Manor, a château of François I.'s time, now erecting by a Mr. Gregory. Yesterday, after the private chapel, we lionised the Castle, which I prefer to Windsor, as the rooms, in proportion to the general edifice, are larger and more magnificent. Afterwards to the Belvoir kennel, which itself required a day.

At the General Election of 1847, Mr. Disraeli, as we have seen, was returned for Buckinghamshire, and in a speech delivered at Aylesbury on the 26th of June, he drew that distinction between Liberal opinions and popular principles, of which his subsequent career afforded many singular illustrations.

For one session Lord George Bentinck, chiefly through the exertions of Disraeli, was the leader of the Protectionist party. But the vote which he gave in 1847 in favour of the Jew Bill cost him his place, or rather evoked remonstrances which led to his resignation of it. Lord Stanley was consulted on the choice of his successor, but refused to interfere, and ultimately, according to Greville, the choice fell upon Lord Granby. But he seems to have been a *roi fainéant*. Lord George Bentinck at the opening of next session took his seat below the gangway, Disraeli still retaining his own on the front Opposition bench ; but the Opposition was in reality " acephalous " as Greville calls it. Throughout this session there was no practical chief. But Disraeli was rapidly showing that there could be only one. On the 20th August he made a speech on Foreign Policy, which even Greville, an unwilling witness, allows to have been a " very brilliant one." Ten days afterwards he spoke again, on the " Labours of the session,' and it was this speech to which he himself always attributed his being invested with the leadership after the death of Lord George Bentinck. This took place in September 1848, and had Lord Granby really been leader, Lord

George's death would have made no difference—would have occasioned no necessity, that is, for choosing a new one. Such however, was its consequence. And on January 1849 the party met for that purpose. Lord Granby himself was one of the first to propose Disraeli. The Duke of Newcastle, the Duke of Richmond, Mr. Miles, and Mr. Bankes, are also named in his letter to his sister, as having urged his qualifications on Lord Stanley. Disraeli himself says "the only awkward thing now is Stanley's position in consequence of his first rash letter." That letter may be conjectured to have been the one which he wrote when applied to the year before on the resignation of Lord G. Bentinck. At page 165 of vol. iii. of the *Croker Papers* is to be found a letter from Lord George Bentinck to Croker, of the date of March 2nd, 1848, from which it might be inferred that Lord Stanley was at that time opposed to the pretensions of Mr. Disraeli. Lord George, after a high encomium on Mr. Disraeli's oratory, records his conviction that, "in spite of Lord Stanley" and others, it will end in Disraeli being leader of the party before two sessions are over. The prediction was fulfilled in less than half the time. And Lord Stanley very soon saw that he was the right man in the right place, and for the remainder of his life never failed on every occasion to do justice to his genius and his character.

In 1849, then, he took his seat in the House of Commons as the acknowledged Leader of the Opposition; and now began his great work—the reconstruction of the Conservative Party. The following is his own account of the steps which he took for that purpose. After the General Election of 1847, the number of supporters on whom the Leader of the Opposition could rely hardly exceeded one hundred and fifty. On his motion on Irish Railways, in 1848, the great trial of strength for the session, Lord George Bentinck only carried a hundred and eighteen members into the lobby with him. But there were still more than a hundred Peelites who belonged to the landed interest, and who, on all subjects but one, were still thorough-going Conservatives. To accustom them to find themselves in the same lobby with their former associates was Disraeli's first object, and he began with a motion for a Select Committee to inquire into the " Burdens upon Land," on the unequal pressure of taxation on the agricultural classes. The existence of considerable distress among the farmers was admitted on both sides of the House. The Peelites, as country gentlemen, were deeply interested in obtaining compensation for their tenantry. Any project of this kind, undarkened by the shadow of Protection, they were bound to support; and when the division took place it justified Mr. Disraeli's foresight, as it gave him an increase of forty votes over the best division which the Conservatives had to show since the dissolution. The speech which he made upon this occasion is perhaps the most truly eloquent of all his great speeches on the subject. It breathes what are rarely found together, genuine feeling combined with brilliant rhetoric.

The agriculturists [he said] have not forgotten that they have been spoken of in terms of contempt by Ministers of State—ay, even by a son of one of their greatest houses : a house that always loves the land, and that the land still loves. They have not forgotten that they have been held up to public odium and reprobation by triumphant demagogues. They have not forgotten that their noble industry, which in the old days was considered the invention of gods and the occupation of heroes, has been stigmatised and denounced as an incubus upon English enterprise. They have not forgotten that even the very empire that was created by the valour and the devotion of their fathers has been held up to public hatred, as a cumbersome and ensanguined machinery, only devised to pamper the luxury and feed the rapacity of our territorial houses.

You think that you may trust their proverbial loyalty. Trust their loyalty, but do not abuse it. Their conduct to you has exhibited no hostile feeling, notwithstanding the political changes that have abounded of late years, and all apparently to a diminution of their powers. They have inscribed a homely sentence on their rural banners; but it is one which, if I mistake not, is already again touching the heart and convincing the reason of England—"Live and Let Live."

Your system and theirs are exactly contrary. They invite "union." They believe that national prosperity can only be produced by the prosperity of all classes. You prefer to remain in isolated splendour and solitary magnificence. But, believe me, I speak not as your enemy, when I say that it will be an exception to the principles which seem hitherto to have ruled society, if you can succeed in maintaining the success at which you aim without the possession of that permanence and stability which the territorial principle alone can afford. Although you may for a moment flourish after their destruction— although your ports may be filled with shipping, your factories smoke on every plain, and your forges flame in every city—I see no reason why you should form an exception to that which the page of history has mournfully recorded: that you, too, should not fade like the Tyrian dye, and moulder like the Venetian palaces. But united with the land, you will obtain the best and surest foundation upon which to build your enduring welfare. You will find in that interest a counsellor in all your troubles, in danger your undaunted champion, and in adversity your steady customer. It is to assist in producing this result, Sir, that I am about to place these resolutions in your hands. I wish to see the agriculture, the commerce, and the manufactures of England, not adversaries, but co-mates and partners, and rivals only in the ardour of their patriotism and in the activity of their public spirit.

In the following year, on the 19th of February 1850, he returned to the charge with resolutions recommending a large remission of local taxation. On this occasion he enlisted the support of Mr. Gladstone, and, on a division, the numbers were 273 to 252, a majority of only 21. In 1851, the agricultural distress being acknowledged in the Queen's Speech, Mr. Disraeli on the 11th of February, moved that Ministers should be called on to introduce some remedial measures in conformity with the language which they had advised Her Majesty to employ; and on this occasion the Ministerial majority sank as low as fourteen—267 members following Mr. Disraeli's banner, and 281 the Government. The Opposition strength had now risen from 189 in 1849 to 267 in 1851. Lord John Russell became anxious to escape from a position which was no longer either necessary to the public or creditable to himself, and he seized the opportunity presented by his defeat on the County Franchise question, to place his resignation in Her Majesty's hands. The Queen sent for Lord Derby, who, not without some slur, as it was thought, upon his own colleagues in both Houses, declined to take office, and the Whigs held on for another session.

But Mr. Disraeli had achieved his task. He had raised the Conservative Party from the dust, and restored its energy, its self-respect, and its status in the country as a great political connection. And he had done this under disadvantages such as no other statesman engaged in a similar undertaking had ever experienced before. Sir Robert Peel's reconstruction of the party after 1832 certainly cannot be compared to it. Half the great statesmen whom the country had looked up to for years were his colleagues or confederates. The Church, disgusted by the ecclesiastical policy of the Whigs, was on his side to a man. Popular distress resulting in Chartism, also told against the Government. In 1848 every one of these advantages was on the other side. The experienced Conservative statesmen whom Peel had trained to affairs stood sullenly aloof; a large and influential section of the Church of England believed itself represented by these gentlemen. The agricultural

distress which undoubtedly prevailed at that time made
the victorious interests of the country still more jealous
of Lord Derby. In the teeth of these difficulties,
he had restored to the shattered and dispirited remnant which still called itself the Conservative Party,
something like the dimensions, the cohesion, and the
dignity of a regular Opposition, who were now not
unwilling to try a fall with their opponents, or to
take the judgment of the country on their respective
merits.

In 1850 and 1851 the letters to Sarah Disraeli contain
a good deal of social matter as well as political, that is of
much interest. In January he went again to Belvoir,
where he seems to have witnessed, for the first time, the
spectacle of the hunting-men dining in their red coats.
From Belvoir he went on to Burghley, which he
admired very much. "The exterior of Burghley is
faultless, so vast, and so fantastic, and in such fine
condition, that the masonry seems but of yesterday.
In the midst of a vast park, ancient timber in profu-
fusion, gigantic oaks of the days of the Lord
Treasurer, and an extensive lake. The plate marvellous." By the end of March he was at Hughenden,
where some hitch seems to have occurred in his Parliamentary position. He writes, "If I cannot lead the
party after the holidays, I had better retire altogether."
This probably refers to some obscure party discussion,
which is now forgotten, though no doubt men were
busy at work trying to trip him up during the whole
three years which preceded 1852. In May we find
him at the house of Sir William Jolliffe near Petersfield,
"a beautiful home, and a still more beautiful family
of all ages from three to twenty, and all good-look-
ing."

In September 1850 he receives two immense chests from the Duke of Portland, containing Lord George Bentinck's papers, and in October he has made a good start with the Biography. His letters are dated from Hughenden, and tell of the beautiful autumn, and the gorgeous tints of the beech-woods which girdled his country home.

In January 1851, Lord Stanley, the present Lord Derby, came to stay with him in Buckinghamshire, and found it very charming " after Lancashire." At this time, Mr. and Mrs. Disraeli, oddly enough, kept no horses, and the statesman and his guest had to make their excursion on foot. They visited Great Hampden, Wycombe Abbey, Denner Hill, and other places of interest, and returned to town for the meeting of Parliament in February. In a letter dated February 26th, there is an allusion to the speech of the 11th, which has been already described, coupled with an anecdote of Croker, which reminds one of *Coningsby.* " Croker met me and nearly embraced me. I hardly recognised him. He said the speech was 'the speech of a statesmen, and the reply was the reply of a wit.' How very singular," adds the writer. After the portrait of Mr. Rigby, it certainly was.

The Life of Lord George was published at the end of December 1851, and independently of the great interest attaching to the political career of this very singular man, the work contains a portrait of Sir Robert Peel which has often been thought the painter's masterpiece, and a chapter on the Jews, in which he unfolds the views first propounded in *Coningsby* and *Tancred* with even more precision, more earnestness, and greater power of argument than he places in the mouth of Sidonia. He winds up the character of Peel in the following memorable words :—

One cannot say of Sir Robert Peel, notwithstanding his unrivalled powers of despatching affairs, that he was the greatest minister that this country ever produced, because, twice placed at the helm, and on the second occasion with the Court and the Parliament equally devoted to him, he never could maintain himself in power. Nor, notwithstanding his consummate parliamentary tactics, can he be described as the greatest party leader that ever flourished among us, for he contrived to destroy the most compact, powerful, and devoted party that ever followed a British statesman. Certainly, notwithstanding his great sway in debate, we cannot recognize him as our greatest orator, for in many of the supreme requisites of oratory he was singularly deficient. But what he really was, and what posterity will acknowledge him to have been, is the greatest Member of Parliament that ever lived.

He anticipates the conversion of the Jews, or rather, to use his own words, that they will accept the whole of their religion instead of only the half of it, as they gradually grow more familiar with the true history and character of the New Testament. And he lays great stress on the fact that the non-Christian Jews at the present day are for the most part descendants of the earlier exiles, whose ancestors never heard of Christ till centuries after the crucifixion, when His religion approached them in the guise of a persecution. "It is improbable," he thinks, "that any descendants of the Jews of Palestine exist who disbelieve in Christ." His appeal to men of his own race is an example in his best style :—

Perhaps, too, in this enlightened age, as his mind expands, and he takes a comprehensive view of this period of progress, the pupil of Moses may ask himself whether all the princes of the house of David have done so much for the Jews as that Prince who was crucified on Calvary? Had it not been for Him, the Jews would have been comparatively unknown, or known only as a high Oriental caste which had lost its country. Has not He made their history the most famous in the world? Has not He hung up their laws in every temple? Has not He vindicated all their wrongs? Has not he avenged the victory of Titus and conquered the Cæsars? What successes did they anticipate from their Messiah? The wildest dreams of their rabbis have been far exceeded. Has not Jesus conquered Europe and changed its name into Christendom? All countries that refuse the Cross wither, while the whole of the New World is devoted to the Semitic principle and its most glorious offspring the Jewish faith; and the time will come when the vast communities and countless myriads of America and Australia, looking upon Europe as Europe now looks upon Greece, and wondering how so small a space could have achieved such great deeds, will still find music in the songs of Sion and solace in the parables of Galilee.

Disraeli did not think that Lord George Bentinck would have succeeded as a party leader. Though without vanity, he was remarkable for obstinacy. His mind, he said, had little flexibility. He was no orator, and his early education had not been of a kind to qualify him for Parliamentary distinction. His clear head, his strong memory, his wonderful powers of acquisition, and his undaunted courage and perseverance, made him a very useful leader of the Protectionists in the time of their trials, but would not have been sufficient for the permanent leadership of a party.

In 1852 occurred the famous quarrel between Lord John Russell and Lord Palmerston on the subject of the *Coup d'état*, followed by the retirement of the latter from the Foreign Office. Lord Palmerston did not mince matters. He made no secret of his intention to " have his tit-for-tat with John Russell "—and an opportunity occurring on the Militia Bill, introduced by Government, he put him in a minority and out of office at the same time. Now comes the first Derby Ministry, and a very memorable chapter in Mr. Disraeli's life. The change of Government took place at the end of February, and the new arrangements were very speedily completed.

Mr. Disraeli became Chancellor of the Exchequer and Leader of the House of Commons. His colleagues in the lower House were, with one or two exceptions, men whom he had silently singled out, during the past four or five years, as well qualified for office; nor was his knowledge of human nature at fault. In Mr. Henley and Sir John Pakington especially he found two as able administrators as could be found among the veterans of the Opposition. It was unfortunate that Lord Derby was comparatively unacquainted with the *personnel* of his party in the lower House. It is said that of some of the gentlemen recommended by the leader of that assembly he had never even heard the names. Eleven of them were sworn in Privy Councillors on the same day. And it was owing to this circumstance that Lord Derby always seemed to think it impossible that he could carry on a Government without the help of Mr. Gladstone or Lord Palmerston. His followers were justly mortified, as may be read in the Memoirs of Lord Malmesbury, who now becomes our most trustworthy authority for the Parliamentary history of the period. The new Chancellor of the Exchequer, however, had no such misgivings. He was in the highest spirits, and declared that "he felt like a girl going to her first ball." The new Ministry was constituted as follows:—

First Lord of the Treasury, Earl of Derby.
Lord Chancellor, Lord St. Leonards.
Chancellor of the Exchequer, Mr. Disraeli.
President of Council, Earl of Lonsdale.
Privy Seal, Marquis of Salisbury.
Foreign Secretary, Earl of Malmesbury.
Home Secretary, Mr. Spencer Walpole.
First Lord of the Admiralty, The Duke of Northumberland.

Colonial Secretary, Sir John Pakington.
President of Board of Customs, Mr. Herries.
First Commissioner of Works, Lord John Manners.

These were the Cabinet. Mr. Henley was President of the Board of Control ; and the Law Officers of the Crown were Sir Frederick Thesiger and Sir Fitzroy Kelly.

The new Ministry ought not to have been the object of any special hostility. They had not taken office till it was forced upon them. The previous Administration was not turned out ; it fell to pieces of its own accord. The change was not due to any personal intervention of the Sovereign, as in 1834, or to any stroke of party vengeance, as in 1846. The Ministry of Lord John Russell was too weak to carry on the Government, and nobody was better aware of the fact than Lord John Russell himself. He was even anxious to escape from his position, yet no sooner were the leaders of the Opposition seated on the Treasury Bench than they were assailed by a fire of invective from Whigs, Peelites, and Radicals, as if they had been guilty of some gross breach of Parliamentary morality. Lord Derby, in 1851, had held out the olive branch to Mr. Gladstone. He had, with Mr. Disraeli's consent and approbation, offered the lead of the House of Commons to Lord Palmerston. Neither would join him, though neither could allege any difference of principle between himself and the new Prime Minister, except on the one question of the Corn Laws ; and the possibility of these being revived by two such men as Lord Derby and Mr. Disraeli was too remote to have influenced the minds of any practical man. Their union with the Ministry would have brought the Conservatives the strength which they required. But each, in fact, was playing for his own hand; and they judged, perhaps rightly, that the course of events was likely to bring the ball to their feet under more favourable circumstances than then presented themselves. But this was no excuse for the flood of vituperation poured upon the heads of the new Government by the Opposition and their organs in the press; and when remarks are made on the bitterness of Disraeli's satire, and the cutting irony in which he spoke of some at least of the Peelite leaders, we should do well to remember his provocation. Of the malignity of which he himself was the object, it is difficult to speak, even at this distance of time, with common patience or forbearance. If it is said that he brought it on his own head by his treatment of Sir Robert Peel; the answer is that it is only among savages that the rights of revenge are held to be inexhaustible, and that in all civilised morality there is, so to speak, a statute of limitations, under which the *lex talionis* expires after a certain time. Even with Juno's unrelenting hate Jupiter interferes at last. The more than feminine fury of the Peelites was alike insensible to justice and incapable of satiety; and knowing the splendid position which Lord Beaconsfield afterwards attained, and the love, honour, and troops of friends which attended him to his grave, it is difficult to note the language in which he was spoken of five and thirty years ago, and believe that we are reading of the same man, the same English people, and the same century.

During the early part of the session of 1852, the Government was thought to have done well. They carried a Militia Bill which gave general satisfaction, and Mr. Disraeli astonished the world by the capacity which he displayed as Finance Minister.

On the 30th of April he introduced his first
Budget, which, says Greville, "was a great performance, very able, and received with great applause
in the House." The frank acceptance of the principles of Free Trade which it contained gave offence
to some of his supporters, and was denounced by the
Opposition as an unparalleled act of tergiversation.
But no one who had given any intelligent consideration
to his speeches during the previous twenty years had
any right to be surprised or shocked. He had always
been in favour of Free Trade conducted upon equitable
principles, which the principles of the League were not.
He had quite recently declared that the country having
deliberately endorsed the policy of Sir Robert Peel, the
farmers' friends must look for compensation rather than
restitution.* This was all he said in the Budget. It
was quite open to him to recognise the beneficial effects
of Sir Robert Peel's policy, without either condoning
the means by which it had been carried out, or ignoring
the injustice which it had inflicted on a large and most
important interest. Mr. Disraeli said that this might
be remedied without flinging back the injustice upon
the shoulders of any other class. And the local
taxation reformers of 1888, including men of all parties
in their ranks, are only saying the same thing.

However, Mr. Disraeli had made himself a great
many enemies among the Peelites, who had great
literary talent at their command: and he also had the
Press against him. By far the two most influential
daily papers of that date were the *Times* and the
Morning Chronicle, of which the one was anti-Con-
servative and the other Peelite to the core. The *Morn-*

* Speech in House of Commons, March 8, 1849.

6

ing Post and the *Globe* were Palmerstonian, and the only regular Conservative daily which then existed was the *Morning Herald*, hardly less unfriendly to Mr. Disraeli than any of the other four. Among them he had no chance ; and it is a wonderful tribute to his genius that with these formidable odds against him the battle should have been doubtful for a moment, and that even from a class of adversaries who rarely err on the side of magnanimity he should have extorted, in spite of themselves, a reluctant eulogy.

In July 1852 Parliament was dissolved, and a final appeal was made to the country to decide whether it would continue " to fight hostile tariffs with free imports," or pronounce for what is known as Reciprocity. The Conservative candidates won a great many seats— some because they were Protectionists, others because they were Conservatives, and because the public began to be afraid of Lord John Russell and his new Reform Bill : but they did not win enough, as the sequel will show ; and they had to deal with old Parliamentary hands who knew well how to strike when the iron was hot. They perceived that if the Chancellor could be forced to make his financial statement before the expiration of the year, it would be morally impossible for him not to propose something for the farmers, which, in all proba- bility, they would be able to use against him. What they foresaw came to pass.

Mr. Disraeli always regretted that his Party had been obliged to take office at the particular moment when they did. In another year the agricultural distress which had prompted his great speeches in 1849, 1850, and 1851, would have passed away. Could the dissolution of Parliament have been postponed for another nine months, it would have been unnecessary to say anything about

it, and many Conservative Free Traders would have
given their votes for Lord Derby. Even could the financial statement have been deferred to its usual period,
the month of April 1853, he used to say that a Budget
might have been framed which the House of Commons
would have accepted. But the Opposition saw this as
well as he did, and forced his hand. They professed
the most violent alarm lest the Corn Laws were about
to be revived. The Anti-Corn Law League resumed
its sittings, and assumed something of the functions
and importance of a vigilance committee. The Government were compelled to call Parliament together in
November. Resolutions re-affirming the principles of
Free Trade were flung in the face of the Ministry,
and it became clear to Mr. Disraeli that he had better
declare his financial policy and take his chance, than
provoke a vote of want of confidence, which would
almost certainly have been carried against him, or
lost by so small a majority as to have destroyed the
moral influence of the Goverment.

Accordingly, on the 3rd of December 1852, he produced the Budget, which gave the Opposition their
expected opportunity. Its chief features were—the
remission of half the malt tax; the gradual remission
of half the tea duty; the assessment of income tax on
one third of the farmer's rental instead of one half; the
extension of income tax to incomes of £100 a year of
precarious income, and to £50 a year of permanent
income; the extension of the house tax to houses of
£10 a year rateable value, and an increase of the assessment to 1s. 6d. in the pound on houses, and 1s. on shops,
the whole produce being calculated at £1,723,000.

Being compelled to make his statement in December,
instead of in the following April, the reduction of the

6 *

malt tax and the alteration in the assessment of the income tax on agricultural incomes were forced upon him, and to compensate for these remissions he was compelled to resort to the unpopular provisions above mentioned, the extension, namely, of the house tax and the income tax.

The speech in which Mr. Disraeli replied to his critics was delivered on the 16th of December, and, together with Mr. Gladstone's answer to it, will long be memorable. He was convinced to the last, and probably with justice, that the coalition was aimed against himself, and he used to compare his position in 1852 with that of Lord Shelburne in 1783. It was the recollection, indeed, of that historic crisis which inspired his famous words: "This I know, that England does not love coalitions," and encouraged him, perhaps, to utter the prediction which was not long in being fulfilled. But he had in the course of his speech referred to Sir James Graham in terms which seem to have been misunderstood on the Opposition benches, and afforded Mr. Gladstone an opportunity of delivering an indignant rejoinder, which had a great effect upon the House. It was thought that but for this, Ministers might have secured a small majority. As it was, the Coalition counted 305 against the Ministerial 286, and Lord Derby immediately resigned. He was succeeded, after a period of complicated negotiations, by Lord Aberdeen.

The party, however, had scarcely expected to retain office. They had considerably increased their number by the general election. They now reckoned nearly three hundred bayonets. They had held office with credit, had exhibited great administrative abilities, and had taught the public to respect them. They were no longer a despised remnant, afraid to meet their enemy in the gate. They were a powerful and well-disciplined party, and the proper functions of an Opposition, which had been too long in abeyance in the House of Commons, were once more re-established.

All Lord Derby's doubts had now vanished, and henceforth he fully justified the saying of Mr. Disraeli, that " an aristocracy hesitates before it yields its confidence, but never does so grudgingly. Under such circumstances, the social feeling and the principle of honour which governs gentlemen mingle in political connections." Lord Derby gave his entire and cordial confidence to his able lieutenant in the House of Commons, and the Derby-Disraeli connection remained intact until the hour of Lord Derby's death.

CHAPTER V.

MR. DISRAELI AND LORD DERBY.

1852-1868.

The *Press* newspaper—Funeral oration over the Duke of Wellington
—Divisions in the Cabinet—Mr. Disraeli's irony at its expense—
Refusal of Lord Derby to take office—Tactics of the Conser-
vative party in Opposition—The China debate—Defeat of the
Palmerston Government—The second Derby Administration—
The Ellenborough despatch—The Reform Bill—Resignation of
Ministers—The Conservatives in Opposition—Earl Russell's
foreign policy — *Church and Queen*—Mr. Disraeli's financial
speeches—The career and defeat of Earl Russell's Government—
The Reform Bills—Mr. Disraeli leader of the party.

SUCH was the position of Mr. Disraeli and his party
when they resumed their seats on the Opposition
benches in January 1853. And Mr. Disraeli now made
it the business of his life to expose the hollowness of
the foundation on which the Coalition rested. His principal speeches in Parliament were all directed to this
end, and in the summer of 1853 he established for the
same purpose the *Press* newspaper.

The *Press* was a weekly newspaper on the model of
the *Anti-Jacobin,* and designed to write down the ob-
noxious Coalition. The first number appeared in the
summer of 1853, and it remained under the direction

of Mr. Disraeli till 1858, when it was sold to Mr.
Newdegate. When I first knew anything of the *Press*
it was edited by Mr. Samuel Lucas, for many years
connected with the literary department of the *Times*,
assisted by Mr. Shirley Brooks as the writer of squibs
and verses, and by Mr. Disraeli himself and the present Lord Derby as leader writers. Mr. Disraeli wrote
the first leading article in the first number, in which
the head of the Coalition is styled "an austere in-
triguer," and the then Lord Stanley continued to
write pretty regularly. Mr. Disraeli's most confiden-
tial servant, however, was Mr. D. T. Coulton, the
founder of the *Britannia* newspaper, and well known at
that time as the author of a very able article on Junius
in the *Quarterly Review*. Mr. Disraeli had a very high
opinion of Mr. Coulton, who died in 1857, at the early
age of forty-six, and every Friday night, while Parliament
was sitting, used to prime him for the next day's leader
with all the newest arguments and information. Mr.
Coulton used to return to the office in the Strand with
a mass of notes, which he speedily reduced into an article,
remarkable, generally speaking, for point, precision, and
that peculiar weight, more easily understood than described, which marks the combination of literary ability
and special knowledge. The *Press* was much read at
the time, and is often referred to by Lord Malmesbury ;
but it never had a very large circulation, and was chiefly
useful as showing that all the wit, brains, and literary
skill of London journalism were not monopolised by the
Liberals.

In September 1852, while the Conservative Government was still in office, the Duke of Wellington died,
and nobody remained behind to represent the old school
of statesmen, who had been trained in the Revolutionary

war, and possessed that influence with the European
Courts which England had justly acquired by the sacri-
fices made on their behalf.   Both Lord Aberdeen and
Lord Palmerston began their political life early in the
century.   But neither had that personal acquaintance
with the sovereigns of the Continent possessed by men like
Wellington and Castlereagh.   The death of the former removed one of the last pillars of the old system as settled
at the Congress of Vienna; and the effect of it was
soon seen in the attitude of Russia towards Turkey.
It fell to the lot of Mr. Disraeli to pronounce the
funeral oration over the great Duke in the House of
Commons, and he was unlucky enough to introduce into
his speech a passage on the Duke's military character
containing a quotation from Claudian, which he had
read many years before in an article on Marshal St.
Cyr, written by M. Thiers for the *Revue Trimestre* in
1829.   He had once pointed it out to George Smythe,
who quoted it in the *Morning Chronicle* of July 4th,
1848.   And it is needless to say how his.enemies gloated
over the discovery.   The *Times* argued in his defence
that he had copied the passage into his common-place
book, and had forgotten whence it came.

But the death of the Duke of Wellington soon gave
the world more important things to think about than
a quotation from Claudian.   The Crimean War was the
direct result of it, and the Coalition Ministry were, according to Mr. Disraeli, the efficient cause.   It was, so he
urged, the natural consequence of a divided Cabinet and
distracted counsels, and they were now reaping the benefit
of having installed a Government in office which had
no principle or sentiment in common, but hatred of a
particular individual.   The Peelites and the Radicals
held back Lord Palmerston.   Lord Palmerston and

Lord John Russell dragged forward Lord Aberdeen. The result was a complete deadlock, almost equal to the famous one in the *Critic*, and Russia of course seized the opportunity and flew at the throat of her victim. Either the peace party or the war party might have made terms with Russia, but a Government which alternated between the two policies, to-day under the influence of one, to-morrow under the influence of the other, was simply impotent, and the Sebastopol winter was the consequence.

Mr. Disraeli, however, never sought to hamper or impede the Government. He set the example of giving them a patriotic support both through the trying time which preceded the declaration of war, and after hostilities had commenced. But soon after the Government was formed, he had an opportunity of saying what he thought upon the subject without exposing himself to any charge of factious opposition. A speech which he delivered on our relations with France, on the 18th of February 1853, may be considered to be one of his most brilliant performances. The polished irony, the scornful satire, and the genuine humour with which again and again he presses home this main question: What is the foreign policy of this heterogeneous Cabinet, of which the members only a year or two ago were abusing each other like pickpockets? are blended together with the highest oratorical art. The Prime Minister was Lord Aberdeen, the Foreign Secretary was Lord John Russell, the First Lord of the Admiralty was Sir James Graham, and the Home Secretary was Lord Palmerston. How had they described each other and each other's principles in the great debate of 1850? On hearing the ·Government programme, says Mr. Disraeli, in which it was stated that

our foreign policy would be the same as it had been
for the last thirty years—

> I could not forget that the principles of the foreign policy then (*i.e.*
> 1850) pursued, and which has been pursued for years by the Govern-
> ment presided over by the noble Lord the Member for London, had
> been described as unbecoming to the dignity of England and perilous
> to the peace of Europe. I could not but remember that this was the
> language used by one of his colleagues in this Coalition Ministry. I
> could not but recollect that Lord Aberdeen himself, with reference to
> the then foreign policy and the principles on which it was conducted,
> had used an epithet rarely admitted into parliamentary debate, for he
> stigmatised them as "abominable." I could not but recollect, also,
> that the great indictment of the foreign policy of the then Govern-
> ment was opened in this House, with elaborate care and vehement
> invective, by the honourable baronet now First Lord of the Admi-
> ralty.

> I will not be deterred from putting the question I am about to ask.
> I say we have a right to ask Ministers upon what principle our foreign
> policy is to be conducted. Is their system to be one of "liberal
> energy" or of "antiquated imbecility"? When the noble Viscount
> opposite (Lord Palmerston), who was then Foreign Secretary, was
> vindicating himself from attacks, he took credit for the liberal energy
> of his policy, and described the principles recommended by his present
> chief as a system of "antiquated imbecility."

The sarcasm which follows at the expense of "All
the Talents," was really not unjustifiable. It expresses,
in fact, the sober and prosaic truth that the veterans
of the Peel party and the veterans of the Russell party,
supposed to be the only men capable of carrying on
the Government, were already beginning that extraordinary series of blunders which led to the Crimean war.

> The present Government tell us that they have no principles—at
> least not at present. Some people are uncharitable enough to sup-
> pose that they have not got a Party; but, in Heaven's name, why are
> they Ministers if they have not got discretion? That is the great
> quality on which I had thought this Cabinet was established. Vast
> experience, administrative adroitness—safe men, who never would
> blunder—men who might not only take the Government without a
> principle and without a Party, but to whom the country ought to be

grateful for taking it under such circumstances; yet at the very first outset, we find one of the most experienced of these eminent statesmen acting in the teeth of the declarations of the noble lord opposite, and of Lord Grey, made in 1852, and holding up to public scorn and indignation the ruler and the people, a good and cordial understanding with whom is one of the cardinal points of all sound statesmanship.

Events justified Mr. Disraeli's words. Two years afterwards the Coalition Ministry was overwhelmed by a storm of public indignation. But Lord Derby, though with the best intentions, unhappily did not seize the opportunity which was offered to him, and, to the life-long regret of Mr. Disraeli, declined to form another Government. He had everything in his favour. The Free Trade controversy was over, the Reform controversy was dormant. The Conservatives would have come into office unhampered by pledges of any kind. The weight of Protection had turned the scales against them in 1852, but that was now thrown off. All the nation wanted was a strong Government, and a general election would, in the then temper of the country, have been certain to yield a Conservative majority. But the chance was lost and never came again. In 1858 and in 1866 a different class of questions had arisen, as embarrassing to the Conservatives as Protection; and even in 1874, though a change of Government was desired, there was not the same opportunity for distinction, and for responding to a great national demand, as there was in 1855. Lord Palmerston stepped in, assumed the responsibilities which Lord Derby shrank from undertaking, and had the country with him for his life.

All this was gall and wormwood to Mr. Disraeli, who saw the cup dashed from his lips, and the legitimate rewards of public life snatched away from his grasp, when in imagination it had almost closed on them. The party, if we are to believe Lord Malmesbury, was as angry as himself. And both leaders and followers entered on a passage of their history which is not particularly creditable to either. They felt that they had lost a chance which would not present itself again. The party began to lose heart, to become garrulous and mutinous, and, as they were anxious to vent their spleen upon somebody, to vent it on their leader in the Commons. They had steadily kept aloof from any co-operation with the Radicals, though plenty of opportunities occurred. But now they became hopeless and demoralised, and disposed even to be factious. Mr. Disraeli was driven into a method of opposition which will not bear very close investigation. The excuse is that it was necessary to do something to keep up the spirits of the party. The tactics for which he has been blamed often had their origin in this necessity, compelling him at times to fight battles without profit, and to take office without power, solely for the sake of stimulating the energies, and reviving the confidence of his followers. Every general knows what it is to be at the head of a dispirited army, in the face of a superior force, weary of inaction, doubtful of the ability of its leaders, and deteriorating every day in discipline and self-respect. Then if an opportunity offers of inflicting a sharp check upon a presumptuous adversary, and of affording to his own troops the excitement and encouragement of a successful battle, he knows that the moral effect of such a field will more than repay him for the effort, even though the issue bring him no material advantage. Mr. Disraeli in his time fought many a battle of Busaco. At the same time, it must be remembered that Lord Palmerston was kept in power by a confederacy between Whigs and Radicals, based on a theory which had long ceased to be a fact; that the hollowness of this pretence was fully recognised by the Radical leaders; and that, although by a process of dexterous mystification the fiction of a great Liberal party was still kept alive in theory, it had not for many years been a working reality in Parliament. Lord Palmerston was the very man to head such a confederacy, and to oil its hinges when they creaked. But, if the public wish to know what, in 1856 and 1857, Mr. Gladstone thought of the chief whom he preferred to Lord Derby, they need only refer to the *Life of Bishop Wilberforce*. After his return to power in 1859, Lord Palmerston threw off the mask and became virtually a Tory Prime Minister. The Opposition tactics then took another form, and were directed rather against the Chancellor of the Exchequer than the head of the Government. But from 1855 to 1858 this was not the case; and Mr. Disraeli felt that in all his attacks on Lord Palmerston during those three years he had his party with him.

Nor is this statement materially affected by what occurred in 1857. The famous China debate of that year turned on a principle by which both the generosity and common sense of Englishmen are always deeply moved. The doctrine that "the servants of the Crown must be supported" is one that has necessarily grown to be an article of faith with a people whose flag waves on every sea, and whose colonies and commerce extend to every quarter of the globe. Our honour, our interests, and the safety of our countrymen and subjects have to be protected in the remotest and most barbarous regions of the earth, and this never could have been done as it has been done had not every British officer from the highest to the lowest known that he was certain of support at

home, and that, placed in circumstances of difficulty
and danger, and compelled to act on his own responsibility alone, the most favourable construction would
always be placed upon his conduct if ever it should be
called in question.   These are broad general truths
which find an echo at once in the instincts of the British
nation, to which no appeal, so enforced, is ever addressed
in vain. It is to Mr. Disraeli's credit that he quite understood this, that the debate on Mr. Cobden's motion was
none of his seeking, that he took part in it with reluctance, and that he regretted the defeat of the Government. The division took place on the 4th of March
at half-past two in the morning, when for Mr. Cobden's
motion there were 263 and against it 247, the majority
against the Government being 16.   Lord Palmerston
immediately dissolved Parliament, and a rout of his opponents followed comparable only to the rout of the Whigs
in '84.   Mr. Cobden lost his seat for Huddersfield, Mr.
Bright and Mr. Milner Gibson were rejected at
Manchester, Mr. Layard was defeated at Aylesbury,
Mr. Cardwell at Oxford, Lord A. Hervey at Brighton,
Mr. Masterman in London.   Mr. Roundel Palmer did
not venture to stand a contest at Plymouth ; and the net
result was that Lord Palmerston returned to Parliament
with a clear majority of seventy over both Peelites and
Conservatives.   It seemed now as if nothing could
unseat him, for the Radicals had received a sharp lesson,
and the Conservatives had lost thirty seats—nearly all
they had won in 1852.

It was at this time that Mr. Gladstone made his
nearest approach to a reconciliation with the Tory party.
He spoke and voted against Lord Palmerston on the
Chinese question.   He had previously joined Mr.
Disraeli in condemning Sir G. Cornewall Lewis's

Budget, though here again the mutinous Tories refused to follow their leader, who was defeated by a majority of eighty. After the general election of 1857 he still continued to evince a friendly spirit towards Lord Derby. He told Bishop Wilberforce that it was only Mr. Disraeli's Budget which made him oppose the Government in 1852. And the Bishop thought that he was evidently for a Conservative alliance. In the following year, 1858, when an attempt had been made on the life of the Emperor Napoleon, and Lord Palmerston in consequence had introduced the Conspiracy to Murder Bill, Mr. Milner Gibson moved an amendment, regretting that the Government had not previously replied in a fitting manner to the remonstrance addressed to them by the French Minister. In favour of this amendment Mr. Gladstone both spoke and voted; and the Government, being defeated by a majority of nineteen, Lord Palmerston resigned and made way for Lord Derby, with Mr. Disraeli in his old place.

—Before constructing his Administration Lord Derby made proposals to Mr. Gladstone, the Duke of Newcastle, and Earl Grey. But they declined to join him, and the Administration was composed for the most part of the old materials.* It had to en-

---

* The second Administration of the Earl of Derby was composed as follows:—

        Earl of Derby, First Lord of the Treasury.
        Lord Chelmsford, Lord Chancellor.
        Marquis of Salisbury, Lord President.
        Earl of Hardwicke, Lord Privy Seal.
        Mr. Disraeli, Chancellor of the Exchequer.
        Mr. Walpole, Home Secretary.
        Earl of Malmesbury, Foreign Secretary.
        Lord Stanley, Colonial Secretary.
        Colonel Peel, War Secretary.

counter a very bitter opposition, and was nearly wrecked upon the threshold, in consequence of a question arising out of the Indian Mutiny, and relating to a despatch addressed by Lord Ellenborough, the President of the Board of Control, to the Governor-General, Lord Canning, severely censuring his policy towards the landed proprietors of Oude. The despatch turned out to be perfectly justifiable; and Sir James Outram, a valued authority on Indian questions, entirely agreed with Lord Ellenborough. But the British public did not know all this; and the despatch, unluckily, being communicated to members of the late Ministry, formed the basis of an attack on the Government which threatened to be fatal. Lord Ellenborough resigned, but the attack went on. It was defeated in the House of Lords. But a motion of Mr. Cardwell's was debated four nights in the House of Commons, and a majority of eighty in its favour was at one time anticipated. Meanwhile, however, the truth had begun to leak out. The supporters of Government fell away, and what followed we shall tell in Mr. Disraeli's own words :—

There is nothing like that last Friday evening in the history of the House of Commons. We came down to the House expecting to divide at four o'clock in the morning—myself probably expecting to deliver an address two hours after midnight. . . . Our serried ranks seemed to rival those of our proud opponents, when suddenly there rose a wail of distress, but not from us. I can only liken the scene to the

---

Earl of Ellenborough, Board of Control.
Mr. Henley, Board of Trade.
Duke of Montrose, Duchy of Lancaster.
Sir John Pakington, Admiralty.
Earl of Eglinton, Lord Lieutenant of Ireland.
Lord Naas, Chief Secretary.
Lord John Manners, Woods and Forests.

mutiny in the Bengal army. Regiment after regiment, corps after corps, general after general—all acknowledged that they could not march through Coventry. It was like a commotion of nature more than an ordinary transaction of human life. I can only liken it to one of those earthquakes which take place in Catania and Peru. There was a rumbling murmur, a groan, a shriek, a sound of distant thunder. No one knew whether it came from the top or the bottom of the House. There was a rent, a fissure in the ground, and then a village disappeared, then a tall tower toppled down, and the whole of the Opposition benches became one great dissolving view of anarchy.

The above is quoted from Mr. Disraeli's speech at the celebrated Slough banquet, and we may as well add the words in which Lord Derby afterwards criticised it: " Great as was the wit, great as was the clearness, great as was the humour of this most graphic description, that which peculiarly appertained to it was its undeniable truth. There was no exaggeration, even of colouring, for no exaggeration could be applied to that matchless scene at which—I shall remember it to the last day of my life—I had the good fortune to be present."

During the remainder of the session of 1858 the Government carried a Bill for transferring the Government of India from the Company to the Crown, and for the admission of Jews to Parliament. The latter was effected by means of a Bill introduced by Lord Lucan in the House of Lords, and supported by Lord Derby, authorising either House by Special Resolution to alter the form of oath to be taken by a member. And thus Mr. Disraeli had the satisfaction of seeing the cause which he had so much at heart triumph under the auspices of a Conservative Government.

The great question of the day, however, was Parliamentary reform, which Lord Derby, on taking Office, declared himself prepared to deal with. Mr. Disraeli had foreseen and provided against the possibility that the Conservative Party would some day be called upon to settle this question; and he had taken an early opportunity of anticipating the objection that it was not a fitting duty for Conservatives.   In 1848 he had expressed his views upon the subject, and in the interval had frequently declared that, though it was not with his consent that the settlement of 1832 had been disturbed, he reserved to the Conservative Party the full right of dealing with the question, now that their opponents had re-opened it.   It has been too much forgotten that the measure of 1832 was by no means satisfactory to the Conservatives, and that Sir Robert Peel was praised for his patriotism in promising honestly to accept it.   But when their opponents themselves revived the question the case was entirely altered.

Accordingly, on the 28th of February 1859, the Chancellor of the Exchequer explained the provisions of a Bill which the Government were prepared to introduce, its two cardinal provisions being the equalisation of the town and county franchise, both being fixed at £10, and the restriction of the 40s. freeholder in boroughs to a vote for the borough in which he lived, depriving him of his vote for the county in which he did not live.* Mr. Disraeli also broached on this occasion his theory of Parliamentary representation, namely, that it should be the representation neither of population nor of property, but of interests.   It should, he said, "be large enough to be independent, and select enough to be responsible."   To this end he introduced certain fancy franchises, as they were then called, for giving votes to holders of stock, to depositors in savings' banks, to holders of pensions of £20 a year and upwards, and to lodgers paying a rent of 8s. a week.   The educational

---

* The non-resident borough freeholder would have retained his vote for the county.

franchise gave a vote to members of universities, and members of the liberal professions. But the Bill did not satisfy either his own party or the Opposition. Mr. Henley and Mr. Walpole disapproved of identity of suffrage as likely to lead to an " ugly rush," and retired from the Ministry. Lord John Russell condemned what he called the disfranchisement of the borough freeholders, though the Whig Government in 1832 had all but agreed to do the same thing, and the non-reduction of the borough franchise ; and, opposing the second reading on these grounds, defeated it by a majority of thirty-nine. On this occasion, too, Mr. Gladstone supported Lord Derby both by his speech and his vote.

Mr. Disraeli, in his introductory speech, demolishes the mild Conservative policy, which he calls "a feeble and a dangerous policy," of a £20 county, and £6 borough franchise, advocated by the noble lord, the Member for Tiverton, and by his right honourable friends, and he would probably have said even at that time that there was no intermediate halting-place between the £10 franchise and the pure rating franchise. But that he would have preferred the former seems evident from the following very remarkable passage. Mr. Sturt had said, in the course of the debate, that he was not afraid of the people. Mr. Disraeli said :—

Why, Sir, I have no apprehension myself that, if you had manhood suffrage to-morrow, the honest, brave, and good-natured people of England would resort to pillage, incendiarism, and massacre. Who expects that ? But though I would do as much justice to the qualities of our countrymen as any gentleman in this House—though I may not indulge in high-flown and far-fetched expressions with respect to them like those we have listened to, for the people may have their parasites as well as monarchs and aristocracies—yet I have no doubt that, whatever may be their high qualities, our countrymen are subject to the same political laws that affect the condition of all other

7 *

communities and nations. If you establish a democracy, you must in due season reap the fruits of a democracy. You will in due season have great impatience of the public burdens combined in due season with great increase of the public expenditure. You will in due season have wars entered upon from passion and not from reason; and you will in due season submit to peace ignominiously sought and ignominiously obtained, which will diminish your authority and perhaps endanger your independence. You will in due season, with a democracy, find that your property is less valuable, and that your freedom is less complete. I doubt not, when there has been realised a sufficient quantity of disaffection and dismay, the good sense of this country will come to the rally, and that you will obtain some remedy for your grievances, and some redress for your wrongs, by the process through which alone it can be obtained—by that process which may make your property more secure, but which will not render your liberty more eminent.

These are prophetic words, and they expressed Mr. Disraeli's real convictions. For the Reform Bill of 1867, he threw the responsibility first on those who had re-opened the settlement of 1832, and, secondly, on those who rejected the Bill of 1859.

Lord Derby dissolved Parliament, and gained largely at the elections, but he was still left in a minority; and on a vote of want of confidence, moved by Lord Hartington, being carried by a majority of thirteen, the second Derby Ministry was dissolved. Lord Hartington's indictment, however, was not confined merely to the Reform Question. He reproached Ministers with having failed to prevent the war between France and Austria, which had broken out just after the dissolution; a topic handled with still more severity by Lord Palmerston, who implied that they had even threatened France, and encouraged Austria by expressions of sympathy and approval. When the correspondence between Lord Malmesbury and the other Powers came to be published, these imputations were sufficiently refuted. But in the meantime they turned the scale, and led to the downfall of the Government. The strangest thing of all is, that while the debate was still in progress, these papers were actually printed ; and why they were not laid on the table of the House is a mystery to this day. Lord Malmesbury says, in a letter to Lord Cowley, of the 18th of June 1859, that it was because Mr. Disraeli himself *had not read them*, and could not have fought them in debate. But this does not seem to be his matured opinion, since five-and-twenty years afterwards he writes as follows : —

Thus fell the second administration of Lord Derby. With a dead majority against him, it is evident that he could not for long have maintained his ground, but it is equally certain that he would not have been defeated on the Address if Disraeli had previously laid on the table the Blue Book containing the French and Italian correspondence with the Foreign Office. Why he chose not to do so I never knew, nor did he ever explain it to me; but I presented it to the House of Lords at the last moment, and at least twelve or fourteen Members of Parliament who voted against us in the fatal division came out of their way, at different times and places, to assure me that had they read that correspondence before the debate they never would have voted for an amendment which, as far as our conduct respecting the war was concerned, was thoroughly undeserved, we having done everything that was possible to preserve peace. Mr. Cobden was one of these, and expressed himself most strongly on the subject.*

Such also seems to have been the opinion of Mr. Delane, the editor of the *Times*, who, after reading the Blue Book, wrote to Lord Malmesbury, as follows :—

DEAR LORD MALMESBURY,

. . . I sincerely believe that if you had published your despatches a fortnight earlier they would have had a very important influence on the division, and I think it has been sufficiently proved how I would have done you justice irrespective of party interests.

Faithfully yours,

JOHN T. DELANE.

---

* *Memoirs of an ex-Minister*, vol. ii., p. 189.

Mr. Disraeli told me himself, a few weeks after the division, that the papers were not ready. But how this statement is to be reconciled with Lord Malmesbury's I do not pretend to say.

The Chinese Vote of 1857, the unsuccessful Reform Bill, and the mismanagement, as was supposed, of the Debate on Lord Hartington's amendment weakened for a time the confidence of the Opposition in Mr. Disraeli's powers ; and the next five years were not the happiest period of his Parliamentary career. Many members of the Tory party thought Lord Palmerston a better leader than their own ; and when the latter had planned an attack, which, if properly supported by the Opposition, would have turned out the Government, he had the mortification of seeing the officer to whom it was entrusted refuse to fight when he understood what the consequences would be. The question was reduction of expenditure, and the debate occurred the day before the Derby. Mr. Disraeli said :—

I see several amendments on the paper which are offered for the purpose of attaining it [a reduction]. With most of them I am obliged, for one reason or another, to differ ; there remained that of my right honourable friend, which I was disposed to prefer to them all. To-morrow I believe we shall all be engaged elsewhere. I daresay that many honourable gentlemen who take more interest than I do in that noble pastime will have their favourites. I hope they will not be so unlucky as to find their favourites bolting. If they are placed in that dilemma they will be better able to understand and sympathise with my feelings on this occasion.

I have been told that, during the greater part of Lord Palmerston's second administration, Mr. Disraeli was a good deal isolated from his party. And in point of fact, the policy of Lord Palmerston left very little for the leader of the Opposition to do. It was a time of peace, to which many old Conservatives looked back after his death, as Tories of the older school looked back after

the Reform Bill, to the halcyon days of Lord Liverpool. Throughout the whole of it foreign affairs
were the principal subject of interest. Lord Russell was
Foreign Secretary, and, in the absence of domestic topics,
Lord Russell and Italy, Lord Russell and Savoy, Lord
Russell and the Pope, Lord Russell and Denmark, Lord
Russell and the Emperors of Russia, Austria, and France,
afforded an inexhaustible fund of amusement every
session to both Houses of Parliament. The "rich
harvest of autumnal indiscretions," as Mr. Disraeli
facetiously termed the annual results of Lord Russell's
work in the recess, supplied the leader of the Opposition with food for many brilliant efforts ; and scat-
tered up and down the volumes of *Hansard* during
these five years are to be found some of the most
masterly speeches on the foreign policy of England which
Parliament can boast, and which make one sometimes
regret that so important a department of public affairs
had never been committed to one who, in many circumstances of his career as well as in his conception of
English interests, so closely resembled Canning.

Some of his best speeches on domestic subjects were
delivered during the same period. Among them may be
mentioned a speech on Commercial Treaties on the 17th
of February 1863, one on Reform in 1865, and four
speeches on the Church of England in the year 1861,
1862, 1863, and 1864 respectively. The gist of his
remarks on Commercial Treaties was that they could do
us very little good now, when, owing to our Free Trade
policy, we had nothing left to give in exchange. His
speeches on the Church of England, taken together,
constitute a little treatise, and were collected and published in pamphlet form under the title of *Church and
Queen.* The first was spoken on the 14th of November

1861, at the meeting of the Oxford Diocesan Church Societies, with the Bishop of Oxford in the chair. // In this speech the statesman addresses himself to what he conceives to be the want of union in the Church, which prevents her from showing that irresistible front to her opponents, which, under other circumstances, she might present. He traces the disunion to three causes: a feeling of perplexity arising out of the state of parties in the Church, a feeling of distrust arising out of the existence of scepticism within her pale, and a feeling of discontent arising out of her relations with the civil power.

Mr. Disraeli said that there had always been parties in the Church, that the scepticism was stale and oft-repeated scepticism, and the connection with the State conferred a benefit on the Church, for which she would do well to endure all its inconveniences. Mr. Disraeli, however, forgot that though there may always have been parties in the Church, they were not always at open hostilities with each other. Between the Reformation and the Restoration they were so, neither believing that the other had any lawful footing in the Church of England. And we know what followed. But from the Restoration to the Oxford Revival such was not the case. The High Church and the Low Church parties existed alongside of each other, without either wishing to exterminate the rival school. But the quarrel between the Ritualists and Evangelicals seemed at one time likely to develop into something almost as dangerous as that between Puritan and Anglican. As for the scepticism, it mattered little whether it was old or new, if it continued to unsettle men's minds and shake their faith in the sincerity of the clergy. It was in that speech that Mr. Disraeli passed his famous judgment upon the Essayists and Reviewers, saying that though he was "all for free enquiry, it must be by free enquirers." He was quite right, however, in the conclusion to which he was leading up, namely, that union among Churchmen only could avert the disestablishment of the Church. The clergy must not be deceived by the victories of the Conservative Party in the House of Commons on the question of Church rates. The enemies of the Church might be only a minority, " but the history of success is the history of minorities."

The second of these speeches was delivered at High Wycombe, at a public meeting held in aid of the Society for the Augmentation of Small Benefices, on the 30th of October 1862, and in this and in the fourth of the series, he sketches out the means by which the Church may assert her nationality, in the face of the fact that so large a part of the nation is estranged from her communion. His suggestions are eight in number. The Church must educate the people. She must increase the episcopate. She must jealously maintain her existing parochial constitution. She must invite the co-operation of the laity in Church government. She must endeavour, as far as possible, to place the pecuniary position of the clergy on a more satisfactory footing. Convocation should be constituted on a broader basis, with a better representation of the parochial clergy, and, perhaps, a union of the two provinces. The relations of the Colonial Church with the Metropolitan must be improved. And, finally, a satisfactory Court of Appeal in ecclesiastical causes must be established.

In all these recommendations we can see the laborious effort of a powerful and acute intellect to throw itself into a cause which appeals to the speaker's head more than to his heart; an effort which, we cannot help saying, is not entirely successful. There is something artificial in the earnestness with which he presses these counsels on the Church; and, more than all, there is an absence of what elsewhere never fails him—that tone of originality and freshness with which his remarks, even on the most hackneyed topics, were usually characterised. At the same time, his suggestions are practical and sensible, and most of them are now numbered among recognised ecclesiastical necessities. There are, moreover, in the last of these speeches, some striking and eloquent passages, principally in relation to the new school of scepticism which was then developing itself. Mr. Disraeli asks—

Will these opinions succeed? Is there a possibility of their success? My conviction is that they will fail. I wish to do justice to the acknowledged talent, the influence, and information which the new party command; but I am of opinion that they will fail, for two reasons. In the first place, having examined all their writings, I believe, without any exception, whether they consist of fascinating eloquence, diversified learning, and picturesque sensibility—I speak seriously what I feel—and that, too, exercised by one honoured in this University, and whom to know is to admire and to regard; or whether you find them in the cruder conclusions of prelates who appear to have commenced their theological studies after they had grasped the crozier, and who introduce to society their obsolete discoveries with the startling wonder and frank ingenuousness of their own savages; or whether I read the lucubrations of nebulous professors, who seem in their style to revive chaos; or, lastly, whether it be the provincial arrogance and the precipitate self-complacency which flash and flare in an essay or review, I find the common characteristic of their writings is this—that their learning is always secondhand.

All that inexorable logic, irresistible rhetoric, bewitching wit, could avail to popularise those views, were set in motion to impress the new learning on the minds of the two leading nations of Europe—the people of England and the people of France. And they produced their effect. The greatest of revolutions was, I will not say, occasioned by those opinions, but no one can deny that their promulgation largely contributed to that mighty movement popularly called the French Revolution, which has not yet ended, and which is certainly the greatest event that has happened in the history of man. Only the fall of the Roman Empire can be compared to it; but that was going on for centuries, and so gradually, that it cannot for one moment be held to have so instantaneously influenced the opinion of the world. Now, what has happened? Look at the age in which we live, and the time when these opinions were successfully promulgated by men who, I am sure, with no intention to disparage a new party, I may venture to say were not unequal to them. Look at the Europe of the present day, and the Europe of a century ago. It is not the same Europe; its very form is changed; whole nations and great nations which then flourished have disappeared. There is not a political constitution in Europe existing at the present time which then existed. The leading community of the Continent of Europe has changed all its landmarks, altered its boundaries, erased its local names. The whole jurisprudence of Europe has been subverted. Even the tenure of land, which of all human institutions most affects the character of man, has been altered. The feudal system has been abolished. Not merely manners have been changed, but customs have been changed. And what has happened? When the turbulence was over, when the shout of triumph and the wail of agony were alike stilled; when, as it were, the waters had subsided, the sacred heights of Sinai and of Cavalry were again revealed, and amid the wreck of thrones and tribunals, of extinct nations and abolished laws, mankind, tried by so many sorrows, purified by so much suffering, and wise with such unprecedented experience, bowed again before the decisive truths that Omnipotence in His ineffable wisdom had entrusted to the custody and the promulgation of a chosen people.

The simile at the end of this passage occurs in Canning's speech in proposing the vote of thanks to the Duke of Wellington after the battle of Vittoria. Sir Walter Scott has also introduced it in his *Life of Napoleon*. But Lord Beaconsfield has embellished it, and applied it with increased effect.

This, too, is the speech in which another memorable phrase occurs:—"What is the question now placed before society with a glib assurance the most astounding? The question is this: Is man an ape or an angel? My Lord, I am on the side of the angels."

The following remark, again, is well worthy of being recorded :—

There is another point in connection with this subject which I cannot help noticing on the present occasion. It is the common cry—the common blunder—that articles of faith and religious creeds are the arms of a clergy, and are framed to tyrannise over a land. They are exactly the reverse. The precise creed and the strict article are the title deeds of the laity to the religion which has descended to them; and whenever these questions have been brought before Parliament, I have always opposed alterations of articles and subscriptions on this broad principle—that the security and certainty which they furnish are the special privileges of the laity, and that you cannot tell in what position the laity may find themselves if that security be withdrawn.

In the year 1862 Mr. Disraeli re-published, in the form of a pamphlet, two financial speeches, one delivered in February 1860, on the introduction of the Budget, the other on the 8th of April 1862, on a similar occasion. The two together form a summary of Mr. Gladstone's financial policy from 1853 to 1862, and events have to some extent justified Mr. Disraeli's criticism. They certainly tend to modify the somewhat extravagant estimate which had been formed of Mr. Gladstone as a financier, and to suggest that his highly popular projects were more showy than safe.

The General Election of 1865 was unfavourable to the Conservatives, and after Lord Palmerston's death in the autumn of that year Earl Russell succeeded to the Treasury with a nominal majority of seventy. But a considerable proportion of these had been returned to support the late Premier, and in the admission of Mr. Bright to the confidence of the new Cabinet they saw little guarantee for the further continuation of his policy. A Reform Bill was introduced by Mr. Gladstone, dealing only with the franchise, and postponing to a more convenient season the redistribution of seats. The objection to this plan is obvious. If the Ministry were allowed to carry their Franchise Bill by itself, they would be able to dissolve Parliament and appeal to the enfranchised classes on the question of redistribution only. Thus they would be sure of a majority, and could manufacture their electorate as they pleased.

Disaffected supporters and keen-witted opponents were not likely to lose this opportunity. The plan was defeated by a combined movement of the two—the present Duke of Westminster and the present Earl of Derby being the mover and seconder of a hostile resolution. Now was formed the celebrated " Cave "—a body of seceders from the Ministerial Party likened by Mr. Bright to the inmates of the Cave of Adullam. They included the present Duke of Westminster, Lord Wemyss, and Lord Sherbrooke, all three at that time in the House of Commons, the Earl of Lichfield, his brother, Major Anson, Member for Lichfield, and numbered altogether some twenty or thirty votes, sufficient, as it proved, to support the Conservative Government in their Reform Bill of the following year. But though Ministers, left with a majority of only five, abandoned their proposal and brought in a complete measure, they never recovered from the shock, and, after a protracted struggle, marked by various vicissitudes, they fell before a resolution of Lord Dunkellin's, affirming the superiority of a rating to a rental franchise.

Had these events happened but one year earlier —had Lord Palmerston died in the autumn of 1864, and Lord Russell's Government been defeated before the General Election of 1865—how different our history might have been! The Tories in that case would have dissolved their own Parliament; all the Conservative public feeling which went to support Lord Palmerston would have gone to swell their own ranks, and instead of losing, as they did, nearly twenty seats, they would probably have gained double, and have returned to Parliament with a clear working majority. But it was not to be, and for the third time Mr. Disraeli found himself Leader of the House of Commons with only a minority at his back.*

Under these circumstances, the policy of the Tory Cabinet was spirited and sagacious. It might certainly have been desirable, had it been possible, that the settlement of 1832 should remain undisturbed, though founded on no principle, and exposed to criticisms against which the argument from experience, however brilliantly enforced, was always felt to be inadequate. But it was not possible. The Whig-Radical Party had committed themselves to a further change; and they could have turned out any Tory Government at a months' notice, which declared itself hostile to reform.

The third Derby Administration was composed as follows :—
First Lord of the Treasury, Earl of Derby.
Chancellor of the Exchequer, Mr. Disraeli.
Lord Chancellor, Lord Chelmsford.
Home Secretary, Mr. Walpole.
Foreign Secretary, Lord Stanley.
Colonial Secretary, Lord Carnarvon.
Secretary for War, General Peel.
Secretary for India, Lord Cranbourne.
Lord Lieutenant of Ireland, Marquis of Abercorn.
Chief Secretary, Lord Naas.
First Lord of the Admiralty, Sir J. Pakington.
Lord President, Duke of Buckingham.
Lord Privy Seal, Earl of Malmesbury.
Commissioner of Works, Lord John Manners.
President of the Board of Trade, Sir S. Northcote.
President of the Poor-Law Board, Mr. Gathorne Hardy.
Postmaster-General, Duke of Montrose.

There was but one thing to do. The Conservative
leaders saw from the first that if you could not defend
the £10 test, you could not defend any other equally
arbitrary one. The existing franchise had acquired
some prescriptive sanctity. Parliaments returned by it
had done great things. If the people would not hold
by that, what chance was there that they would long
endure a £7 franchise with no such titles to their reverence ? Lord Derby and Mr. Disraeli thought the £10
franchise worth a fight ; and they fought in its defence
a gallant and well-contested action. But having once
been beaten on it they treated that result as final, and
resolved to have no more to do with it. Mr. Henley, a
typical Conservative, took the same view ; and even
Lord Sherbrooke himself acknowledged that there was
no permanent resting-place between the £10 franchise
and household suffrage.

Mr. Disraeli, however, determined, if he could, to
remove the question from the domain of party, and to
make the whole House of Commons assist him in the
work. This was the meaning of his celebrated thirteen
" Resolutions," by means of which he hoped to ascertain the collective opinion of the House, so as to frame
a measure which could not be assailed on pure party
grounds. As the success of this proposal would have
had the effect of disarming the Opposition, its leaders,
of course, refused it, and the Cabinet was compelled to
bring in a Bill at once. Mr. Disraeli proposed a £15
county franchise, and a borough franchise based on
household rating, combined with two years' residence
and personal payment of rates. But between the introduction of the Resolutions on the 11th of February and
the further discussion of them on the 25th, doubt arose
in the minds of Lord Cranborne, Lord Carnarvon, and

General Peel with regard to the rating suffrage, and on
Sunday the 24th they placed their resignation in the
hands of Lord Derby.   They consented to remain on
condition that a different measure was proposed; and
the "Ten Minutes' Bill," substituting a £6 franchise in
the borough, was adopted.   Mr. Disraeli had literally
hardly more than an hour to prepare himself for this
sudden change of front, and he offered to resign office
rather than undertake a task so much to his own dis-
taste.   However, he was overruled.   At three o'clock
on that Monday afternoon, February 25th, he had eaten
nothing, and, after taking a single glass of wine in
Downing Street, he went down to the House, there to
discharge his allotted task with an air of depression
and deprecation which surprised everyone who heard
him.   The Bill, naturally, was only born to perish, and
the Government and the Conservative Party had now to
consider what course they should pursue.   The Government, however, was not left to decide.   A meeting was held
at the Carlton Club, the result of which was to inform the
Prime Minister and the Chancellor of the Exchequer
that the Tory Party now would support the original
scheme and no other.   Thus, so far from Mr. Disraeli
having dragged an unwilling party after him, the party
itself insisted upon his acting as he did; and he had no
sincerer supporters through the desperate struggles
which ensued than some of those very county members
whose trust he was said to have abused.

Whatever may have been thought of the policy of
the Government measure, there is no doubt that Mr.
Disraeli's parliamentary reputation was enormously
enhanced by his conduct of it.   So bitter and ruthless
an opposition has rarely been met by such consummate tact, such immovable good temper, such alert

logic, and such perfect self-possession. His humorous comments on Mr. Gladstone's bursts of passion delighted both sides of the House; the easy good-humour with which he expressed his satisfaction at having had the table between himself and Mr. Gladstone, during one of that gentleman's diatribes, destroyed its whole effect in a moment. His description of Mr. Lowe, after that gentleman had referred, in illustration of his own position, to the Battle of Hastings and the Battle of Chæronea, as an "inspired school-boy"; and his retort on Mr. Beresford Hope, who refused to support an Asian mystery, that in his severest sarcasms there was a "Batavian grace" which robbed his words of all their sting, will never be forgotten, either by those who heard him at the time, or those who treasure up the traditions of Parliamentary eloquence and wit.

Nor were his graver efforts less surprising. One night he wound up a great debate, answering the House all round in a speech of three hours duration, without a single note; and it was allowed on all sides that he had not missed a point, nor failed to make the most of an argument throughout the whole of it. When after his first great division against the whole might of Mr. Gladstone, which he won by a majority of twenty-one, Tory members crowded up to the Treasury Bench to shake hands with and congratulate him, they only expressed the feeling of three-fourths of the House, who would have liked to pay the same tribute of admiration to so genial and gallant an antagonist.

The Franchise clauses of the Bill itself, as originally introduced by its author, will be found in the Appendix. It was greatly altered for the worse in Committee. But Mr. Disraeli is not responsible for

8

the consequences. As it originally stood, it was a much more Conservative measure than in its final form. The abolition of the compound householder, and the change of two years residence for one, destroyed two of its principal securities.

The year 1868 brought to Mr. Disraeli, in his sixty third year, the prize to which he had aspired from his early manhood, and for which he had served as few have ever served before him. He had fought his way by his eloquence and his wit, and, on the resignation of Lord Derby in March 1868, he was at once recognised by all competent judges as his only possible successor. His speech on taking his seat as Prime Minister in the House of Commons was brief and dignified; and so was his tenure of the office. But it must always be regarded as one of the most important events in modern history, as it undoubtedly had the effect of re-opening the Irish Question, and entailed on us the long and disastrous train of consequences which seem still to be unexhausted. If we allow Mr. Gladstone's Irish Resolutions of 1868 to have been a legitimate party move, the fact remains that but for Mr. Disraeli's elevation to the Premiership, and his prospects of a majority at the next General Election, these resolutions would never have been introduced, and the terrible struggle of the last eight years would have been either postponed or averted altogether.

CHAPTER VI.

MR. DISRAELI AS LEADER OF THE PARTY.

1868–1881.

Mr. Gladstone's Irish Resolutions—Mr. Disraeli's speech on the Abyssinian war—General Election of 1868—Mr. Disraeli's speeches in Opposition—Death of Lady Beaconsfield—Refusal to take office in 1873—Mr. Disraeli Lord Rector of the University of Glasgow —The Conservative reaction—Mr. Disraeli and the masses—The Cabinet of 1874—The Public Worship Regulation Bill—*Sanitas sanitatum*—Social legislation—Educational measures—Ecclesiastical questions—The Royal Titles Act—Mr. Disraeli becomes Lord Beaconsfield—Foreign policy of his Administration—The Eastern Question—The Bulgarian Atrocities—The March Protocol—Declaration of War by Russia—The treaty of San Stephano and its consequences—The Treaty of Berlin—Its results—The The Anglo-Turkish Convention— Peace with Honour—The Affghan war—Unpopularity of the Government—The General Election of 1880—Lord Beaconsfield's last appearances in Parliament—His illness and death—Grief of the nation—The funeral at Hughenden—Visit of the Queen—The Primrose League— Tributes to Lord Beaconsfield's memory.

HENCEFORTH we have to regard Mr. Disraeli and Mr. Gladstone as the two rival chiefs of Conservatism and Liberalism, towering by a head and shoulders over all their contemporaries, and converting party warfare into a duel between the two heroes. It was in 1868 that Mr. Gladstone brought in the first of his Irish

8 *

Resolutions, which, after a long debate and a powerful reply from the Prime Minister, was carried by a majority of sixty-five. Mr. Disraeli then said that as the appeal was ultimately to the nation he would not give the House the trouble of dividing upon the others. But he was not allowed to escape without a severe cross-examination, conducted by Mr. Bright and Mr. Gladstone, whose contention was that he ought to have resigned at once. But his position was this: he would not allow that the existing House of Commons was a fair judge of the question. When an adverse vote may fairly be taken to express the opinion of the country, a constitutional minister resigns; when there is a doubt upon the point, he dissolves Parliament, and puts the question directly to the people. These are the two constitutional courses, one or other of which a minister is bound to adopt. Now, what had been the recent history of the Irish Church question up to that period? Shortly before the last General Election, Mr. Gladstone himself had spoken of the Irish Church as a question " out of the domain of practical politics," as surrounded with "immense difficulties," and as not likely to come forward in his own time—exactly as he speaks of the Church of England now. With these statements staring the country in the face, the question of the Irish Church could have had no influence whatever in determining the choice of the constituencies. The existing House of Commons, therefore, was no adequate reflection of public opinion on the subject; consequently it was no part of Mr. Disraeli's duty to resign office.

The legitimate alternative was to advise Her Majesty to dissolve. This, then, was the course which he adopted, coupling his advice, however, with a tender of resignation should it seem more conducive to Her Majesty's personal convenience. Pestered with inquiries as to whether he had recommended an appeal to the present constituencies or the new ones, Mr. Disraeli said his advice had been quite general, and would include an appeal to either, but that he hoped it might be possible to make his appeal to the latter in the following autumn. With this statement, the Opposition was obliged to be contented, and with a few lingering growls, their anger gradually subsided. But it is perfectly clear that Mr. Disraeli had only followed the course prescribed by the Constitution in taking the opinion of the country before he retired from the helm. Had he been forced by the factiousness of Opposition to dissolve before the new system was completed, and so necessitate two general elections, one upon the heels of the other, that would have been their fault, not his.

Before the Session of 1868 was over, it fell to Mr. Disraeli's lot to propose a vote of thanks to the troops engaged in the Abyssinian war, which had been undertaken in 1867 to obtain the release of some Englishmen kept in prison by the King of that country. In the course of his speech the Prime Minister said that Englishmen must take a peculiar interest in the fact that "the standard of St. George had been hoisted on the mountains of Rasselas." It has been alleged that Johnson was not thinking of the real mountains of Abyssinia when he wrote *Rasselas.* The objection would be hypercritical in any case. But in my edition of Lord Beaconsfield's speeches, will be found some information supplied by Lord Stanley of Alderley, which makes it almost certain that Johnson *was* thinking of the real mountains when he wrote.*

* See *Speeches*, vol. ii. p. 129.

On the eve of the General Election of 1868, Mr. Disraeli issued an address to his constituents, brief indeed, but expressing a great truth with that terse and concise gravity which is the highest excellence of that kind of composition.

So long as there is in this country the connection through the medium of a Protestant Sovereign between the State and the National Church, religious liberty is secure. That security is now assailed by various means and on different pleas; but admidst the discordant activity of many factions there moves the supreme purpose of one power. The philosopher may flatter himself he is advancing the cause of enlightened progress; the sectarians may be roused to exertion by anticipations of the downfall of ecclesiastical systems. These are transient efforts, vain and passing aspirations. The ultimate, triumph, were our Church to fall, would be to that power which would substitute for the authority of one sovereign the supremacy of a foreign prince, to that power with whose traditions, learning, and discipline, and organization our Church alone has hitherto been able to cope, and that, too, only when supported by a determined and devoted people.

Mr. Disraeli, however, had overrated the strength of his own position, and the comparative force of the different opinions which were arrayed against each other in the country. On the one hand was the strong Protestant feeling of England and Scotland, and the support which might reasonably be expected from the newly enfranchised classes. On the other lay the combined armies of Nonconformity and Popery, laying aside their mutual hostility as they have done before in their common hatred of the Establishment, and both backed up by the rising strength of the Radicals, who are naturally in favour of all revolutions, whether civil or ecclesiastical. The event proved that the latter combination was the stronger. Mr. Disraeli, at the Mansion House dinner on the 9th of November, predicted a victory, and boasted that the " arms of precision "

—whatever he may have meant by the expression—
were on the Conservative side. He was doomed to
disappointment, and the verdict of the country consigned him once more to five years of opposition.

On this period of his life we need not linger long.
He did not take a very prominent part in the debates
on either the Irish Church Bill or the Irish Land Bill.
He had said what he had to say about the Church in
his speech on Mr. Gladstone's Resolution, when he
referred to the words which he had used in 1844, and
which had been turned against him in the debate—" an
alien church, a starving population, and an absentee
aristocracy." He said the situation was changed now,
for the people were no longer starving, and the proprietors were no longer absentees. As to the alien
church, of course, he could say nothing, and his views
on that subject will be deferred to a later chapter.

During the session of 1869–70, he seemed, in fact,
to be "lying by." But the breaking out of the French
and German War in 1870, and the question of the
neutrality of Belgium which arose out of it, drew forth
from Mr. Disraeli, on the 1st of August, perhaps one
of the most powerful speeches on foreign affairs which
he ever delivered. After calling on the House of
Commons to take note that there were " vast ambitions
stirring in Europe," he went on to remind it of what
took place in 1853, and it is important to quote these
words because of what occurred in 1876,* and because
of the light which they throw on what Mr. Disraeli
meant by the " armed neutrality," which he recommended
England to observe. Admitting the advantage of possessing a strong Government at such a moment, composed of able and experienced men, he said that in

* See page 140–43.

1853 we had a still stronger Government, composed of still abler men, and yet what happened? "It was at this very period of the year, at the end of July, that, after two months of hesitation, Russia crossed the Pruth, and we have it upon record, we have it upon authoritative and authentic evidence, that Russia would not have crossed the Pruth had England at that time been decided; had she told Russia that it was a question of war with England. . . . What did it end in? In the March of next year you had to go to war with Russia, because she had crossed the Pruth in the preceding July, and involved herself in war with Turkey." A word in time would have prevented the Crimean war. But for a neutral power to be able to speak that word, her neutrality must be an armed neutrality. What he, therefore, wished to impress upon the public was that, if we desired to prevent the violation of the treaties guaranteeing Luxemburg and Belgium, our neutrality must be an armed neutrality, for it was evident from the secret treaty that both France and Prussia would have violated them without remorse.

In the following year, however, when the two great Irish measures had been passed, Mr. Disraeli descended into the arena again with all his wonted vigour. At the commencement of the session he spoke twice on the Treaty of Paris,* with great force and great mastery of the question. On the famous Westmeath Committee he attacked the Government with an energy of sarcasm which reminded one of the Peelite period.

The right honourable gentleman opposite (Mr. Gladstone) was elected for a specific purpose: he was the Minister who alone was

* Russia had announced her intention of abrogating of her own accord the article in the Treaty of Paris providing for the neutralisation of the Black Sea. *Select Speeches*, vol. p. ii. 133.

capable to cope with these long-enduring and mysterious evils that had tortured and tormented the civilisation of England. The right honourable gentleman persuaded the people of England that with regard to Irish politics he was in possession of the philosopher's stone. Well, Sir, he has been returned to this House with an immense majority, with the object of securing the tranquillity and content of Ireland. Has anything been grudged him? Time, labour, devotion —whatever has been demanded has been accorded, whatever has been proposed has been carried. Under his influence and at his instance we have legalised confiscation, consecrated sacrilege, condoned high treason; we have destroyed churches, we have shaken property to its foundation, and we have emptied gaols; and now he cannot govern a country without coming to a parliamentary committee! The right honourable gentleman, after all his heroic exploits, and at the head of his great majority, is making government ridiculous.

Mr. Disraeli opened the Session of 1872 with declaring that during the whole of the preceding autumn Ministers had lived in "a blaze of apology." And when the Ballot Bill was introduced he declared that the time had gone by when the country stood in need of the ballot. The Prime Minister had, he said, "passionately embraced a corpse."

It was during the Easter holidays of this year, 1872, that Mr. Disraeli paid a long-promised visit to Lancashire, and delivered a long speech at Manchester, shortly after Mr. Gladstone had been present at a great Liberal reception in the same city; a circumstance which furnished the subject of a cartoon to *Punch* illustrating a quotation from Bombastes :—

> I too have heard on inky Irwell's shore
> Another lion give a louder roar,
> And the first lion thought the last a bore

The gist of this speech lies in the one sentence. "The programme of the Conservative party is to maintain the institutions of the country." We have then an exhaustive consideration of the various component parts of that Constitution, and the advantages of each, especially of the monarchy, which had then been recently attacked in a lecture at Newcastle by Sir Charles Dilke. Some remarks on the union of Church and State follow; then comes the condition of the people, both agricultural and manufacturing, with some reference to the doctrines of Fenianism; and the speech concludes with a description of the Ministry and their conduct of foreign affairs, which, whatever its justice, will long be remembered for its felicitous imagery and biting satire.

It was in this speech that the following passage occurs, which really has more literal truth in it than the jocular rhetoric of Mr. Disraeli invariably possessed :—

> But, gentlemen, as time advanced, it was not difficult to perceive that extravagance was being substituted for energy by the Government. The unnatural stimulus was subsiding. Their paroxysms ended in prostration. Some took refuge in melancholy, and their eminent chief alternated between a menace and a sigh. As I sat opposite the Treasury Bench the Ministers reminded me of one of those marine landscapes not very unusual on the coasts of South America. You behold a range of exhausted volcanos. Not a flame flickers on a single pallid crest. But the situation is still dangerous.

This speech was followed up by another at the Crystal Palace on the 24th of June, which was in some respects a repetition of the former, laying down the Conservative programme as the "maintenance of the Empire, the preservation of our institutions, and the improvement of the condition of the people."

Before the end of the year it became apparent that the Gladstone Ministry had lost its hold upon the country. But "the perfect wife," who had cheered so many of her husband's darker hours, was not spared to witness the brilliant dawn that was at hand, "to share the triumph or partake the gale." Mrs. Disraeli, whom Her Majesty had created Lady Beaconsfield in 1869, died in the winter of 1872, and Mr. Disraeli might almost have said with Johnson that success came to him at last when he was old and could not enjoy it, when he was solitary and could not impart it. Deprived of her active sympathy, he seems still, however, to have been sustained by her memory; and certainly his judgment was never more conspicuous than in the Ministerial crisis of 1873. Defeated on the Dublin University Bill by a majority of three, Mr. Gladstone at once resigned, and Her Majesty, without a moment's delay, summoned Mr. Disraeli to her councils. Contrary to the judgment of some of his friends at the time, he declined to take office, assuring Her Majesty at the same time that he should have no difficulty in constructing an Administration, but that he could not undertake to do so with the existing House of Commons. Nor did it suit Mr. Disraeli to take office and dissolve Parliament. As he pointed out to the House in his explanatory statement, a new Government on coming into office cannot dissolve at once. The mere formation of the Ministry is a work of time. The time necessary for obtaining that accurate knowledge of the state of our foreign relations, and of our financial prospects, which is accessible only to men in office, and without which an incoming Ministry can hardly appeal to the country on any definite principles, is still greater. Practically, said Mr. Disraeli, he should have to finish the Session before he could dissolve Parliament, and what would happen in the interval? He knew only too well from bitter experience.

We should have what is called "fair play," that is to say, no vote of want of confidence would be proposed, and chiefly because it would be of no use.   There would be no wholesale censure, but retail humiliation.   A right honourable gentleman will come down here, he will arrange his thumb-screws and other instruments of torture on this table—we shall never ask for a vote without a lecture ; we shall never perform the most ordinary routine office of government without there being annexed to it some pedantic and ignominious condition.

I wish to express nothing but what I know from painful personal experience.   No contradiction of the kind I have just encountered could divest me of the painful memory ; I wish it could.   I wish it was not my duty to take this view of the case.   For a certain time we should enter into the paradise of abstract resolutions.   One day honourable gentlemen cannot withstand the golden opportunity of asking the House to affirm that the income-tax should no longer form one of the features of our Ways and Means.   Of course a proposition of that kind would be scouted by the right honourable gentleman and all his colleagues ; but then they might dine out that day, and the resolution might be carried, as resolutions of that kind have been.   Then another honourable gentleman, distinguished for his knowledge of men and things, would move that the diplomatic service be abolished. While honourable gentlemen opposite were laughing in their sleeves at the mover, they would vote for the motion in order to put the Government into a minority.   For this reason.   Why should men, they would say, govern the country who are in a minority ? totally forgetting that we had acceded to office in the spirit of the Constitution, quite oblivious of the fountain and origin of the position we occupied.   And it would go very hard if on some sultry afternoon some honourable member should not "rush in where angels fear to tread," and successfully assimilate the borough and the county franchise.   And so things would go on until the bitter end—until at last even the Appropriation Bill has passed, Parliament is dissolved, and we appeal to those millions who, perhaps six months before, might have looked upon us as the vindicators of intolerable grievances, but who now receive us as a defeated, discredited, and degraded Ministry, whose services can be neither of value to the Crown nor a credit to the nation.

Mr. Gladstone seemed inclined to lay down the doctrine that no leader of Opposition is entitled to give a vote calculated to defeat the Minister unless he is prepared to take his place.   Such a doctrine, if generally acted on,

would make all effective criticism impossible. A statesman strong enough to take the Minister's place would
not long remain in Opposition, and one not strong
enough would have no right to exercise the power which
alone makes an Opposition formidable. Mr. Gladstone
resumed office, and the session came to a close without
any further incident of importance.

In the autumn of 1873 Mr. Disraeli was chosen Lord
Rector of the University of Glasgow, an honour which
was renewed in 1874, when he defeated Mr. Emerson
by a majority of two hundred. The Tory party had
now for the time become the popular party in the
country. Of that there could be no doubt. The
measures of the Government had produced considerable irritation in the nation, which was not diminished either by their administrative failures,* or by
certain equivocal transactions, which produced a great
sensation at the time, though it is needless to recapitu-
late them now.

The vague floating discontent thus gradually engendered resulted in a state of public opinion, towards the close of Mr. Gladstone's Government,
which was sufficient to account for its overthrow,
even had the nation been indifferent to Toryism. But
it was not. Concurrently with the active dislike of Mr.
Gladstone's policy, both foreign and domestic, had grown
up a feeling that some injustice had been done to the Conservatives. The country had enjoyed five years for reflection. People saw that after all the Conservatives *had*
been the party which effected the extension of the

---

* Mr. Disraeli's Bath letter, in which he described the policy of the
Government as one of " plundering and blundering," was thought no
exaggeration at the time.

franchise, let them have thought about it what they might. It was brought home to the working classes that the Conservatives were the authors of that beneficent factory legislation which the Liberals had so strenuously resisted, and they began to understand too that Conservative principles of foreign policy might be more advantageous to the people than Liberal ones. The Church also, during these five years, had made great progress among the working classes. Many old prejudices had been dissipated, and many new ideas had dawned upon the labouring population, when the General Election of 1874 revealed the fact that the existence of the Conservative working man was not a dream.

Add to this that, by skilfully taking advantage of every opportunity that occurred, and of every mistake committed by his opponents, in order to draw out those ingenious and suggestive contrasts between Conservatism and Liberalism, which for nearly thirty years formed so marked a feature in all his political addresses, Mr. Disraeli had succeeded in disturbing very materially the vulgar conception of Toryism which had prevailed in England from the Peace to the middle of the present century, and we shall understand that other causes were at work besides weariness of sensational legislation to ensure the Conservative victory of 1874. Of the contrasts to which reference has been made, though the effect might be heightened by that dexterous manipulation of phrases in which he was so great an adept, the foundation was sufficiently real to secure for them a place among the recognised topics of the party; and, though they might be too fine-drawn for middle aged men of business, there is no doubt that over the minds of a younger generation, always pleased with what is subtle and adroit, they exercised considerable influence.

Her Majesty dissolved Parliament in January 1874, Mr. Gladstone promising the people that if he was again returned to power he would abolish the income tax. The answer to his appeal was a Conservative majority of fifty. The result was largely due to the action of the working-classes in the towns, and Mr. Disraeli's severest critics were forced to admit that he had taken the measure of the British workmen more accurately than themselves. The fact is, that those who denied the possibility of the Conservative working man, proceeded on the assumption that all his instincts were selfish. They knew that he had been taught to associate cheap food, high wages, and reduced taxes with the political creed represented by Mr. Bright and Mr. Gladstone, and they reasoned that no counter attraction could possibly be strong enough to detach him from the Liberal Party. The elections of 1868, of course, strengthened the conviction. But it was seen in a very short time that such views were entirely superficial, and that in relying on the existence of a deeper chord of feeling in the working classes, which would respond at once to appeals of a more generous character, Mr. Disraeli had shown his knowledge of human nature and of English human nature in particular. He spoke to them of England; of her glory and her duty; of the imperial inheritance which their ancestors had won, and which they must transmit to their posterity; of the proud position which she occupied among the nations of the world, and of the divine mission which it was her privilege to fulfil in the spread of civilisation and religion. In an age of economy and materialism, of cheap breakfast tables, and bread and butter prosperity, these accents fell upon the public ear, long unaccustomed to such sounds, with thrilling power. It may be perfectly true that in these appeals to the popular imagination, and to the poetic and romantic element of which almost every man has some small share in his composition, Mr. Disraeli was occasionally bombastic, grandiose, or turgid, But through all the gorgeous vapours and fantastic shapes in which his eloquence occasionally clothed itself, a real truth was always visible, and ever and anon flashed out with startling and convincing brightness. This was the secret of Mr. Disraeli's power with the masses: and that they should not understand it who believed that the people of England were incapable of rising to any loftier conception of national life than had been propounded by the Manchester school, was natural enough.

It is also to be remembered that Mr. Disraeli, even when he could not secure the votes, always commanded the admiration of the English people. They liked his pluck, his humour, his cynicism, his audacious eccentricity, and the blows he had levelled at the " big-wigs." They regarded him, at the same time, as a man of the people, whose escutcheon was his pen, and who had fought his own way to greatness and power through tremendous obstacles.

Thus, from whatever point of view he was regarded, whether judged by his opinions, his character, or his history, personally, politically, or socially, he was eminently an *interesting* man. And the interest which he excited himself was communicated in some measure to the party of which he was the leader. Toryism began to appear the more picturesque creed of the two. The people were tired of the whitey-brown monotony of middle-class Liberalism. " I 'm all for the nobs," says the factory girl in *Sybil*, " if we can't have our own man." And the sentiment is perfectly natural. Toryism and Socialism have this in common, at all events, that they both lift us out of the region of the commonplace, and appeal to ideas, though the conclusions derived from them may be absolutely contradictory of each other.

As soon as Mr. Gladstone saw that the elections left him no hope of a majority, he followed Mr. Disraeli's example in 1868, and hastened to resign his office, without waiting for the meeting of Parliament. Mr. Disraeli was now commissioned by the Queen once more to undertake the task of forming a Conservative Administration.

Melioribus opto
Auspiciis, et quæ fuerit minus obvia Graiis.

He received Her Majesty's commands on the 18th of February, and in about three weeks all his arrangements were completed. The following composed the Cabinet :—

Mr. Disraeli, First Lord of the Treasury.
Lord Cairns, Lord Chancellor.
The Duke of Richmond, President of the Council.
The Earl of Malmesbury, Privy Seal.
The Earl of Derby, Foreign Secretary.
Marquis of Salisbury, Secretary for India.
Earl of Carnarvon, Colonial Secretary.
Mr. Gathorne Hardy, Secretary for War.
Mr. R. A. Cross, Home Secretary.
Mr. Ward Hunt, First Lord of the Admiralty.
Sir Stafford Northcote, Chancellor of the Exchequer.
Lord John Manners, Postmaster-General.

Among the members not in the Cabinet, Mr. Disraeli found efficient colleagues in Lord Sandon, Mr. Sclater

9

Booth, Mr. Clare Sewell Read, Lord George Hamilton, and Mr. Bourke.

He had now, as it seemed, a fair chance of realising some of his favourite ideas. It is true, he was sixty-eight years of age. But he was seven years younger than Lord Palmerston when he became Prime Minister for the second time in 1859, and a year younger than Lord Aberdeen when he went to the Treasury in 1853. He had always been considered a man of vigorous constitution, and his frame was well built and robust. Yet certain it is that no sooner was he in office than he seemed rather disposed to rest upon his laurels, and leave the active work of legislation to his colleagues. Unfortunately for himself, however, he had not been in office more than two months before a Bill was introduced by the Archbishop of Canterbury which affected Mr. Disraeli during the whole remainder of his life. This was the Public Worship Regulation Bill, which was brought in on the 20th of April, and read a third time in the House of Lords on the 25th of June. In the House of Commons the measure was entrusted to Mr. Russell Gurney, and it was uncertain almost to the last moment which side Mr. Disraeli would espouse. So far the Government had treated it as an open question; and the Marquis of Salisbury, the new Secretary of State for India, had not concealed his dislike of it. In the House of Commons, Mr. Hardy (Lord Cranbrook), spoke in the same strain; and it was not till Mr. Disraeli rose on the 15th of July that the Anti-Ritualists knew what a powerful ally they were to find. We read in the *Life of Bishop Wilberforce* that the Prime Minister only made up his mind to support the measure on the morning of the day when informed that all the Bishops were in favour of it, and that if it was rejected, disestablishment must very speedily follow. His first impulse was to oppose it; and had he been the Mr. Disraeli of *Coningsby* and *Sybil* he certainly would have done so. As it was, he made the unfortunate declaration that this was a Bill "to put down" Ritualism, and that he intended to support it with that object. These words were remembered against him to the day of his death, and made him enemies among the clergy, who had only too many opportunities of influencing the popular vote. In reality Mr. Disraeli meant no harm. He was very careful to distinguish between the High Church, of which he spoke in terms of high eulogy, and the Ritualist party, which he conceived to be an excresence from it, small in point of numbers and ability, and deliberately adopting practices symbolical of those Romish doctrines which the Church of England has condemned. This is what he meant. That he did not understand Ritualism is more than probable. But the Ritualists did not choose to accept this hypothesis in extenuation of the offence which he had given them; and remained his bitter enemies to the last.

It is neither necessary nor possible to discuss at any length the series of domestic measures passed by Mr. Disraeli's Administration during its six years' lease of office. When he laid down that one of the cardinal doctrines of the Conservative policy was the improvement of the condition of the people he was thoroughly in earnest. In the speech at Manchester in 1872, to which I have already referred, occurs the *sanitas sanitatum omnia sanitas*, which one of his oponents soon after derided as "a policy of sewage." Mr. Disraeli retorted on him in his speech at the Crystal Palace with merited severity, pointing out how deeply interested the working classes were in this matter, and promising the honour-

9 *

able gentleman that the laugh would soon be turned
against himself.   Accordingly when he came into office
he lost no time in fulfilling the pledges which he had
given in Opposition ; and between 1874 and 1879 he
placed upon the Statute Book no less than fifteen Acts
of Parliament, all directed to the benefit of the public
health, the improvement of the condition of the poor,
and the removal of the special grievances under which
they believed themselves to be suffering.   These are the
Factories Act and the Licensing Act (1874), the Conspiracy and Protection to Property Act, the Masters and
Workman's Act, the Artizans' Dwellings Act, the Public
Health Act, the Friendly Societies Act (1875), the
Commons Act, the Pollution of Rivers Act, the Mer-
cantile Shipping Act (1876), the Canal Boats Act, and
Poor Law Amendment Act (1877), the Factories and
Workshops Act, the Cattle Diseases Act (1878), and the
Artizans' Dwellings Act Amendment Act (1879).

To the farmers he gave the Agricultural Holdings
Act, which changed the presumption of law in favour
of the tenant, though it was forgotten in subsequent
discussions that Mr. Disraeli himself always spoke of
it as an experiment, which could be amended afterwards
if necessary.   To the local ratepayers he afforded a
large instalment of that relief to which he had admitted
them to be entitled ; while our system of local administration was greatly improved by the Rating Act,
the Highways Act, and the Prisons Act, of which the
first seem to have given general satisfaction,
though it must be owned that some clauses of the last
interfere more than was desirable with that local
authority and jurisdiction which Mr. Disraeli himself
was always so anxious to maintain.

Two efforts were made to reform our whole system of

county government on a very much larger scale, by the establishment of " County Boards," and two Bills were brought in by Mr. Sclater Booth, the present Lord Basing, with that object. Both, however, were withdrawn, as the time was not ripe for a compromise between the supporters of the existing system, and those who would subvert it altogether; and Mr. Disraeli was not destined to add the settlement of this very important question—more important than it seems at first sight—to the list of his achievements. But his Ministry, on the whole, can show a record of social legislation which will contrast very favourably with that of any other Government during the present century. Many of these measures were warmly appreciated by the working classes. Mr. Macdonald, the working class member for Stafford, spoke to that effect, and the prosy details of ordinary politics are lighted up for the moment with a gleam of real poetic interest as we think of the author of *Sybil* being publicly thanked in the House of Commons by the representatives of Labour.

In the field of education a measure was carried through by Lord Sandon to amend some of those provisions in the Act of 1870, which pressed unjustly on denominational schools, and some educational measures for Ireland can also be added to the list. But the chief Bill of this description was the Universities Bill, intended to meet the views of that class of University Reformers who desired to see the restoration of university teaching, as distinct from the collegiate or tutorial system; and likewise to encourage among resident members the pursuit of learning and scholarship for their own sakes. To make Oxford a centre of learning, as well as a great seat of education, was

the object of the new school, and they had the sympathies of Mr. Disraeli, or, as we must now call him,
Lord Beaconsfield, on their side. Opinions may differ
with regard to the operation of the new system, but
nobody can doubt that it was honestly intended to pro-
mote the interests of literature and culture, or that it
had the warm approval of a statesmen who used to
boast that he was born in a library.

The chief ecclesiastical questions with which the
Ministry of 1874–80 will be remembered, besides the
Public Worship Regulation Bill, are the Abolition of
Lay Patronage in Scotland in 1874, the Bishoprics
Bills of 1877 and 1878, and the attempt made by Lord
Salisbury in the House of Lords to settle the Burials
Question. The two Bishoprics Bills, in conformity with
which the six new sees of Truro, St. Albans, Liverpool,
Southwell, Newcastle, and Wakefield have been erected,·
were described by the Archbishop of Canterbury as
the greatest ecclesiastical reform since the Reformation, and the Church of England may venerate the
memory of Lord Beaconsfield for this good action, at
all events, if for no other. Here, too, he was only
pursuing when in office the policy he had sketched in
opposition, an extension of the Episcopate having been
recommended by him fifteen years before the time when
he was actually able to undertake it.

The attempt to settle the Burials question in 1876
was unfortunately frustrated by the action of the late
Archbishop of Canterbury, Dr. Tait, who, by suddenly
accepting an amendment moved by Lord Harrowby,
compelled the Government to abandon the measure.
But we may fairly doubt whether, had it become law,
the agitation would have been permanently quelled.

Last but not least on our list is the Act of Parliament

by which Mr. Disraeli has linked his name for ever with the style and dignity of the English monarchy. The Royal Titles Act, enabling Her Majesty to assume the title of Empress of India, was passed in the Session of 1876, and was resisted by the Opposition with a degree of warmth which at this distance of time appears absolutely childish. Mr. Lowe, the present Lord Sherbrooke, made himself particularly conspicuous in declaiming against it, and actually stated, in a speech made at Retford during the Easter recess, that the Queen had solicited two previous Prime Ministers for the same title, and that both had refused to recommend it; but that now, having found a more pliant instrument, she had succeeded in her object. It can readily be understood how Mr. Disraeli handled this atrocious fiction, and a few days afterwards Mr. Lowe was compelled to apologise, and to acknowledge that his reference to the Queen was a breach of parliamentary decorum.

Before passing on to the foreign policy of Lord Beaconsfield's Government, we must remind our readers that on the 12th of August 1876 it became known to the public that Mr. Disraeli's place in the House of Commons, in which he had played so great a part for nearly forty years, would know him no more. His health and strength seemed no longer equal to the daily-increasing labour of leading the popular assembly, though high medical authorities have hazarded the conjecture that by retiring from it when he did, he rather shortened his life than prolonged it. Had he retired ten years sooner, says the leading medical journal of the day, he might have experienced great benefit from the change. As it was, it came too late: when constant excitement would, perhaps, have sustained his vital energies longer than comparative repose.

On the 11th of August he delivered his last speech in the House of Commons, under circumstances which may, perhaps, have suggested to his mind a striking contrast to his first. The House now hung with rapt attention on every word that fell from him ; and on this occasion they were, as it was fitting they should be, words of no ordinary weight. "We are always treated," he said, "as if we had some peculiar alliance with the Turkish Government, as if we were their peculiar friends, and expected to uphold them in any enormity they might commit." There was not one jot or one tittle of evidence to support such an assumption. "We are, it is true, the allies of the Sultan of Turkey ; but so is Austria, so is Russia, so is France. We are also their partners in a Tripartite Treaty,* in which we not only generally but singly, guarantee the integrity of Turkey. These are our engagements, and engagements which we endeavour to fulfil ; and if these engagements, renovated and repeated only four years ago by the wisdom of Europe, are to be treated by the honourable and learned gentleman † as idle wind and chaff, and we are to be told that our political duty is to expel the Turks by force to the other side of the Bosphorus, then politics ceases to be an art, statesmanship becomes a mere mockery, and the House of Commons, instead of being faithful to its traditions, had better resolve itself into one of those revolutionary clubs which settle all political and social questions with as much ease as the honourable and learned gentleman himself."

Next day the secret was out, and Mr. Disraeli exchanged the name by which he had been known to the

---

* 1856.   † Sir W. Harcourt.

public for nearly fifty years, and the place endeared to him by a thousand interesting and elevating associations, for the title of Lord Beaconsfield and the leadership of the House of Lords.

The foreign policy of Lord Beaconsfield will be judged, of course, by his policy on the Eastern Question. The Indian and African troubles which arose during his administration were provincial and colonial, not foreign ; and no other European question troubled the horizon between 1874 and 1880.

It was a fixed idea, not only with Lord Beaconsfield, but with a large portion of the British people, that since the death of Lord Palmerston, England had lost her old place among the nations of Europe, and that the great Powers of the Continent were inclined to take very little account of her in considering the forces with which they had to reckon in the execution of their own plans. The paramount necessity of convincing them that England was still the England of Palmerston, Canning, and Pitt, weighed, perhaps, with Lord Beaconsfield almost as much as the duty of defending British interests. But it may come to be suspected hereafter that the demeanour of the Opposition was more to blame for the encouragement which it gave to Russia, than the policy of Lord Beaconsfield for the encouragement which it gave to Turkey.

The Eastern Question, which Lord Beaconsfield's evil genius called up to trouble him in his declining years, occupied the attention of England and of Europe for about three years—that is, from July 1875 to July 1878. It was in the summer of the first-mentioned year that disturbances had broken out in the European provinces of Turkey, but it was not till late in the autumn that they seemed likely to lead to serious results. Lord Beaconsfield, however, was one of the first to appreciate their importance. On the 9th of November he told his audience in the Guildhall that they might be fraught with very critical consequences. And so they were. The first attempt on the part of the Powers to aid in composing these disturbances was made through Count Andrassy, the Austrian foreign minister, who proposed a scheme of administrative reform to the Porte which the revolted provinces might accept. This came to nothing, chiefly, as Lord Beaconsfield said, because it was "inopportune"; in other words, because a country plunged in bankruptcy, as Turkey then was, and struggling with almost insuperable financial difficulties, was not in a position to carry out a great scheme of administrative reform.

England signed the Note, but expected very little from it. The project fell through, and the insurrection continued with varying success; till at length, in the following May 1876, the Berlin Memorandum was drawn up, calling on Turkey, more imperatively and menacingly than in the Andrassy Note, to undertake these reforms. To this Memorandum England refused to be a party, because, as Lord Beaconsfield explained, in case these reforms were not executed within a given time, it implied the right of the Powers to enforce them by armed intervention, a right which Lord Beaconsfield repudiated as a violation of those treaty engagements which had been solemnly renewed and sanctioned so recently as 1871. Lord Beaconsfield was treading exactly in the footsteps of both Mr. Canning and the Duke of Wellington. His language on the Berlin Memorandum might have been taken direct from some of Canning's despatches on the Greek Question in 1826 and 1827.

In the meantime, however, reports had been brought
to this country, grossly exaggerated as they afterwards turned out to be, of the cruelties and outrages
of the Turkish irregular troops in suppressing the
rebellion. " The Bulgarian Atrocities " were taken up
by the Leaders of the Opposition, and flaming speeches
delivered from one end of the kingdom to the other,
denouncing alike the ruffians who committed them, the
Turks who connived at them, and our own Government
who were loudly accused of laughing at them. A speech
delivered by Mr. Disraeli on the 26th of June was
twisted into the most absurd perversion of its natural
meaning. Referring to the tortures alleged to have
been inflicted on Bulgarian prisoners, the Prime
Minister merely said he was inclined to doubt the truth
of these stories, because among the Turks "a more ex-
peditious mode of business was generally adopted."
These words were instantly seized upon by a school of
writers and talkers in this country who have done more
to make earnestness ridiculous than a whole legion of
cynics, and held up to public execration as a specimen
of cold-blooded frivolity. The country rang with
furious denunciations of the savages in Turkey and
their sympathisers in Downing Street, which unques-
tionably had the effect of prolonging the resistance of
the insurgents, and especially of the Servians, who continued in arms till the following October. Then came
the Russian Ultimatum demanding an armistice, which
the Porte granted, and then the Conference of Constantinople in December, which Lord Salisbury attended
as Plenipotentiary, but which proved abortive as all
foresaw, the Turks steadily refusing to accept a High
Commission nominated by foreigners to carry out
internal reforms in the Turkish Empire.

The whole account of the negotiations and transactions of the year 1876 is to be found in an admirably
clear and concise form in Lord Beaconsfield's Guildhall
speech on the 9th of November, where we find stated
more plainly than elsewhere the real reason of his
refusal to accept the Berlin Memorandum.

So matters went on till the following March, when
finally a Protocol was drawn up and signed by the Great
Powers, expressing a hope that, peace now being restored,
Turkey would at length set about the business of reform
in good earnest. "The Powers," it was said, "propose
to watch carefully the manner in which the promises of
the Ottoman Government are carried into effect ; and if
their hopes should once more be disappointed . . .
they reserve to themselves to consider in common as to
the means which they may deem best fitted to secure
the well-being of the Christian population and the interests of the general peace." These are nearly the
terms of the Treaty of London of 1827 ; and two things
things are clear from them : one that Turkey was to be
allowed some time for carrying out these reforms, which
in her then financial state could not be effected in a
day; the other, that should it ever become necessary
for the Powers to take further action, they must do so
"in common." This condition was in accordance with
the Treaties of 1856 and 1871. But what followed ?

Three weeks afterwards Russia declared war against
Turkey, of her own accord, without either consulting
her co-signatories, or giving any further notice to the
Porte. A more flagrant insult to the other Powers, or
a clearer violation of the law of nations, can scarcely
be imagined. Lord Derby, on the 1st of May, wrote
an indignant despatch to the Russian Government,
characterising its conduct as it deserved. But the

English Government did not think it necessary to treat it as a *casus belli.*

Lord Beaconsfield always kept before his mind two great principles of foreign policy; first, that no engagement by which all the members of an alliance are equally bound can be set aside by one without the consent of all the rest; secondly, that every State must be held to be the judge of its own interests, and has a right to interfere between belligerents when those interests are threatened. The violation of the first of these principles justifies any one of the contracting Powers in armed interference, but does not impose it as a duty unless the others are prepared to join in it. As regards the second, States as well as individuals are bound by the rule of law so to use their own as not to injure what belongs to others; and accordingly Lord Beaconsfield informed Russia, when the war broke out, that the neutrality of England must be "conditional neutrality," dependent on the observance of this rule by the belligerents. As soon as it was set at defiance by the Treaty of San Stephano, which became known in England at the beginning of March 1878, he took immediate steps for recalling Russia to the due observance of her obligations. He insisted that the Treaty should be laid before the other Powers, that, in the words of the Protocol, they should consider it "in common," and that the pacification of Eastern Europe should be the work of all.

English interests being seriously menaced at the same time, Lord Beaconsfield did not hesitate for a moment to inform the Russian Government that, with or without allies, England was resolved to go to war unless these terms were immediately complied with.

Russia paused in her path, and " stared with her foot
on the prey." Lord Beaconsfield called out the Reserves,
and a division of our Indian Army was ordered to the
Mediterranean.   Then Russia saw we were in earnest,
and loosened her grip upon the victim.   By our
steady and determined attitude, the rights of Europe
had been vindicated, and the interests of England secured ; and since the first heat of factious opposition
has subsided, the wisdom and courage displayed by
Lord Beaconsfield at this particular crisis has been
universally acknowledged.   It cost him the services
of two of his most able colleagues, Lord Derby and
Lord Carnarvon, who thought that the object to
be gained was not worth the risk we ran of being plunged
into a war with Russia.   Lord Beaconsfield probably did
not think the risk so great.   England, he said, at the
Lord Mayor's dinner to which I have already referred,
if compelled to go to war, will not be obliged to ask
herself whether she can bear a second or a third cam-
paign.   He knew at the same time that this was a
question which Russia would be obliged to ask herself.
And it is more than probable that after the Shipka Pass
and the siege of Plevna had told their tale on the in-
vaders, the first redcoat that set foot in Bulgaria would
have been the signal for Russia to recross the Danube.

Of course there were other contingencies to be
taken into consideration, but so there always will
be in every dispute in which we may be entangled
with Russia.   And, at all events, Lord Beaconsfield's policy succeeded.   Russia was compelled to
give way, Constantinople was again saved, and the
Turkish Empire in Europe, though shorn of its original proportions, was still a fact.   The " calm pride
of England," which Mr. Matthew Arnold notices in

the despatches of Lord Grenville, had again done its work.

Lord Beaconsfield complained that the doctrine of English interests had been stigmatised as selfish. It is, he said, "as selfish as patriotism," and I may here perhaps be allowed to introduce a letter of Mr. Canning's on the same subject which on the 5th of November 1822 he wrote to Sir Charles Bagot, our ambassador at Constantinople, "You know my politics well enough to know what I mean when I say that for Europe I shall be desirous now and then to read *England*."

As soon as Russia had agreed to submit the Treaty of San Stephano to a European Council—a concession, be it remembered, extorted from her exclusively by Lord Beaconsfield—it was arranged that a Congress should assemble at Berlin, whither accordingly Lord Beaconsfield and Lord Salisbury repaired about the middle of the month of June 1878. Of the Treaty of San Stephano, and of the Treaty of Berlin which superseded it, I can only say in other words what has already been said so often that the world, I fear, is weary of the subject. By the first of these treaties, extorted from the Turk with a halter round his neck, Turkey in Europe was virtually annihilated, and a new and independent province of Bulgaria (the "big Bulgaria") was constituted, extending from the Danube to the Ægean, and stretching inland to the western boundaries of Macedonia. It left only a narrow strip of coast-line to Turkey, Constantinople being thus completely cut off from the outlying provinces of Bosnia and the Herzegovina; and as the new province was to be placed entirely under the control of Russia, it was clear that from the moment this Treaty became law, Russia would be mistress of the

Balkan provinces and the Black Sea, with a firm hold on the Ægean at the same time, the Sultan being left only, as a writer of the day expressed himself, with a palace and a garden.

There were other provisions in the Treaty of a very mischievous and menacing tendency. But the "big Bulgaria" was the real giant to be slain, and it was soon found, when boldly confronted, that if his head was of brass his feet were only of clay. The Congress of Berlin simply tore the Treaty up; and whoever wishes to understand the magnitude of the change which it effected should consult two speeches of Lord Beaconsfield's: one delivered soon after his return from Germany, on the 18th of July 1878, and another in reply to the Duke of Argyll, on the 16th of May 1879. The general results may be briefly summarized as follows:—The Bulgaria of San Stephano extended from Widdin to Salonica, from Mangalia to Mount Grammos. It completely cut off, as we have pointed out, the seat of Government in Turkey from the outlying provinces. It handed over large populations of Greeks and Mussulmans to Sclav rule, it strangled the small districts left to the Turks about Constantinople in its embraces. It contained 50,000 square miles, and a population of four millions. Its definitive frontiers were to be traced by a Russo-Turkish Commission, before the evacuation of Roumelia by the Russian army. The Bulgaria constituted by the Treaty of Berlin embraces an area of but 20,000 square miles, and a population of about a million and a half. It is thrust back more than a hundred miles from the Ægean, it loses the valuable port of Bourgas on the Black Sea—the only safe port in that sea—and is separated from Turkey by the Balkans; a line of defence which is left to the Turks, and which they may make impregnable.

The Treaty, of course, was severely criticised at the time; that was only to be expected. I can only refer my readers to the Parliamentary debates on the subject; and then remind them, as Lord Beaconsfield continually did remind the public, that its results, if not all that could be wished for, had been gained without the cost of war. They were the fruits of skilful and courageous diplomacy. But, of course, they were not all which might have been extorted at the point of the sword, after a long and sanguinary struggle. The only question to be answered is whether the lesser advantages which we were able to secure with peace were not to be preferred to the larger ones which might have been obtained by war? Two answers may be given to this question, and it is difficult to say which of them Lord Beaconsfield would have given had he spoken from the bottom of his heart. But the fact remains that the Treaty of Berlin cost us nothing; and whatever securities it provided against the terrible scenes that must ensue if ever the dismemberment of Turkey shall become the avowed object of any European Power, were so much clear gain.

On the familiar question of the "integrity of the Ottoman Empire," Lord Beaconsfield's views were traditional, but not superannuated. His primary object was to bar the advance of Russia to the Mediterranean, and to ensure that when the day comes,

As come it must,
When Troy's proud temples shall be laid in dust,

the Power to step in and occupy the vacant place shall not be the Muscovite. The best means to that

10

end lay in the creation of a powerful independent
State between the Adriatic and the Black Sea. But
such a State could not be established in a day. It
must be really, as well as nominally, independent; a
free Power, and not a Russian province. Lord Beaconsfield fully recognised the superiority of such a
barrier over any other that could be created against
Muscovite aggression. But in 1878 no materials
existed for such an edifice. If we turn back to what
Mr. Canning told the Greeks in 1826, and the conditions on which he was prepared to acknowledge their
independence, we shall see that he, at all events, would
have recognised the futility of attempting in 1878 to
erect an independent kingdom out of the ruins of the
Turkish Empire in Europe. With reference to the
possible establishment of commercial relations with
Greece, and other steps preliminary to a recognition of
her independence, he distinctly asserted that this could
not be done till Greece showed herself capable of
maintaining an independent existence, of carrying on a
Government of her own, and of controlling her own
military and naval forces.*

But Lord Beaconsfield's policy was distinctly shaped
with a view to the realisation of this idea at some future
time. For this purpose the grasp of Russia must at
once be loosened from these provinces, and leisure
must be secured for them to develop their internal
resources, and gradually fit themselves for the independence which it was hoped would one day be their portion. To this end precise instructions were given to
our ambassador at Constantinople, and to Mr. Michel,
our representative at Sofia, to nurse the spirit of na-

* Mr. Canning to Prince Lieven, Nov. 21, 1826.

tionality wherever they found it among the inhabitants of these countries, and to encourage them by every means in their power to acquire the faculty of self-government. In carrying out these instructions, they naturally gave umbrage to the many Russian officers who still lingered on the spot, and as soon as Lord Beaconsfield was driven from office, and the complaints of Russia reached the ears of Mr. Gladstone, Sir Henry Layard and Mr. Michel were recalled.

As an independent State could not at that time be formed, it was necessary, in the meantime, to take other steps for providing against Russian conquest, and the only alternative was to persevere in the support of Turkey, and to strengthen the hands of Austria. Should it eventually turn out that no new State could be constructed, and that the territory in question must be absorbed into one or other of the adjoining empires, it was better that it should not be Russia. An Austrian empire, stretching from Ragusa to Varna and from the Carpathians to the Balkans, or possibly farther still, should keep the Cossack from the Mediterranean for as many generations as statesmen are called on to forecast.[*]

Lord Beaconsfield, in the speech already quoted (Nov. 9th, 1877), explained the nature and origin of the Anglo-Turkish Convention, which was simply a precaution adopted by this country for the security of the Euphrates Valley. She had given the Sultan her guarantee for the integrity of his Eastern possessions in Asia Minor, and had occupied Cyprus to enable her the more readily to carry out the engagement. She also undertook to urge on Turkey those administrative reforms

---

[*] *History of Toryism*, p. 386.

10 *

in her Asiatic provinces, which should take away all cause for Russian interference in future. The Anglo-Turkish Convention was, in fact, an Indian rather than a Turkish affair, and must stand or fall by its expediency as a safeguard to our Indian Empire. The other Powers would co-operate with us in all the other branches of the Eastern Question, because they were interested in them themselves; but not in this one, in which England, accordingly, must look to "her own resources only." It did not increase our responsibilities. It only lightened them by anticipating them.

The meeting of Lord Beaconsfield with the other European statesmen who assembled at the Congress of Berlin, must have been a deeply interesting event to almost all of them. His fame, of course, had gone before him, and it seems that the reality rather exceeded than fell short of their expectations. Lord Beaconsfield always addressed the Congress in English, and the combination of dignity and power which marked his best style of speaking seems to have made a profound impression on the group of continental statesmen. Whenever he mingled in Berlin society, what struck the company most deeply was the well-known characteristics so familiar to us all in England, namely, his imperturbable demeanour. But he does not seem to have left behind him any specimens of his colloquial powers, such as made him famous among his countrymen, for the few repartees which rumour attributes to him are too poor to have been really his. As soon, however, as he touched the shores of England on his return journey, the peculiar rhetoric of which he was so fond again came into play, and "Peace with Honour," which he told the people of Dover he had brought back with him, soon became a household word.

His return to London was one long ovation. At Charing Cross he was met by the Lord Mayor in his robes of office, and an assemblage of all that was most brilliant in the worlds of politics, of beauty, and of fashion. Dense crowds of working men thronged every inch of the way from the station to Downing Street to pay their tribute of homage to the hero of the hour. Banners waved, and triumphant arches stretched from house to house to greet the great statesman who had raised aloft again the name of England and re-burnished her bedimmed escutcheon.

He made his entry into London on the 16th of July, and on the 27th he and Lord Salisbury were entertained at a great banquet by the members of the Conservative party in the Riding School at Kensington. A few days afterwards the freedom of the City was conferred upon them both by the London Corporation, and another grand banquet in their honour was held at the Guildhall. The speeches of both plenipotentiaries on both these occasions threw additional light on the settlement effected by Lord Beaconsfield. And it must not be forgotten that in the second of these two speeches Lord Beaconsfield confessed his belief that a more resolute attitude on the part of England in 1876 would have prevented the war altogether, as a similar display of firmness in 1853 would have prevented the Crimean war. He said, very generously, that he accepted his full share of the responsibility ; but it was an open secret that the responsibility did not rest with him, unless it is thought that he ought to have resigned office rather than continue to sanction a policy of which he disapproved. But the public dwelt more, perhaps, on the humour and the sarcasm with which the Prime Minister retorted on his assailants than on the facts and arguments which were set before them.   One Opposition statesman was described as " inebriate with the exuberance of his own verbosity " ; to others was imputed " the hare-brained chatter of irresponsible frivolity."   The world was contented to laugh without reflecting much on either the propriety or the taste of these sallies, and exultant "jingoism," as it was the fashion to call the warlike spirit of the day, carried everything before it, and exalted Lord Beaconsfield to as high a pinnacle of fame as has ever been reached perhaps by any English minister since the days of Chatham.

> Aspice ut insignis spoliis Marcellus opimis
> Ingreditur, victorque viros supereminet omnes.

So said Mr. Gladstone in the House of Commons in reference to the crowning moment in Lord Beaconsfield's career ; and though the gale of popular favour was destined very soon to change, it needed but the dignity of adversity to restore him to a still higher place in public estimation than that which he had occupied before, a place which he will now possess for ever.

His foreign policy must be considered as a whole, and the occupation of Cyprus, the purchase of the shares in the Suez Canal, and the " scientific frontier " of Affghanistan, were really all part and parcel of one great scheme for the security of our Indian Empire. It was indispensable that England should possess some control over the new highway opened up to her Asiatic provinces, and the nation was not less satisfied with this stroke of policy on Lord Beaconsfield's part, than with the Treaty of Berlin, or the Convention which was its necessary supplement.

Of the policy of the Affghan war of 1878–9 the best accounts are to be found in Lord Beaconsfield's speech in the House of Lords on December 10th, 1878, the speech at the Lord Mayor's dinner in the previous November, and in his speech on the evacuation of Candahar on the 4th of March 1881. It was to this last speech that Lord Granville referred a few months afterwards,* when he said that he had known him swallow drugs in order to allay for a time the pangs of neuralgia, which would otherwise have prevented him from addressing the House of Lords with the necessary clearness and animation. In the speech at Guildhall he described " the scientific frontier," which had now been secured for us ; and in the House of Lords he explained the difference between a scientific frontier and a haphazard frontier very pithily by saying that the former was one which could be defended by five thousand men, while the other would require a hundred thousand. But in a volume like the present we can take account only of general principles, and perhaps the following remarks will place Lord Beaconsfield's ideas before the public as clearly as anything else. They are taken from the December speech :—

My Lords, you have an old policy with regard to the relations of this country, India, and Afghanistan, which has been approved by all public men. Lord Lawrence, whom we all speak of with great respect, though the Lord Privy Seal says we systematically insulted him, was most decided in his policy that there should be an English interest in Afghanistan, and that Russian influence in it should not for a moment be tolerated. Well, what is your policy now? Where will English interests be when you have evacuated Afghanistan? What will be the state of Afghanistan? It will be a state of anarchy. We have always announced, as a reason for interfering in Afghanistan, that we cannot tolerate a state of anarchy on our frontiers. Is not that an argument as good for Russia as for us ? Will not the Russians say, " Afghanistan is in a state of anarchy, and we cannot go on civilising Turkestan when Afghanistan is in a state of anarchy"?

* House of Lords, May 9th, 1881.

Therefore you are furnishing Russia with an occasion for advancing. When I speak of this policy of Russia, I do not speak of it in a hostile spirit. Russia has a right to its policy as well as England, Russia has as good a right to create an empire in Tartary as we have in India. She must take the consequences if the creation of her empire endangers our power. I see nothing in that feeling on the part of England which should occasion any want of friendliness between this country and Russia. We must guard against what must be looked upon as the inevitable designs of a very great Power When Lord Palmerston carried one of the greatest measures of his life—the fortification of the Channel, which was of much more importance than the retaining of Candahar—was that looked upon as a symbol of hostility to the French people? Everyone knows that Lord Palmerston was very friendly to the French alliance, and yet that was an operation directed immediately against France, for the purpose of putting an end to the continual fluctuations of bluster and fear which such a situation as England was in at that time must necessarily entail.

What I see in the amendment is not an assertion of great principles, which no man honours more than myself. What is at the bottom of it is rather that principle of peace at any price which a certain party in this country upholds. It is that dangerous dogma which, I believe, animates the ranks before me at this moment, although many of them may be unconscious of it. That deleterious doctrine haunts the people of this country in every form. Sometimes it is a committee; sometimes it is a letter; sometimes it is an amendment to the Address; sometimes it is a proposition to stop the supplies. The doctrine has done more mischief than any I can well recall that have been afloat in this century. It has occasioned more wars than the most ruthless conquerors. It has disturbed and nearly destroyed that political equilibrium so necessary to the liberties of nations and the welfare of the world. It has dimmed occasionally for a moment even the majesty of England. And, my lords, to-night you have an opportunity, which I trust you will not lose, of branding these opinions, these deleterious dogmas, with the reprobation of the Peers of England.

In a passage in *Coningsby* the author says of Mr. Rigby that he had persuaded the world that he was not only clever, but also that he was always in luck, a quality which many people appreciate even more than capacity. Now one may surely assert that the result of

a long course of events had been to produce the contrary
impression with regard to Lord Beaconsfield and the
Tories. Many instances could be produced in support of
this assertion. But it will be enough to remark on
the very unfortunate conjunction of adverse circumstances which closed round the last years of Lord
Beaconsfield's Administration. The Zulu War, which
ought to have been no more than one of those petty
expeditions such as are almost inseparable from the
possession of a great colonial empire, was swelled by
mismanagement into an affair of the first magnitude,
and all the disgrace and all the grief occasioned by
Isandula were visited on the head of Lord Beaconsfield. At the same time, the favourable condition,
of trade and agriculture, which had lasted almost
without intermission from the repeal of the Corn
Laws to the resignation of Mr. Gladstone, rapidly
declined from that date; and an unparalleled series of
bad seasons and miserable harvests, combined with an
ever-growing foreign competition, helped to generate
wide-spread distress among the agricultural classes, with
its natural concomitants of discontent, irritability, and
a blind belief that any change must be for the better.
But three very favourable elections occurring about
the same time at Sheffield, Liverpool, and South-
wark, shed a delusive ray of popularity over the
Conservative Government, and persuaded Lord Beaconsfield's colleagues that now or never was the time to
appeal to the people. Just before the dissolution he
addressed a letter to the Duke of Marlborough, the
Lord Lieutenant of Ireland, dwelling on the dangerous
condition of that country, which was much censured at
the time, but the truth of which was speedily acknowledged. However, the people were bent upon a change.

The Conservative Party lost one hundred and eleven seats. And Lord Beaconsfield, who had never been sanguine of the result, retired once more to his old position without any external signs of chagrin or disappointment.

He was now in his seventy-sixth year, and time and toil and trouble had done their work upon him. But the dignity with which he bore his change of fortune, and the wise and moderate counsels by which, for the brief period still left to him, he regulated the counsels of his party, were the theme of general remark. To distract his own attention, as much perhaps as for any other purpose, he went back to literature, and as he had solaced himself after the great reverse of 1868 with the composition of *Lothair*, so did he now with the composition of *Endymion*, which was published in November 1880, and of which what I have to say will be found in a subsequent chapter. But at the opening of Parliament in January 1881 he appeared in his place, apparently in his usual health, and spoke both on the Address (January 6th), and on Lord Lytton's policy in India as effectively as ever. This, however, was his last great speech in Parliament, and it is interesting to know that his last words were uttered in defence of the great Empire, and the great principles of government, of which he had all his life been the faithful soldier and servant.

I saw him for the last time at a London party one evening in March, and he then seemed to be quite as strong and well as a man of his age could be expected to be. But on the 23rd it became known that he was suffering from an attack of bronchitis, and as the symptoms grew more serious, the sympathy and anxiety of the public became general and profound. Of the four weeks that followed, during which Lord

Beaconsfield's condition was in every heart and on every tongue, a detailed account is to be found in the newspapers of the period, and need not be repeated here. His illness fluctuated with the changes of the weather, which was generally, however, unfavourable to his complaint, and the complication of gout and bronchitis made the treatment of it proportionably difficult. All day long his door in Curzon Street was besieged by a succession of visitors eager to see the latest medical report, or to testify their respect and affection for the illustrious patient. The Queen and the Prince of Wales were constant in their inquiries, and groups of working men assembled every morning in Curzon Street, deeply interested in the life of one whom they recognised not less as the benefactor of their own order than as the vindicator of their country's honour.

During the progress of his illness Lord Beaconsfield retained his cheerfulness, and conversed occasionally upon public affairs with his usual spirit. The only friends, however, who were admitted to his bedside were Lord Rowton, Lord Barrington, and Sir Philip Rose, who were sometimes surprised at the apparent strength and vivacity which he exhibited. Towards the end of the second week in April the weather grew comparatively mild, and hopes were entertained that the strength of Lord Beaconsfield's constitution might still enable him to rally. On the 17th, however, the wind turned to the north-east, and the cold once more became severe. On the 18th, Easter Sunday, the effect of it on the patient was very visible, and towards night became alarming. About midnight he sank into a stupor, and at half-past four on the morning of Tuesday the 19th he died, his right hand in the clasp of his dear

friends Lord Barrington and Lord Rowton, and his left
in that of Dr. Kidd.

So passed away one of those extraordinary characters
who appear only at intervals of centuries. No such
public grief has been witnessed in England since the
the death of Mr. Pitt, and even that was confined to a
narrower circle, and chiefly to the people of Great Britain. But the death of Lord Beaconsfield affected all
classes and all countries. The peasant and the artizan,
the middle classes, the aristocracy, and the Court were
stirred by a common sorrow, while some of the most
touching tributes to Lord Beaconsfield's character and
genius, and most accurate estimates of the great loss
which England had sustained, are to be found in the
columns of Contineual journals, the conductors of
which well knew that it was not England alone on whom
the blow had fallen.

Lord Beaconsfield was buried on Monday the 28th of
April in the vault of Hughenden Church, by the side
of Lady Beaconsfield, and not far from one who had
left her fortune to the great statesman whom she vene-
rated, on the romantic condition that in death at least
they should not be divided. The day will long be remembered by Hughenden, by Buckinghamshire, and by
England. The Prince of Wales, the Duke of Con-
naught, and Prince Leopold saw his coffin lowered into
the grave; and the surrounding circle included the
Marquis of Salisbury, the Marquis of Exeter, Count
Munster, Sir Stafford Northcote, Lord John Manners,
Lord Beauchamp, Lord Lytton, Sir Frederick Leighton,
Lord Henry Lennox, Mr. Cecil Raikes, Lord Laming-
ton—"peers of every degree, the representatives of the
greatest sovereigns of the world, and men whose names
are part of the history of England." Lord Rowton

and Lord Barrington stood on the right hand of the clergyman, and next to them Mr. Ralph Disraeli with his son Coningsby Disraeli, then a boy of twelve years old, and the future owner of Hughenden. But not the least interesting feature of this interesting and melancholy day was the assembly gathered together on the road outside the church, consisting of the statesman's humbler friends and neighbours in his Buckinghamshire home, farmers and labourers and tradesmen, women and children, all, if not in black, at least with some token of mourning displayed upon their persons. It may be said that till the day of his death England hardly knew how much she had loved the deceased statesman, and that she might almost have exclaimed, with the child mourning for his brother, that while he was still spared to her she could have wished that she had loved him more.

On the 30th of April Her Majesty and the Princess Beatrice paid a visit to Hughenden, when the Queen, having descended into the vault, and placed another wreath of white camelias on Lord Beaconsfield's coffin, took a last farewell of the loyal and trusted Minister, who, whatever his faults and errors, had always been true to herself, and to all that he believed most conducive to the glory of the English monarchy.

Lord Beaconsfield was very fond of flowers, and of them his favourite was the primrose. After his death it became the emblem of the principles which he represented, and the badge of all those who wished to be considered his disciples. A Primrose League was established for the propagation of "that new creed which is the old," the Toryism which he had cleared of its excrescences, and restored to its pristine popularity; and Primrose Clubs sprang up in abundance with the same

object in view.   The day of his death is still observed
as Primrose Day, and it has now long been evident
that the love and admiration with which he had
inspired the English people was no fickle or evanescent
passion excited by a showy and meretricious policy, and
ending with the phenomena that produced it, but a
deep and lasting sentiment, founded on a firm belief in
the greatness of his character, the power of his intellect, and the important services which he had rendered
to the Constitution and the Empire.

In both Houses of Parliament graceful and eloquent
tributes to his memory were paid by the Leaders of
both parties.   Lord Granville said, " My Lords, it is
impossible for anyone to deny that Lord Beaconsfield
played a great part in English history.   No one can
deny his rare and splendid gifts, and how continuous
have been his services with regard to the Crown and
Parliament."   The Marquis of Salisbury said :—

That his friends and colleagues should mourn his loss and revere
his memory is only too natural. I have not the same title to speak on
this subject as many of those beside me, because my close political
connection with him was comparatively recent. But it lasted through
anxious and difficult times, when the character of men may be plainly
seen by those who work with them. And to me, as I believe to all
others who have worked with him, his patience, his gentleness, his
unswerving and unselfish loyalty to his colleagues and fellow-
labourers, have made an impression which will never leave me so long
as life endures. But these feelings could only affect a limited circle
of his immediate adherents. The impression which his career and
character have made on the vast mass of his countrymen must be
sought elsewhere. To a great extent, no doubt, it is due to the peculiar character of his genius, to its varied nature, to the wonderful
combination of qualities he possessed, and which rarely reside in the
same brain. To some extent, also, there is no doubt that the circumstances to which the noble Earl has so eloquently alluded—that is, the
social difficulties which opposed themselves to his early rise, and the
splendid perseverance by which they were overcome—impressed his
countrymen, who love to see exemplified that career open to all

persons, whatever their initial difficulties may be, which is one of the characteristics of the institutions of which they are most proud.

Zeal for the greatness of England was the passion of his mind. Opinions might, and did, differ deeply as to the measures and steps by which expression was given to the dominant feelings, and more and more, as life drew near its close, as the heat and turmoil of controversy were left behind, as the gratification of every possible ambition negatived the suggestion of any inferior motives, and brought out into greater prominence the purity and strength of this one intense feeling, the people of this country recognised the force with which this desire dominated his actions.

In the questions of interior policy which divided classes he had to consider them, he had to judge them, and to take his course accordingly. It seemed to me that he treated them always as of secondary interest, compared to this one great question—how the country to which he belonged might be made united and strong.

Mr. Gladstone said :—

The career of Lord Beaconsfield is, in many respects, the most remarkable one in Parliamentary history. For my own part, I know but one that can fairly be compared to it in regard to the emotion of surprise, and when viewed as a whole, an emotion, I might almost say, of wonder; and that is the career, and especially the earlier career, of Mr. Pitt.

There were certain great qualities of the deceased statesmen on which I think it right to touch. His extraordinary intellectual powers are as well understood by others as by me, and they are not proper subjects for our present commendation. But there were other great qualities—qualities not merely intellectual, in the sense of being dissociated from conduct, but qualities immediately connected with conduct, with regard to which I should say, were I a younger man, that I should like to stamp the recollection of them on myself for my own future guidance, and with regard to which I will confidently say to those who are younger than myself, that I would strongly recommend them for notice and imitation. They were qualities not only written in a marked manner on his career, but possessed by him in a degree undoubtedly extraordinary. I speak, for example, of such as these—his strength of will, his long-sighted persistency of purpose, reaching from the first entrance on the avenue of life to its very close his remarkable powers of self-government; and last, but not least, of all, his great parliamentary courage, a quality in which I, who have been associated in the course of my life with some scores of ministers have never known but two who could be pronounced his equal.

These two were possibly. Lord John Russell and the late Lord Derby. With this record of opinion from his great antagonist, the narrative of Lord Beaconsfield's public life may be appropriately closed. It remains to speak of his general position as a statesman, an orator, and a man of letters.

CHAPTER VII.

STATESMAN AND ORATOR.

Estimates of Lord Beaconsfield's statesmanship—His foreign policy—
His domestic policy — Theory of popular government—One
opinion of the duties of Conservatism — Lord Beaconsfield's
opinion—Changes in his views—Distrust of the middle class—
Our territorial constitution —The Irish question—Lord Beaconsfield's ecclesiastical views—The monarchichal revival—Idealism
of Lord Beaconsfield—Increased power of the minister—Lord
Beaconsfield's position as an orator—Specimens of his eloquence
—His use of rhetoric—His vein of irony—Famous sarcasms.

OF Lord Beaconsfield's statesmanship various estimates
have been formed. That he was one of the greatest
Party Leaders which our system of government has
produced will be generally admitted. But a man may
be a great Party Leader without being a great statesman; and to determine whether his claims to this higher
dignity are well founded or not, we must consider how
far he comprehends the character of his own age,
whether in his dealings with the contingencies and
emergencies which it thrusts upon him he displays the
qualities of foresight, sagacity, and the power of taking
broad views of political affairs, or whether, so to speak,
he only lives from hand to mouth, and is satisfied

with so adjusting public questions as to suit the temporary exigencies or prejudices of his own party without looking farther ahead.   Lord Beaconsfield has been accused of doing this ; of sacrificing Conservative principles for the sake of place and power, and of inflicting deep wounds on the Constitution for selfish and ambitious objects.   It may be permitted us on the present occasion to examine the validity of this charge with some little attention, since it is doubtful even now whether the delusion in which it had its origin has ever been properly exposed.

Of Lord Beaconsfield's statesmanship in the department of Foreign Affairs, it is sufficient to say that he followed the traditional policy of Chatham, Pitt, Grenville, Canning, and Palmerston, as distinguished from those theories on the subject which a later school of Radical politicians have more recently introduced. That England, though a small island, is the head of a vast empire, which through its commerce and its colonies is connected by a thousand links with the European system, as firmly and as closely as if it had been conterminous with France, Germany, or Russia ; consequently that our interests are more or less affected by every continental complication, and that alliances and interventions are as much a necessity to ourselves as to any of the great military Powers ; that a policy of isolation is in principle like a policy of disarmament, founded on the belief that it is better to run the risk of ruin than to pay the cost of insurance—such are the few cardinal maxims which have ruled the foreign policy of all our greatest modern statesmen. They lie upon the surface, and require neither defence nor explanation.   But that is not the case with the domestic policy of Lord Beaconsfield, which was based on considerations not, indeed, very abstruse or recondite, but requiring, nevertheless, a little more thought than the Tadpoles and Tapers of the day are generally willing to bestow on them.

In the course of the debates on the Reform Bill of 1867, Lord Beaconsfield pointed out that the objections brought against his measure were fatal in reality to all popular government, since all popular government involved the periodical extension of political privileges. These might, of course, be abused, and made subservient to revolutionary agitators. But that could not be helped. Nobody will maintain at the present day that it would have been possible for any Government, after 1832, to continue to hold power on the avowed principle of resisting all popular innovations. Even the Conservatives of 1867 would hardly have said that. What they did say was this, that it was not for the Conservative Party to undertake such changes, without apparently perceiving that such a doctrine was tantamount to condemning the Conservative Party to perpetual exclusion from office, on any honourable or independent terms. If they come into power on such an understanding, they can only retain it till their opponents have determined what is the next great change that can most advantageously be announced, and what the most popular cry to raise throughout the country. A session is enough for this, and in the meantime a Conservative Government must necessarily be a Government upon sufferance, and therefore an object of contempt. Lord Beaconsfield knew what it was to hold office on sufferance, and the iron had entered into his soul.

There were not wanting Conservatives in 1867 who were willing to face this position and accept the logical result. Let the Conservative Party they said, be hence-

11 *

forth recognised as the Constitutional Opposition, whose business it is to temper, modify, and restrain the Radical tendencies of Liberalism, but never to assume the Government. If popular progress is the order of the day, the proper *régime* is a Liberal Government to introduce organic changes, and a Conservative Opposition to prevent them from going too far. Thus each party will be in its right place, and both perhaps equally useful. The Conservative Party will occupy an intelligible and honourable position, and always be able to act up to its original principles. Unfortunately, however, this theory of Parliamentary Government, if carried a step farther will be found to destroy itself. An Opposition, to discharge the functions here assigned to it, must be powerful, and an Opposition to be powerful must be formidable. But an Opposition which abjured office would have no terrors for any Ministry. It could only fire blank cartridges, and, make as much noise as it would, nobody would be really hurt. In other words, an Opposition which acted on this principle would cease to be an Opposition at all in the Parliamentary sense of the term, and could exercise little or no control over the policy of the Government. What becomes, then, of its pretensions to keep in check Radical proclivities ?

But this is not all. Such an Opposition as this, while it would have no weight with the Ministry, would have no attractions for the public. Clever young men would cease to throw in their lot with a party which made a virtue of renouncing all the prizes of public life. The leaders of the Bar who look to a Parliamentary career as the surest road to professional advancement, would no longer be found on the Opposition benches, and the party would be robbed of a tributary which is now one of its chief elements of strength. Ceasing to be continually reinforced by the best brains in the country, and the fresh energies of the rising generation, the Opposition, would dwindle to a shadow, and become totally incapable of exercising that conservative influence for the sake of which alone it had adopted this self-denying ordinance. For the Conservative Party to fulfil its mission, it must retain the power of attracting into its ranks the young, able, and ambitious men of each succeeding generation, and of holding over the ministers of the day the constant possibility of a change. To do this they must be in a position not only to take office, but to keep it. And to place themselves in this position they must be ready to move with the times, and show themselves capable of satisfying the wants of the nation.

Lord Beaconsfield saw that this rule of action, so far from being a sacrifice of Conservative principles, was really the only way of giving effect to them. Changes which cannot be prevented may be rendered less destructive in Conservative hands than they would be in Radical hands; and Conservatives are acting just as honourable and dignified a part in adopting a policy of which they disapprove in the abstract, that they may render it less mischievous in the concrete, as they would be in resisting it altogether when their resistance is certain to be useless. This was the conviction on which Lord Beaconsfield acted; and it was surely a statesman-like conviction. He knew that we lived in revolutionary times, and he saw that the only way in such times of securing any share of influence to Conservative ideas was that which I have described. With many Conservative Members of Parliament it is simply enough that they dislike a thing, that it seems to them intrinsically undesirable, to make them think it must be doggedly resisted without looking to the right or to the left. They do not consider that, in an age like the present, politics, from the Conservative point of view, are often but a choice of evils. They did not see this in times past, even if they see it now. But Lord Beaconsfield saw it, and proved his statesmanship by acting on it.

It ought to be unnecessary at the present day to argue such a point as this. Parties are always in a state of change. It is the law of their nature. Whigs and Tories, Conservatives and Radicals are always, to borrow a metaphor from Mr. Gladstone, going through the process analogous to that which is constantly taking place in our bodily system. To recognise the truth where others fail to see it, and to act upon it when all around us are resisting it, is one test of statesmanship, as well as of political philosophy, from which Lord Beaconsfield certainly need not shrink. What his Conservative critics would have had him do was a practical impossibility.

In his conception of the English Constitution, and of the relations of parties to each other, Lord Beaconsfield shifted his standpoint, as he gained more practical experience. In the *Life of Lord George Bentinck*, he describes the Whigs as the leaders of the English aristocracy. When he wrote these words he must have meant by the aristocracy the nobility, and have been comparing them with the Tory country gentlemen who did undoubtedly at one time represent popular feeling more accurately than the Whigs. He loved to dwell on the popular character and functions of "the knightly order" and the great part which it had played in history. He himself has told us that between 1783 and 1815 the positions of English parties were reversed. But he seems for a long time to have dwelt on the possibility of their returning to their original positions, and though it is clear that by the year 1873, when he made the speech which is quoted at page 57, he was alive to the fact that both classes of the aristocracy were in the same boat at last, and that the nobility and country gentlemen had no longer any separate interests, but must stand or fall together.

The fact is that Lord Beaconsfield in his library, giving the rein to his imagination, and tracing all kinds of analogies between the past and present state of politics, and Lord Beaconsfield in the House of Commons, dealing with actual circumstances and educating his party upon questions calling for immediate settlement, were two distinct men, leading two lives almost as different from each other as were the two lives led, according to Lockhart, by Sir Walter Scott. In the one he was a Wyndham, a Shippen or a Bromley fighting for the Church, the landed interest, and the poor, against the Whigs, the Dissenters, the moneyed interest, and the mob, deploring the degradation of the Crown and the predominance of a crafty oligarchy. In the other he was the keen and ready-witted leader of the modern Tory Party, including in its ranks the greater part of that very oligarchy, which history taught him to be the natural enemy of Toryism, engaged in the defence of principles never called in question by our ancestors, and responding to watchwords which, to them, would have been wholly unintelligible.

In the one capacity he was as speculative as Hobbes or Harrington; in the other, as practical as the Conservative attorneys who " nibbed their pens and whispered there was nothing like reaction." He lived these two lives separately and alternately till his last hour; but, unlike what might have been expected, they rarely interfered with each other. For the popular Toryism with which he is associated was founded on an acute perception of the character of his own times, and of the only means by which Conservatism could become a real power in the country.

In one respect, and in one only, does he seem to have been always the same, and that was in his distrust of the middle classes as an element of political stability. In his speech on the Chartist petition in 1839 he gave utterance to this sentiment. It is to be found again in a very remarkable speech which he delivered on the 20th of February 1846, and every page of *Coningsby* and *Sybil* is rife with it. He believed that permanent and powerful governments might be founded on either monarchy, oligarchy, or democracy. But he had no faith in a *bourgeoise* constitution.

In his views regarding the peasantry and the artisans, the commercial capitalists, and the rural aristocracy, we may trace the influence of Cobbett. Cobbett believed in our "territorial constitution" as much as Lord Beaconsfield, but he wished to see it rescued from the predominance of dukes, marquises, and nabobs, with their overgrown estates, and sighed for the days when the halls and manor houses, inhabited by country gentlemen of ancient birth and moderate estate, had not yet been bought up by the Tritons and turned into farmhouses. Mr. Disraeli was obliged to handle this part of the question somewhat delicately. But what he thought upon the subject is plainly discernible in *Sybil*, where the very words of Cobbett are occasionally to be discovered.

While, however, we may entirely agree with Lord Beaconsfield in his estimate of our territorial constitution, a conjecture may be hazarded that if, on any point, his statesmanship was the dupe of his imagination, it was on this.   In the speech on the threshold of the great Corn Law struggles of 1846, he said :—

I have now nearly concluded the observations which I shall address to the House.   I have omitted a great deal which I wished to urge upon the House, and I sincerely wish that what I have said had been urged with more ability, but I have endeavoured not to make a more Corn Law speech.   I have only taken corn as an illustration ; but I don't like my friends here to enter upon that Corn Law debate, which I suppose is impending, under a mistaken notion of the position in which they stand.   I never did rest my defence of the Corn Laws on the burdens to which land is subject.   I believe that there are burdens, heavy burdens, on the land ; but the land has great honours, and he who has great honours must have great burdens.   But I wish them to bear in mind that their cause must be sustained by great principles. I venture feebly and slightly to indicate those principles, principles of high policy, on which their system ought to be sustained.   First, without reference to England, looking at all countries, I say that it is the first duty of the Minister, and the first interest of the State, to maintain a balance between the two great branches of national industry.   I repeat what I have said before, that in this country there are special reasons why we should give a preponderance—I do not say a predominance—why we should give a preponderance, for that is the proper and constitutional word, to the agricultural branch ; and the reason is, because in England we have a territorial constitution.   We have thrown upon the land the revenues of the Church, the administration of justice, and the estate of the poor ; and this has been done, not to gratify the pride or pamper the luxury of the proprietors of the land, but because in a territorial constitution you, and those whom you have succeeded, have found the only security for self-government, the only barrier against that centralising system which has taken root in other countries.   I have always maintained these opinions My constituents are not landlords ; they are not aristocrats ; they are not great capitalists   they are the children of industry and toil ; and they believe, first, that their material interests are involved in a system which favours native industry by insuring at the same time real competition ; but they believe also that their social and political interests are involved in a system by which their rights and liberties have been guaranteed ; and I agree with them—I have the same old-fashioned notions.

At page 30 of this little volume will be found a much earlier speech, giving expression to the same opinions in more rhetorical and glowing colours.   But at all periods of his life he was fond of reverting to them, and of speaking of the country gentlemen of England as the natural leaders of the people : and I cannot help thinking that he must have sometimes shut his eyes to the effect of recent changes in our political and social system, which have certainly weakened, though they may not have finally destroyed, the foundations of the ancient *régime.*   Our territorial constitution grew up at a time when all property and all powers were territorial, and though of all the forms in which property and power can be embodied, this is probably on the whole the most beneficial to society, yet with the development of trade and commerce, rival interests and rival aspirations are certain to spring up, jealous of the privileges attaching to the ownership of land, and severely critical on the working of " a territorial constitution."   In England this last has long been declining in importance.   Public offices and public duties once inseparably connected with landed property, have now been severed from it.   The House of Commons is no longer led by members of the territorial class, and though forty years ago it still presented, as it does still, an imposing exterior, the shock given to feudal ideas by the French Revolution, the reduction of aristocratic influence by the Reform Bill of 1832, and the enormous concurrent development of the manufacturing interests, have all been working for the degradation of that great system, the merits of which Lord Beaconsfield did not over-estimate, and which has found one of its warmest eulogists in Mr. Gladstone himself.*

It is open to doubt whether Lord Beaconsfield fully understood this.   He was loth to part with the belief that the country gentlemen of England represented "the

* Cf. p. 65.

popular political confederacy " of this country, and still retained their ancient place in the hearts of the labouring classes. He knew that evil tongues had come between them, but it is uncertain if he appreciated the full extent of the mischief; and perhaps we ought to hope that he died in the faith in which he lived, namely, that the extension of popular privileges could never be injurious to those who deserved well of the people. We have not seen the end yet, and Lord Beaconsfield may have been quite right. His prescience was rarely at fault. He stood alone in his belief in the Conservative working man. His belief in a Conservative peasantry may prove equally well founded. But the circumstances are not analogous, and one need not be an alarmist to think that on this point he may possibly have been over sanguine.

But though he may have miscalculated the force of those hostile agencies which the nineteenth century has developed, it does not follow that his admiration of " the territorial constitution " was not well worthy of a statesman. Lord Beaconsfield believed that the persons most proper to be entrusted with the exercise of local authority and local administration should naturally be looked for in the more conservative elements of society, which have been supposed since the days of Aristotle to reside in the proprietors of the soil. He thought that the administration of justice and the interests of the poor were alike benefited by being confided to the hands of men who had hereditary claims on the respect and affection of the people. Such a system, it is said, lightens the pressure of authority by the influence of immemorial prescription, and dignifies the receipt of charity by imparting to it some flavour of the kindness which springs from a family relationship.

Finally, without underrating the patriotism and self-devotion of the manufacturing and commercial classes, which they have proved on many memorable occasions, Lord Beaconsfield was of opinion that the possession of land intensified the love of country, and invested it with a concrete form which commerce alone could not supply. He thought that in times of trouble more fortitude, resolution, and patience were to be expected from a territorial than from a commercial aristocracy; and it was the avowed intention of the Anti-Corn Law Leaders to substitute the one for the other in this country, which more than anything else made Lord Beaconsfield a Protectionist. These views may be unfashionable. They may be mistaken. But they have a recognised *locus standi* in political philosophy, and well become an English statesman.

On what is now the great question of the day Lord Beaconsfield's opinions varied with the course of events; but there is no doubt that had the settlement of the Irish Question lain with himself from forty to fifty years ago he would have arranged it on broad and equitable principles, which would have saved us all our present difficulties. Let us never forget his memorable words spoken in 1843: "An alien Church, an absentee aristocracy, and a starving people—that is the Irish Question." To establish the Church of the people in Ireland, as we have established the Church of the people in Scotland, was his remedy for the first grievance which lay at the root of the evil. How he would have dealt with the second it is impossible to say. But it is clear enough that a resident Irish aristocracy, such as the wealthy landed proprietors who lived almost entirely in England, would have gone a long way towards improving the condition of Irish agriculture, so as to make starvation, at all events, impossible. But when the Irish Question was at length taken up by Mr. Gladstone it was too late. The Fenian agitation had begun. And although, in Mr. Disraeli's opinion, it was very nearly stamped out when Mr. Gladstone blew up the embers, it practically made it impossible for English statesmen to recur to any such remedies as might have been effective at an earlier period. Mr. Disraeli then said, Leave Ireland alone. Between 1848 and 1865 she had been advancing steadily along the path of social progress. The Fenian movement was essentially a foreign one, fanned by bad management into something much more formidable, but capable at one time of being crushed without any difficulty. Natural causes had removed some of Ireland's difficulties. Time, patience, and perseverance would have done the rest. Mr. Gladstone's Irish measures of 1869 and 1870 seemed to Lord Beaconsfield not to be the cure of an old agitation so much as the creation of a new one.

It was on ecclesiastical subjects that Lord Beaconsfield was seen to least advantage. Of the recent history of the Church of England, and of the true nature of the questions which separate her from Rome and from Geneva, his knowledge was imperfect; and his ideas, in consequence, unlike those which he had formed on politics and society, were not original. He took them from those whom he believed to be well informed upon the subject, and was sometimes deceived by appearances, sometimes converted by clamour, and sometimes made the tool of party. Yet all the time it is difficult to doubt on which side lay his real sympathies. The natural bent of his mind was to see in the Catholic Church only a continuation of the Jewish, and to recognise in her rites and ceremonies the legitimate fulfilment of those which God had ordained in the Old Testament. He tells us that the Romish Church possesses "the old learning as well as the new." When he refers to the Papacy it is not to condemn the Pope, but to suggest that the visible head of the Church should have been seated, not at Rome, but at Jerusalem. Both on the Monarchy and the Church of England the sentiments which he puts into the mouths of Coningsby and Henry Sidney are those of Hurrell Froude.

I believe that these, his earliest expressed opinions, were the most congenial to his mind, as they were certainly most in harmony with the political creed, the primitive Toryism, which he had adopted. But they were not founded on independent study; they were not built upon a rock, and were liable to be shaken by any gust of popular passion which assailed them. No one would ever have thought it likely that the author of *Sybil* could support a Bill "to put down Ritualism"; and we know that Mr. Disraeli's first impulse was to oppose it. But he yielded to representations with which his own information did not enable him to cope, and made one of the greatest mistakes of his life in consequence.

Again, when he said with reference to *Essays and Reviews* that he, too, was for free enquiry, but that it must be by free enquirers, he was not *en rapport* with the general tone and temper of the better class of English clergy. Notwithstanding the truth which the words undoubtedly contain, they jarred on the ears of many men who were as orthodox as Lord Eldon and as firm believers in the literal inspiration of the Bible as Luther. The fact is, the one thing which he did not thoroughly understand in England was the Church. And the clergy, on the other hand, did not understand him. This, unfortunately, was the source of woes unnumbered to the Conservative Party, for which a large share of the responsibility must undoubtedly rest with Lord Beaconsfield. He allowed. himself to fall into the hands of a party with whom at the outset of his career he had no sympathy whatever. But had he been told that the Public Worship Regulation Bill was not in accordance with the principles which " the descendants of the cavaliers" might be expected to espouse,* he would have replied, perhaps, that since he last appealed to those principles " many things had happened," and that it was useless to galvanize a corpse.

Lord Beaconsfield, while Prime Minister, between 1874 and 1880, was frequently accused of attempting "to revive personal government." The charge was absurd enough, but it was eagerly taken up in certain quarters, and men said it was only what was to be expected from the author of *Coningsby.* Now what the author of *Coningsby* had glanced at merely as one mode of escape from the difficulties created by the Reform Bill—difficulties summed up in the Duke's well-known question, How is the King's Government to be carried on ?—was undoubtedly something more than the revival of those monarchical functions which, since the death of William the Third had, with the exception of one brief interval, been practically in abeyance. It was nothing less than the termination of Parliamentary supremacy altogether in favour of a genuine monarchy, controlled by journalism, and assisted in the work of administration by " a vast pile of municipal and local government."

* See Speech in House of Commons, Aug. 9, 1843.

This, we must remember, is a mere speculation, not meant for a moment as a really practical suggestion.

Representation is not necessarily, or even in a principal sense, Parliamentary. Parliament is not sitting at this moment, and yet the nation is represented in its highest as well as in its most minute interests. Not a grievance escapes notice and redress. We must not forget that a principle of government is reserved for our days that we shall not find in our Aristotles, or even in the forests of Tacitus, nor in our Saxon Wittenagemotes, nor in our Plantagenet parliaments. Opinion now is supreme, and Opinion speaks in print. The representation of the Press is far more complete than the representation of Parliament. Parliamentary representation was the happy device of a ruder age, to which it was admirably adapted; an age of semi-civilization, when there was a leading class in the community; but it exhibits many symptoms of desuetude. It is controlled by a system of representation more vigorous and comprehensive; which absorbs its duties and fulfils them more efficiently, and in which discussion is pursued on fairer terms, and often with more depth and information.

He did not think that the settlement of 1832 was likely to be permanent, and if we were "forced to revolution," he preferred a monarchical to a democratic revolution. But he was never wild enough to imagine that personal government could co-exist with a reformed House of Commons, and before 1874 the question raised in *Coningsby* had been answered in another way.

If the charge formally brought against him in 1879 was not absolutely meaningless, it implied that Lord Beaconsfield was suggesting to Her Majesty that she should act upon her own views of foreign and domestic policy without regard to the opinion of Parliament. Unless it meant as much as this, it meant nothing at all. But personal government of this kind, either by the Sovereign or the Minister, as Parliament is at present constituted, is simply impossible, unless the Sovereign is prepared to try conclusions with the majority, and establish a system under which the defeat

of the Government shall not involve its resignation.
If Lord Beaconsfield had any such scheme as this in
contemplation, it is odd that no trace of it should
exist in the history of one who was three times leader of
the House of Commons at the head of a minority, and
once Prime Minister. That a minister in a minority
has a right of appealing to the people before he resigns
office, is of course a truism, and Mr. Disraeli held
office in 1852, in 1859, and in 1867 on that understanding. In 1868 and 1880 he resigned before the
elections were over. But this is not the point at issue.
The only Prime Minister who has ever seriously tried
to conduct the Government of this country in the face
of a hostile majority after, and not before, the appeal
to the people has been made, was not Lord Beaconsfield,
but Sir Robert Peel.

That Lord Beaconsfield was in some respects the
slave of his own fancies may perhaps be granted; and
he may have believed he saw materials for a monarchical revival where none existed. But that he had any
formed design as late as 1874 for attempting to carry
it out, is to my mind a ridiculous supposition. That
the mere charge should have been made, however, undoubtedly points to what was his chief defect as a
statesman. He was too much under the dominion of
ideas, and allowed too little for the force of circumstances, which he strove vainly to reconcile with his
theories. The *Times* once referred to the difficulty of
reconciling Lord Beaconsfield's language with the
world in which we live; and the explanation is what I
have already given, namely, that he lived in two
worlds, and that he sometimes allowed himself, in
talking to the denizens of one, to use the language of
the other. We see the influence of this tendency to

12

idealism in the tenacity with which he clung to his
belief in the stability of our old rural system, after its
foundations had been so severely shaken by the
severance of old ties, by prolonged agricultural distress, and by the indefatigable efforts of a sordid social
democracy to sow dissension in its ranks. We see it
in his failure, with all his marvellous foresight and
insight, to comprehend the moral change which had
come over the English people during half a century of
democratic education, with its pseudo-philanthropy, its
maudlin sensibility, and its Pharisaical hypocrisy. He
knew what the English people once were, and he would
not believe it possible that they should suddenly behave
like women and children. He forgot that democracies
are very like women in their nature; generous, but im-
pulsive, passionate, and intolerant, easily stirred by
emotion, but seldom accessible to argument; and the
clamour against the Bulgarian atrocities for the moment
seems to have confounded him.

In the region of Foreign Affairs we see the same
defect. In much that he wrote about the French Alliance, on the occasions when he still insisted on
it as a practical article of our policy, he forgot
that since the days when the French Alliance was a
reality, a hundred and twenty years of almost constant hostility had intervened; that the system
under which France came to be regarded as the natural
enemy of England, had been rivetted on this country
by the Whigs, and clinched by the Revolutionary war.
He forgot that the Bourbons could never forgive us after
the war of the Spanish Succession, or the loss of India,
or the loss of Canada. He forgot that with the
decline of Spain and Holland, France succeeded to their
place as the great maritime rival of Great Britain,

while in the meantime our connection with Germany
had been relieved of its old burdens and strengthened by
many new ties.

I have already said that these beliefs and speculations had but little influence on his practical policy,
and it may be thought, therefore, that they had
no result at all, and that it is unnecessary to say
anything about them. But that is not exactly true,
for they flavoured Lord Beaconsfield's language when
they did not affect his conduct, and imparted a somewhat fanciful character to what, stripped of these gar-
ments, was often very plain common-sense. This, to
some extent retarded his rise in life, and made those
"sober politicians," whose voice in the long run is
always in this country decisive, distrust and underrate
him. This peculiarity in a statesman whose lot is cast
in a country governed by popular institutions, is certainly
a defect, which all Lord Beaconsfield's marvellous power
of keeping his imagination under the control of his
reason in the practical conduct of affairs was unable to
completely neutralise.

It may be added, in conclusion, that Lord Beaconsfield was, perhaps, the first to perceive that one result
of the overthrow of the old constitution must be to throw
great additional power into the hands of individuals.
He had hoped, no doubt, that the individual to profit
by the tendency would be the Sovereign. Events have
given the power to the Minister, who, with a House
of Commons' majority, at the present day approaches
far more nearly to the position of a dictator than
ever he did under the old system. Then both the
Sovereign, and the aristocracy through their nominees,
possessed some control over him. But now they can
exercise none; and Members of Parliament returned to

12 *

support him by numerous popular constituencies, even if popular opinion runs against him at a particular moment, will scarcely give a hostile vote, because the fickleness of a purely democratic electorate is so great that they can never tell how soon the wind may change, and the majority veer round again to their former unqualified allegiance.   When a great noble saw cause to withdraw his support from the Government of the day it was not till after due consideration, and his resolution was probably permanent.   But that is not the case with a great popular constituency; and, though on occasions of exceptional magnitude and rare occurrence members will still, as ever, act for themselves in spite of all party obligation;   still in ordinary times there is nothing now behind the House of Commons which a minister has to fear during his seven years of office, compared with what there was formerly, and, in this sense of the word, personal government has resulted from what was supposed to be a great measure for the extension of popular power.

As an orator, Lord Beaconsfield stands high, but not perhaps in the first class.   If he does it is in the class to which Pitt and Grenville belonged; not to that which is peopled by Chatham, Fox and Canning.   If to the highest level of oratory a certain fire and impetuosity is indispensable—that white heat which is sometimes perceptible in Mr. Gladstone, that boiling torrent of words which his contemporaries admired in Mr. Fox—then to this level Lord Beaconsfield did not attain.   But if we consider not inferior to this the more stately and measured eloquence, calm and proud, and over-mastering us with the sense of power, which tradition ascribes to the first two statesmen I have named, did Lord Beaconsfield attain to this? Nearer certainly than to the other. In some of the speeches especially which he delivered after his retirement from office in 1880, there is a tone of mingled gravity and dignity, well befitting the political veteran, which is deeply impressive, and often recalls to us what we have heard of the manner of Mr. Pitt. A good specimen is the close of his speech on the Address in January 1881, when the Government which had abandoned the Peace Preservation Act, to mark their sense of Lord Beaconsfield's mis-government, came down to Parliament and asked for similar power for themselves. Lord Beaconsfield, after commenting severely on their conduct, proceeded as follows :—

It may be said, If these are your views, why do you not call upon Parliament to express them ? Well, I do not know anything which would be more justifiable than an amendment to the Address expressing our deep regret that measures for maintaining peace and order, for guarding life and property, and, let me add, liberty, which, I think, is equally in danger in Ireland, were not taken in time, and pointing out that if such measures had been taken in time, an enormous number of terrible incidents might have been averted ; that men would now have been alive who have been murdered ; that houses would now have been in existence that have been burned ; that cases of torture to man and beast would never have happened—for these things, as your Lordships are aware, have mainly occurred within the past two months. But, my Lord, there are occasions when even party considerations must be given up. There are occasions when it may not be wise, even for your Lordships, to place yourselves, as it were, at the head of public opinion in indignant remonstrance at the action of the Ministry. The great dangers and disasters which have been impending, or have happened in this country during the past nine months, have arisen from the abuse of party feeling ; and for that reason alone, if there were no other, I would recommend your Lordships to pause before taking any step which would weaken the movements of the Administration at this moment. I conclude that the Government have come to their determination in a *bonâ fide* spirit. I expect that their Bills when introduced will be found adequate to the occasion, for I am convinced that only ridicule will result if they are not conceived in a comprehensive spirit. I conclude, also, that it is now their intention to proceed with these Bills *de die in diem*, in order that some hope, some courage, may be given to our loyal and long-suffering subjects in Ireland. When those Bills have been passed, we shall be ready to consider any other measures which Her Majesty's Government may bring before Parliament. But I think it utter mockery to discuss any questions connected with Ireland now, except the restoration of peace and order, the re-establishment of the sovereignty of the Queen, and a policy that will announce to Europe that the spirit of England has not ceased, and that, great as are the changes that now environ Ministers, the Parliament of England will be equal to the occasion.

Another example may be quoted from his speech on the evacuation of Candahar in the following March, only six weeks before his death :—

My opinion is that, though such places may not be essential to us, yet that I should regret to see any great military Power in possession of them. I should look upon such an event with regret, and perhaps with some degree of apprehension; but if the great military Power were there, I trust we might still be able to maintain our Empire. But, my Lords, the key of India is not Herat or Candahar. The key of India is in London. The majesty and sovereignty, the spirit and vigour of your Parliament, the inexhaustible resources, the ingenuity, and determination of your people—these are the keys of India.

But a better example still, perhaps, may be found in a much earlier speech, one delivered in May 1865, on the Borough Franchise; and it is perhaps the best example of his graver style of eloquence that can be cited.

Between the scheme we brought forward (*i.e.* 1859) and the measure now brought forward by the honourable member for Leeds, and the inevitable conclusion which its principal supporters acknowledge it must lead to, it is a question between an aristocratic government, in the proper sense of the term—that is, a government by the best men of all classes—and a democracy. I doubt very much whether a democracy is a government that would suit this country; and it is just as well that the House, when coming to a vote on this question, should really consider if that be the issue—and it is the real issue, between retaining the present Constitution, not the present constituent body, but between the present Constitution and a democracy—it is just as well for the House to recollect that the stake is not mean, that what is at issue is of some price. You must remember, not to use the epithet profanely, that we are dealing really with a peculiar people. There is no country at the present moment that exists under the circumstances and under the same conditions as the people of this realm. You have, for example, an ancient, powerful, richly-endowed Church and perfect religious liberty. You have unbroken order and complete freedom. You have landed estates as large as the Romans, combined with commercial enterprise such as Carthage and Venice united never equalled. And you must remember that this peculiar country, with these strong contrasts, is not governed by force; it is not governed by standing armies, it is governed by a most singular series of traditionary influences which, generation after generation, cherishes and preserves, because it knows that they embalm custom and represent law. And, with this, what have you done? You have created the greatest Empire of modern time. You have amassed a capital of fabulous amount, you have devised and sustained a system of credit still more marvellous, and, above all, you have established and maintained a scheme of labour and industry so vast and complicated that the history of the world has no parallel to it. And all these mighty creations are out of all proportion to the essential and indigenous elements and resources of the country. If you destroy that state of society, remember this—England cannot begin again.

There are countries which have been in great danger, and gone through great suffering—the United States, for example, whose fortunes are now so perilous, and who, in our own immediate day, have had great trials; you have had—perhaps even now in the United States of America you have—a protracted and fratricidal civil war, which has lasted for four years; but if it lasted for four years more, vast as would be the disaster and desolation, when ended the United States might begin again, because the United States then would only be in the same condition that England was at the end of the War of the Roses, when probably she had not even 3,000,000 of population, with vast tracts of virgin soil and mineral treasures, not only undeveloped, but undreamt of. Then you have France. France had a real revolution in this century—a real revolution, not only a political, but a social revolution, the institutions of the country were uprooted, the orders of society were abolished—even the landmarks and local names removed and erased. But France could begin again. France had the greatest spread of the most exuberant soil in Europe, and a climate not less genial. She had, and always had, comparatively, a limited population, living in the most simple manner. France, therefore, could begin again. But England—the England we know, the England we live in, the England of which we are proud—could not begin again."

These, and other passages which might be quoted, flash out great truths, and elevated sentiments in the

language most appropriate to them, the language of
perfect simplicity.   But Lord Beaconsfield at the same
time was a great master of rhetoric, and some of his
greatest effects were produced by the dexterous employment of it.   His description of the landed interest in
1849, which has been already quoted,* is a good illustration of his powers.

Another highly-wrought passage is the peroration to
that speech of 1848 which, as stated above,† secured
him the leadership of his party in the House of Commons.   The subject is the failure of legislative power
in that Assembly, which the orator attributes to the
absence of authority in the Government, and the breaking up of the House into a number of small cliques.

After all their deliberations, after all their foresight, after all their
observation of the times, after all their study of the public interest,
when their measures are launched from the Cabinet into this House,
they are not received here by a confiding majority—confiding, I mean,
in their faith in the statesmanlike qualifications of their authors, and
in their sympathy with the great political principles professed by the
members of the administration.   On the contrary, the success of their
measures in this House depends on a variety of small parties, who, in
their aggregate, exceed in number and influence the party of the
ministers.   The temper of one leader has to be watched; the indica-
tion of the opinion of another has to be observed; the disposition of a
third has to be suited; so that a measure is so altered, remoulded,
remodelled, patched, cobbled, painted, veneered, and varnished, that
at last no trace is left of the original scope and scheme; or it is withdrawn in disgust by its originators, after having been subjected to
prolonged and elaborate discussions in this House.

Men in their situation will naturally say, "What is the use of taking
all these pains, of bestowing all this care, study, and foresight on the
preparation of a measure, when the moment it is out of our hands it
ceases to be the measure of the Cabinet, and becomes essentially the
measure of the House of Commons?"   And, therefore, measures are
thrown before us with the foregone conclusion that we are to save the
Administration much care and trouble in preparing the means of
governing the country.   Thus it happens that the House of Commons,

* P. 71.   † P. 69.

instead of being a purely legislative body, is every day becoming a mere administrative assembly. The House of Commons, as now conducted, is a great committee, sitting on public affairs, in which every man speaks with the same right, and most of us with the same weight: no more the disciplined array of traditional influences and hereditary opinions—the realised experience of ancient society and of a race that for generations has lived and flourished in the high practice of a noble system of self-government—that is all past. For these the future is to provide us with a compensatory alternative in the conceits of the illiterate, the crotchets of the whimsical, the violent courses of a vulgar ambition, that acknowledges no gratitude to antiquity, to posterity no duty; until at last this free and famous Parliament of England is to subside to the low-water mark of those national assemblies and those provisional conventions that are at the same time the terror and the derision of the world.

But undoubtedly when we think of Lord Beaconsfield as an orator, we think rather of his wit, his humour, and his sarcasms, than of his higher and more serious flights of eloquence. On the lower ground he has no superior, and it may be doubted if he ever had an equal. But it is impossible to preserve the spirit and flavour of eloquence of this description when the circumstances which gave it point and purpose have either lost interest or are totally forgotten. Even Townsend's " champagne speech," now that the cork has been drawn so long, would probably read very flat could we have it restored in its integrity. And so it is with some of Lord Beaconsfield's most celebrated witticisms, and still more with that matchless vein of irony in which he loved to address the members of the hated " coalition." To give any fair idea of its quality we should have to quote whole speeches, since the effect is often not produced by felicitous images or pungent epigrams, but by one continuous flow of elaborate mockery, which does not admit of being broken up, and which cannot be appreciated even as it stands without a minute acquaintance with the political and Parliamentary circumstances to which it is addressed. For such as wish to judge for themselves, I may mention his speech of February 18th, 1853, as perhaps the most perfect specimen of the kind I have already mentioned.

I have quoted, at p. 61, perhaps the finest of all his sarcasms levelled at Sir Robert Peel. But one more must still be added : —

Sir, I must say that such a Minister may be conscientious, but that he is unfortunate. I will say, also, that he ought to be the last man in the world to turn round and upbraid his party in a tone of menace. Sir, there is a difficulty in finding a parallel to the position of the right honourable gentleman in any part of history. The only parallel which I can find is an incident* in the late war in the Levant, which was terminated by the policy of the noble lord opposite. I remember when that great struggle was taking place, when the existence of the Turkish empire was at stake, the late Sultan, a man of great energy and fertile in resources, was determined to fit out an immense fleet to maintain his empire. Accordingly a vast armament was collected. It consisted of some of the finest ships that were ever built. The crews were picked men, the officers were the ablest that could be found, and both officers and men were rewarded before they fought. There never was an armament which left the Dardanelles similarly appointed since the days of Solyman the Great. The Sultan personally witnessed the departure of the fleet ; all the muftis prayed for the success of the expedition, as all the muftis here prayed for the success of the last General Election. Away went the fleet, but what was the Sultan's consternation, when the Lord High Admiral steered at once into the enemy's port ! Now, Sir, the Lord High Admiral on that occasion was very much misrepresented. He, too, was called a traitor, and he, too, vindicated himself. "True it is," he said, "I did place myself at the head of this valiant armada ; true it is that my Sovereign embraced me ; true it is that all the muftis in the empire offered up prayers for my success : but I have an objection to war. I see no use in prolonging the struggle, and the only reason I had for accepting the command was that I might terminate the contest by betraying my master."

* The delivery of the Turkish Fleet to Mehemet Ali by Achmet Pasha, the Turkish High Admiral, June 30th 1839

With one more quotation I must hasten to conclude this chapter. It is from a speech delivered at Edinburgh in October 1867, which was an exhaustive presentation of his case on Parliamentary Reform :—

I see many gentlemen here who have been, no doubt, inspectors like myself, as magistrates, of peculiar asylums, who meet there some cases which I have thought at the same time the most absurd and the most distressing ; it is when the lunatic believes all the world is mad, and that he himself is sane. But to pass from such gloomy imagery, really those " Edinburgh " and " Quarterly " Reviews, no man admires them more than myself. But I admire them as I do first-rate, first-class posting-houses, which in old days for half a century or so—to use Manchester phrase—carried on a roaring trade. Then there comes some revolution or progress which no person can ever have contemplated. They find things are altered. They do not understand them, and instead of that intense competition and mutual vindictiveness which before distinguished them, they suddenly quite agree. The " boots " of the " Blue Boar " and the chamber-maid of the " Red Lion " embrace, and are quite in accord in this—in denouncing the infamy of railroads.

Between the effect of this raillery, when delivered by the orator himself with all the advantages of voice, eye, and gesture, when the subject-matter of it was a topic of daily conversation, and the effect of it reproduced in print twenty years afterwards, the difference is almost as great as between a living man and his portrait. *Quid si ipsum tonantem audivisses.* The difference is peculiarly marked in passages of wit and humour arising out of temporary incidents, and dependent for their flavour on their freshness.

CHAPTER VIII.

LORD BEACONSFIELD AS A MAN OF LETTERS.

Lord Beaconsfield's works—His earlier novels—Plots of *Coningsby* and *Sybil*—*Tancred, Lothair* and *Endymion*—Three prose burlesques—Political writings—Lord Beaconsfield's style.

LORD BEACONSFIELD was the author of eleven novels, namely, *Vivian Grey* published in 1826, the *Young Duke* in 1831, *Contarini Fleming* in 1832, *The Wondrous Tale of Alroy* in 1833, *Henrietta Temple* in 1836, *Venetia* in 1837, *Coningsby* in 1844, *Sybil* in 1845, *Tancred* in 1847, *Lothair* in 1870, and *Endymion* in 1880. Besides these he published the *Rise of Iskander* in 1833, the *Revolutionary Epic* in 1834, and *Count Alarcos*, a tragedy, in 1839. His three burlesques. namely, *Popanilla, Ixion in Heaven*, and the *Infernal Marriage*, were given to the world between 1828 and 1833. The political pamphlets which bear his name appeared in the following order:—*What is He?* in 1833, *The Crisis Examined* in 1834, *The Vindication of the British Constitution* in 1835, and the *Letters of Runnymede* and the *Spirit of Whiggism* in 1836. In 1852 appeared his *Life of Lord George Bentinck*.

Vivian Grey as the production of a youth of one and twenty, has been deservedly extolled, and at the time of its publication its originality and its audacity took the world by storm. But we have got used to Lord Bea-

consfield since then, and *Vivian Grey*, which amazed
his contemporaries, is not so entertaining to ourselves.
It has no plot deserving of the name, and the political
intrigues described in it betray the age and inexperience
of the writer, and are almost unreadable at the present
day. What remains is a dashing smartness and neat-
ness in the dialogue, and some brilliant bits of social
satire, derived, however, more from books than from
nature, and only showing by their popularity the low
ebb to which fashionable fiction must have fallen sixty
years ago. Mrs. Felix Lorraine and Cleveland, the
wicked intriguante and the disappointed, half-maddened
politician, are the two best characters in the book. To
one who is not depicted in the brightest colours he,
curiously enough, assigns the title of Lord Beaconsfield.
In the latter part of it, the scene is laid entirely abroad.
There are some amusing sketches of the gaming tables.
But the story is silently dropped, and the hero disappears
in a deluge.

The *Young Duke* is inferior to *Vivian Grey* in that
particular quality for which we can find no better name
than "rattle," and which carries off a multitude of errors.
But it is a better story and introduces us to more interesting people. It is a specimen of what used to be called
the novel of high life—the noble young millionaire
who spends half his fortune in licentious dissipation,
and, when he is tired of it, settles down respectably on the
remainder, and marries a girl much too good for him.

Of his earlier novels, *Contarini Fleming*, I think, is
decidedly the best. *L'enfant incompris* is a character
of which, in most hands, one soon grows weary. But
in the analysis of passion and the development of
character presented to us in *Contarini Fleming*, there is
such a vivid reality, that it reads like a personal ex-

perience, as, for what we know, it may be. In the incidents and plot there is nothing incredible or fantastic.
The love scenes are natural and touching, and it seems
to afford much better evidence of the author's intellectual
power than either of its two predecessors.

The *Wondrous Tale of Alroy* is an Oriental fiction
founded on a Hebrew tradition concerning the "Princes of
the Captivity "—rulers whom the Jews continued to elect
from among the descendants of the House of David even
after the dispersion. Alroy is one of them, who, after
a long interregnum, possessing himself, by supernatural
assistance, of the sceptre of Solomon, establishes the
Hebrew monarchy on the ruins of the Caliphate of Bag-
dad. His life is of course short, and his reign much
shorter. But his adventures are told with great spirit.
The whole narrative is brilliantly coloured; and in tales
of this kind, in which heroes compel genii to do their
bidding, and we pass backwards and forwards from the
natural to the supernatural by such frequent and easy
transitions that we hardly know one from the other,
nothing, of course, can be called either monstrous or
extravagant.

The *Rise of Iskander* is a tale of the Turkish wars of
Amurath II., and on reading it through a second time,
I find I have nothing to say about it. It is short and
interesting enough for an ordinary magazine story.

An interval of four years separates *Alroy* from Lord
Beaconsfield's next work of fiction, which is a marked
advance on his more juvenile productions. *Henrietta
Temple*, indeed, is of his non-political novels by far the
best. The love passages remind one of *Romeo and Juliet*,
and the scene in the sponging-house might have been
written by Fielding. The picture of the ancient family,
proud in their decay, and clinging with desperate tena-

city to their mortgaged estates, is an interesting and touching one. It has been said that Count Mirabel was a bad portrait of Count D'Orsay.

Venetia is chiefly remarkable as an attempt " to shadow forth, though as in a glass darkly, two of the most renowned and refined spirits that have adorned these our latter days." The two are Byron and Shelley. Had these been likenesses, the novel would have been better known. But the attempt to reproduce literary characters in novels has rarely been successful. Kings, statesmen, and soldiers are men of action, and lend themselves readily to all the requirements of fiction. But in the case of men of letters, it is what they thought, not what they did, which requires to be reproduced if the picture is to interest us. To describe such men merely by their external characteristics or habits is to trifle with the reader. The attempt to imitate their conversation betrays, generally speaking, only the inferiority of the imitator. Byron's actions, no doubt, afford plenty of materials for romance; but then it is impossible to separate the champion of the Greeks, from the satirist of the English, or the practical philanthropist from the literary misanthrope. *Venetia*, on the whole, is perhaps, the least interesting of all Mr. Disraeli's fictions.

With *Coningsby* and *Sybil* we turn over a new chapter in Mr. Disraeli's literary career. He now reverts to the political novel which he had essayed twenty years before, and very wisely relinquished till he had acquired some actual experience of the men and manners to be depicted. His object in these celebrated works was simply to reproduce, in the form of fiction, those political and constitutional theories which he had originally touched in the letters and essays to which I shall presently revert. What these were has already been sufficiently explained. We have now only to consider the literary and dramatic merit with which they were introduced to " the new generation."

The plot in *Coningsby* is, I think, Mr. Disraeli's best, the secret being well kept, and the catastrophe and *denouement* both skilfully contrived. The story has, in part, been anticipated.* The hero is introduced to us while he is still a boy at Eton, in that memorable month of May 1832, when Lord Lyndhurst and the Duke of Wellington were engaged in the last expiring effort of the Tory Party to defeat the Whig Reform Bill. His grandfather, the Marquis of Monmouth, returns to England as Coningsby is leaving Eton in 1836, and our young hero *en route* for Coningsby Castle, pays a visit to his friend Lord H. Sidney at Beaumanoir (Belvoir). On his way from Beaumanoir to Coningsby, he visits Manchester and the factories of Millbank senior, who invites him to dinner, and introduces him to his daughter, a beautiful girl of sixteen.

To amuse his guests at Coningsby, among whom are numbered the Prince and Princess Colonna and their daughter Lucretia, the Marquis engages a company of French actors, under the management of Villebecque, whose daughter Flora makes her first appearance on the castle stage. Flora is a pretty delicate girl, who breaks down as an actress, but remains as a kind of companion to the Princess Lucretia, and experiences many little acts of kindness at the hands of Coningsby, who often noticed, and endeavoured to relieve, the somewhat awkward and forlorn position in which she found herself.

Having introduced the principal persons, the remainder of our sketch may be shortened. There is a

* p. 40.

long-standing feud between the Marquis and Mr. Millbank, who beats Rigby for the Marquis's pocket
borough, steps in and buys an estate on which he had
set his heart, and thwarts and annoys him in every possible manner. Coningsby and Miss Millbank, of course,
fall in love with each other, the result being that Millbank forbids him his house and his grandfather disin-
herits him. The Marquis had married the Princess
Lucretia, who conspired with Rigby to do Coningsby
this injury by representing his connection with the Millbanks in the worst possible light : Coningsby having
previously offended the Marquis by refusing to stand
for Darlford against Edith's father. But they do not gain
much by their manœuvres. When the Marquis's will is
opened, it is found that he has left the bulk of his immense property to Flora, who turns out to be his natural
daughter. Now Flora had been secretly in love with
Coningsby ever since they met at the Castle, and, when
she dies of consumption, leaves her whole immense property to the hero, who, however, has been reconciled to
the Millbanks and engaged to Edith before the turn in
his fortunes.

This plot has always seemed to me a very good one,
better than that of *Sybil*, because the events are brought
about more naturally and without any touch of melo-
drama, of which *Sybil*, exquisite as the story is, presents
here and there a slight suspicion. In *Sybil*, however,
the plot is sufficiently ingenious, while the story and the
character make it even more interesting than *Coningsby*.
Sybil herself is one of the most exquisite creations
which the hand of fiction ever drew. But the description of factory life and the cruelty and extortion to
which the working classes were exposed at the hands
of their employers, scenes described from personal

13

observation, are the most striking portion of the book, as well as the most humorous and graphic.

But apart from the story, we have both in *Coningsby* and *Sybil* a collection of political and social sketches, to which we doubt if English literature contains anything that is superior: Rigby himself; Mr. Ormsby, the man of society who has "forty thousand a year paid quarterly," and whose world is bounded by Mayfair, St. James's, and Pall Mall; Tadpole and Taper, the two political underlings; Lord Marney, the thoroughly selfish, able man, who believes he can go through life on the principles of Helvetius—are beyond all praise as types of the class they are intended to represent, with its mingled cynicism and good nature, its common sense, its addiction to gossip, and its perfect satisfaction with the little world in which it lives, outside of which it knows nothing.   Of all these, perhaps Lord Marney is the most original.   I can think of nothing like him in any other English novel; and yet we have all met such men, men in whom selfishness is so complete and so candid as almost to excite our admiration, and in whom the love of contradiction amounts to monomania.   "The great difficulty with Lord Marney," says the author, "was to find a sufficient stock of opposition; but he lay in wait, and seized every opportunity with wonderful alacrity.   Even Captain Grouse could not escape him; if driven to extremity, he would even question his principles on fly-making."   On these two characters Mr. Ormsby and Lord Marney, Mr. Disraeli may stake his reputation.   Tadpole and Taper have, of course, become household words; but they are interesting chiefly for the political satire of which they are the vehicles.   They are not finished off with the delicacy of Mr. Ormsby and Lord Marney, who are interesting exclusively as specimens of human nature quite irrespective of politics.

The dialogue in which these various characters are revealed to the reader is equally good. Mr. Ormsby's remarks on Lord Monmouth's separation from his wife, and Lord Marney's conversation with the clergyman, Mr. St. Lys, in *Sybil*, may be taken at random as examples of the author's art in making his characters speak for themselves. We might mention beside a host of minor personages redolent of that humour which Mr. Disraeli has borrowed from nobody. Mr. Cassilis, the elderly dandy, who, upon hearing of Young England, and understanding that " it requires a doosed deal of history and all that sort of thing," gravely observes that " one must brush up one's Goldsmith," Devilsdust, Stephen Morley, Baptist Hatton, Lady St. Julian, Lady Deloraine, Lady Firebrace, and last, not least, that finished portrait, Lord Eskdale, form a gallery which would alone have made the painter famous had he no other title to distinction.

Of *Tancred* the great merit lies in the description of Syria, and of life in the mountain and the desert, in which it abounds. Tancred is a high-born youth dissatisfied with modern society, yearning for the restoration of faith, and resolving to visit the land in which the Creator had conversed with man as being the only spot in which it is at all likely that illumination or inspiration will be vouchsafed to him. The story of his adventures is told with wonderful spirit and beauty. But the vision of Tancred on Mount Sinai is the application of fiction to purposes for which it never was intended, and even of those who have no religious feelings to be wounded by it, the taste is likely to be shocked.

Between the publication of *Tancred* in 1847, and

13 *

the publication of *Lothair*, a much longer interval
occurred. *Lothair* was not written till the author was
sixty-five, and had already been Prime Minister. But
it shows no falling off in his humour and powers of
description. Lothair, like the young duke, is a noble
millionaire succeeding to an immense fortune after a
long minority, but whose character and career are very
different. The Roman Catholic Church and the Revolutionary Societies run a race against each other for
his money, which is won by the latter, chiefly through
the influence of an American lady who is the inspiring
spirit of the Italian patriots.* His adventures with
both parties, and his final escape to England, where he
recovers his senses, saves the remainder of his fortune,
and marries the Lady Corisande, need not be narrated
here. Many of the characters in the story are in the
author's best manner. Mr. Phœbus the painter, who
" has always been of opinion that reading and writing
are very injurious to education "; Mr Putney Giles,
the wealthy solicitor; Lord St. Aldegonde, who de-
clares in the presence of two bishops that " he hates
Sunday," are inferior only to the characters already
singled out for praise in *Coningsby* and *Sybil*.

Endymion was published in 1880, and in this the
signs of advancing age are visible. It is an exclusively
political story, and it is odd that his first and his last
novel should in some respects be more like each
other than those which came between. Endymion's
father reminds one of Cleveland; Endymion is very
unlike Vivian Grey in point of character and judgment,
and he does not rise in life by the same tactics which
caused Vivian Grey to fall; but there is the same air

* Since the above was written it has been stated by Mr. Froude
that the " General " in *Lothair* was meant for General Cluseret.

of unreality about the incidents recorded, and the fact
that more than one leading character is compounded of
several originals, without much care being taken in the
blending of the colours, helps still further to confuse
the reader. For all that, however, the book bears
unmistakable marks of its author's genius, and the
account of "the crisis" in 1834 and the bitter disappointment of Travers, is as interesting and as powerful
as anything he has ever written.

It has been said that a common thought runs through
all Lord Beaconsfield's novels from first to last; the
struggles of some youth of genius, striving to emancipate
himself from the tryanny of custom, whether it be social
or political. That several of Lord Beaconsfield's heroes
are in some degree reflections of himself may be admitted,
and it follows, therefore, that what he was doing in life,
they seem to be doing also. But if this was a favourite
idea with Mr. Disraeli, it was not universally embodied
in the creations of his fancy, not in *Alroy*, not in
Henrietta Temple, not in *Endymion*. It is an idea
very likely to occur to any young man of great intellectual power, who finds his station in life not equal to
his ambition. And that it should have had a great
fascination for Benjamin Disraeli is only what we
might expect.

The three prose burlesques deserve to be better known
than they are. The *Infernal Marriage* and the *Voyage
of Popanilla* are both political squibs, descriptive of the
state of parties at the time they were written. In the
first, Proserpine is taken to Elysium, that is, goes to
Court, and becomes a great lady and a leader of society.
The Gods and the Giants are the Liberals and the Tories
during the ministry of Mr. Canning, so that Mr. Trollope
was not original in his application of these names to them.

The Duke of Wellington is then Enceladus, and Sir Robert Peel, Hyperion. But in *Popanilla*, when he becomes Prime Minister, he is Chiron the Centaur, who can use his heels as well as his head. *Ixion in Heaven* is rather social than political; a not ill-natured satire on the Court and society. Jupiter is George the Fourth, with " an immortal waist." Apollo is Byron, calling for soda-water and biscuits, which they do not keep in Olympus, and finally consoling himself with something much more substantial. It is very amusing, the dialogue extremely clever, and sixty years ago, when many of the minor characters and more obscure allusions. would have been appreciated, should have attained some celebrity. By-the-by, when Ixion is asked to write something in Minerva's Album, he writes: " Adventures are to the adventurous," clearly proving that the omniscient Sidonia was acquainted with this *jeu d'esprit*. *Popanilla* is a professed imitation of *Gulliver's Travels*, but is very fresh, sparkling, and original, for all that.

Lord Beaconsfield is the author of certainly two, and possibly three works in verse, the *Modern Dunciad*, of which enough has been already said; the *Revolutionary Epic*, and *Count Alarcos*. The *Revolutionary Epic* contains some really fine passages. The plan of the poem is simply this: Magros, the genius of Feudalism, creates the Teutonic races, and establishes that system in the world, and about one-third of the poem is a description of its virtues. Then arises upon earth a destructive monster called " Change," whose deeds pave the way for Lyridon, the genius of Federation, who in his turn sings the praises of liberty, fraternity, and equality. The concluding portion of the piece is the conquest of Italy by

Napoleon. Productions much inferior to the *Revolutionary Epic* have caused their authors to be enrolled among English poets. But only the very best can bear the blaze of Lord Beaconsfield's fame, and anything less than that seems so totally unworthy of it as to be consigned to a lower place in literature than perhaps, on its merits, it deserves.

The tragedy of *Alarcos* is founded on the Spanish ballad of the same name, said by Ticknor to be " one of the most beautiful and touching in any language." It has been translated by Lockhart, and no less than four Spanish plays have been founded on it ; but as I have not read them I cannot say how far, if at all, Lord Beaconsfield was indebted to them. His own Play is well written and contains some characteristic lines :—

> Aye—ever pert is youth that baffles age.

And these still more so—

> The COUNTESS.
>
> Hast thou still **foes?**
>
> The COUNT.
>
> I trust so : I should not be what I am,
> Still less what I will be, if hate did not
> Pursue me, as my shadow.

Of the four political compositions which I have already enumerated the first in order of time is a short piece entitled *What is He?* written in 1833, shortly after his first contest at High Wycombe, in order to explain what Tory Radicalism meant. In it he says that as neither the Whigs* nor the Tories can carry on the Government with the new machinery, a new party is required. That must be either aristocratic or democratic.

* See Letters of Peel in Croker Papers.

Aristocratic, however, it cannot be, for the aristocratic principle perished out of the Constitution when the Lords gave way on the Reform Bill. It could not be restored by force: nor yet for more than a very brief period by a coalition between the Whigs and Tories, and it therefore becomes the duty of the Tory party to coalesce with Radicals. He says here what he repeats in *Coningsby*, that "it was not the Reform Bill itself which has shaken the aristocracy of the country, but the means by which it was carried." *The Crisis Examined* is the substance of a speech delivered by him at High Wycombe, December 16th, 1834, and is to be found at page 8. In this we find that the views expressed in the previous pamphlet had already undergone some modification. In *What is He?* he told us that the Whigs *have* succeeded in overpowering the House of Lords, and the aristoratic principle is destroyed. He now speaks of what *might* have happened if they had done so. The rally of the Tory party under Peel and Wellington seems to have shaken his convictions and led him to suspect that his prophecies had been premature.

It was in the following year, 1835, after the resignation of Sir Robert Peel's short-lived but able administration, that Mr. Disraeli published his *Vindication of the English Constitution*, wherein are laid down in a more formal manner the majority of those political precepts, which were afterwards reproduced in a more popular shape in the dialogues between Coningsby and Sidonia. The rise and progress of the English Parliament, the nature of the Plantagenet Monarchy, its alteration by the Tudors and Stuarts, and its attempted revival by the aristocracy in the reign of Charles the First; the origin of the "Venetian" Constitution, the refusal of William to submit to it, and the struggles of the Georges to escape from it; the democratic or popular Toryism which was always opposed to the oligarchy, and which enabled George the Third to bridle it; the distortion of English history which the Whigs have so sedulously fostered, and which the Tories have been too indolent to combat; all these, with many auxiliary speculations which did not so readily fall in with the plan of a novel, are to be found in the *Vindication,* drawn out with great clearness and ingenuity, and expressed in language at once vigorous, precise, and elegant, qualities for which Mr. Disraeli's English prose is not invariably conspicuous.

It is needless to defend its accuracy at every point, and against all comers. The question is whether this epitome of our Constitutional history is true in the spirit. It is remarkable, indeed, that we do not find in *Coningsby* the same construction placed on the resistance to Charles the First which we find in the *Vindication.* In the latter the author's sympathies are with the Parliament, in the former they are with the King. But the discrepancy, perhaps, is more apparent than real. For of the entire struggle which lasted from 1627 to 1714, though Lord Beaconsfield may have varied in his opinion of it at particular stages, the ultimate result is condemned alike both by the essay and the novel. The following extract from the *Spirit of Whiggism* shows, perhaps, the real harmony which underlay this seeming inconsistency :—

When Charles the First, after a series of great concessions, which ultimately obtained for him the support of the most illustrious of his early opponents, raised the royal standard, the constitution of the Plantagenets, and more than the constitution of the Plantagenets, had been restored and secured. But a portion of the able party which had succeeded in effecting such a vast and beneficial revolution was not content to part with the extraordinary powers

which they had obtained in this memorable struggle.   This section of
the aristocracy were the origin of the English Whigs, though that title
was not invented until the next reign.

That is to say, one section of the Parliamentary
party, seeing more power within their reach than they
had originally aimed at, resolved to make a spring at it,
and their descendants, in 1714, pretty nearly succeeded
in securing it.

The *Letters of Runnymede,* published also in 1836,
are nineteen in number, and are dedicated to Sir Robert
Peel.   They appeared at intervals between the 18th of
January and the 15th of May, and were addressed
chiefly to the leading members of the Government.
One, however, was addressed to Sir Robert Peel, one to
Lord Stanley, one to " the People," and two to the
House of Lords.   They all relate to the politics of the
day, and though witty and occasionally wise, are less
able and less dignified than the *Vindication of the
British Constitution.*   The invective and the satire
are too laboured; and, though part of what seems
far-fetched to ourselves probably did not seem so to
contemporaries well acquainted with every incident
referred to, they cannot be considered on the whole
a favourable specimen of Lord Beaconsfield's literary
powers.

Lord George Bentinck: a Political Biography, was
published in 1852, and of all his works, not being
works of imagination, it is the one most likely to be
known and admired by posterity.   I say nothing of
the economical opinions expressed in it, though the
wheel of time and the course of events may again
bring them into fashion.   But that wonderful study of
Sir Robert Peel, which the greatest masters of literary portraiture have never surpassed, those glowing

and graphic scenes of Parliamentary warfare, where every combatant stands out in bold relief, and every change of fortune is as visible as to spectators in the gallery, will surely live for ever, or as long as men continue to take an interest in the history of senates and the romance of politics. We have also in the same work two most interesting dissertations, one on the growth of English Parties since the end of the Revolutionary war; the other on his own people and his father's house, in which he gives in a more connected form the same account of the Jewish race as first surprised the world in *Coningsby.*

It cannot be said that Lord Beaconsfield's prose style is conspicuous for elegance or purity. Exceptions may be named, no doubt. I think the letter to the *Times,* quoted at page 14, is one such. The Vindication is another. But he is not, as a general rule, sufficiently careful to confine words in their proper signification ; his constructions are often harsh, and he does not always display the art or skill we might have expected from him in the disposition of his sentences. That the writer whose natural bent is towards warmth, brilliancy, and richness, should sometimes be guilty of the excess to which these qualities are prone, and become florid or fantastic, is by no means wonderful ; and Lord Beaconsfield's taste for all that is bright, glowing, and gorgeous, both in nature and art, was well known. He used to say that he never wondered at the sun-worshippers. But I think that, for splendour of style, unblemished by a word that is either tawdry or meretricious, the description of Jerusalem in *Tancred,* and of the Queen's first Council in *Sybil,* may be mentioned with some confidence that the critical judgment of posterity will not disallow their claims.

The council of England is summoned for the first time within her bowers. There are assembled the prelates and captains and chief men of her realm; the priests of the religion that consoled, the heroes of the sword that has conquered, the votaries of the craft that has decided the fate of empires; men grey with thought, and fame, and age, who are the stewards of divine mysteries, who have toiled in secret cabinets, who have encountered in battle the hosts of Europe, who have struggled in the less merciful strife of aspiring senates; men too, some of them, lords of a thousand vassals and chief proprietors of provinces, yet not one of them whose heart does not at this moment tremble as he awaits the first presence of the maiden who must now ascend her throne.

A hum of half-suppressed conversation which would attempt to conceal the excitement, which some of the greatest of them have since acknowledged, fills that brilliant assemblage; that sea of plumes, and glittering stars, and gorgeous dresses. Hush! the portals open; she comes; the silence is as deep as that of a noontide forest. Attended for a moment by her royal mother and the ladies of her court, who bow and then retire, VICTORIA ascends her throne; a girl, alone, and for the first time, amid an assemblage of men.

In a sweet and thrilling voice, and with a composed mien, which indicates rather the absorbing sense of august duty than an absence of emotion, THE QUEEN announces her accession to the throne of her ancestors, and her humble hope that divine Providence will guard over the fulfilment of her lofty trust.

The prelates and captains and chief men of her realm then advance to the throne, and kneeling before her, pledge their troth, and take the sacred oaths of allegiance and supremacy.

Allegiance to one who rules over the land that the great Macedonian could not conquer; and over a continent of which even Columbus never dreamed: to the Queen of every sea, and of nations in every zone.

It is not of these that I would speak; but of a nation nearer her footstool, and which at this moment looks to her with anxiety, with affection, perhaps with hope. Fair and serene, she has the blood and beauty of the Saxon. Will it be her proud destiny at length to bear relief to suffering millions, and, with that soft hand which might inspire troubadours and guerdon knights, break the last link in the chain of Saxon thraldom?

The materials for the picture were supplied to the artist by Lord Lyndhurst, who took Mr. Disraeli with him in his carriage to Kensington Gardens, and on their return journey gave him a full account of the impressive scene which he had witnessed.

For the passage in *Tancred,* I must refer my readers to the work itself. But, before quitting the subject, I shall give one specimen of his more highly-decorative style, which has been supposed to violate the laws of taste, but which, though it belongs to the arabesque, can scarcely be called vicious :—

The summer twilight had faded into sweet night; the young and star-attended moon glittered like a sickle in the deep purple sky ; of all the luminous host Hesperus alone was visible ; and a breeze, that bore the last embrace of the flowers by the sun, moved languidly and fitfully over the still and odorous earth.

The moonbeam fell upon the roof and garden of Gerard. It suffused the cottage with its brilliant light, except where the dark depth of the embowered porch defied its entry. All around the beds of flowers and herbs spread sparkling and defined. You could trace the minutest walk ; almost distinguish every leaf. Now and then there came a breath, and the sweet peas murmured in their sleep ; or the roses rustled, as if they were afraid they were about to be roused from their lightsome dreams. Farther on the fruit trees caught the splendour of the night ; and looked like a troop of sultanas taking their garden air, when the eye of man could not profane them, and laden with jewels. There were apples that rivalled rubies ; pears of topaz tint ; a whole paraphernalia of plums, some purple as the amethyst, others blue and brilliant as the sapphire ; an emerald here, and now a golden drop that gleamed like the yellow diamond of Gengis Khan.

It is, however, in his colloquial style, that I think he shows to most advantage. As with his speeches, so with his novels, his humour is superior to his eloquence ; and of the language of society, the language of clubs, lobbies, and drawing-rooms, he was a perfect master.

CHAPTER XI.

CONCLUSION.

His Public and Private Character—Not an Adventurer—Devotion
to Politics—Love of Nature, and of Animals, and of Children—
Stories of his early Eccentricities—Life at Hughenden—Popularity in the Neighbourhood—His Scholarship—His Library—
Lady John Manners's Reminiscences.

LORD Beaconsfield has been called a "political adventurer," and if, to be a political adventurer, is to enter
public life without patrimony or connections, and to
rise only by the force of merit, he may have deserved
the name. But, at that rate, many eminent men whose
memory is still cherished must answer to the charge as
well. Burke, Canning, Cobbett, must all be styled
political adventurers. While, if we glance at the ranks
of living statesmen, we shall see one among them
who, while answering to this description more closely
than any we have named, is yet conspicuous for honesty,
frankness, and singleness of purpose above his fellows:
need I name Mr. John Morley. Surely a political
adventurer, like a military adventurer, is one who makes
his principles subservient to his interests, and transfers
his allegiance from side to side as advantage or convenience dictates, indifferent to the cause which he is

required to defend, and concerned only with the fulfilment of his duties and the receipt of his stipulated fee.
English history is no stranger to such men, though they
have usually played a secondary part. But there is no
definition of the term "adventurer" which will embrace
at once Lord Beaconsfield and such men as these. Lord
Beaconsfield never changed either his principles or his
party. He was a Tory of the type which I have described, from the first address which he issued to the
electors of High Wycombe to the last speech which he
delivered in the House of Lords half a century afterwards. Insulted, distrusted, and calumniated by the
very men who should have been the first to welcome
him, he never swerved for a moment in his attachment
to the cause which he and they had at heart. He
served the Tory party as no man except the younger
Pitt had ever served it. He served it through poverty,
adversity, and unpopularity, without ever losing heart
or hope, or allowing his own private circumstances to
affect his political conduct.

And he had his reward at last. In the life of Lord
George Bentinck there is a passage * which I have
always thought a very interesting one, as it applied
prophetically to himself: "An aristocracy hesitates
before it yields its confidence, but never does so
grudgingly." In his own case it hesitated long, and
with additional circumstances not wholly creditable to
itself But it ended by trusting him completely. Lord
Derby set a noble example. He, too, had hesitated.
But if asked at any later period why nobody trusted
Mr. Disraeli, he would indignantly declare that it
was false, adding, proudly, "*I* trust him." The English aristocracy seeing this, laid aside their prejudices

* Already quoted at p 85.

by degrees. His character became better understood.
A younger generation grew up familiar with his writings,
and with those views of the English Constitution and
English Parties, which reconciled so many of the seeming contradictions of his life : and long before he
became Prime Minister with real power, his political
integrity and his party loyalty were as fully and as
freely recognized as that of any living statesman.

Of Lord Beaconsfield's private life there is comparatively little to tell, and of that little so much has been
already told, that I cannot hope to impart any freshness or novelty to these concluding pages. Lord
Beaconsfield lives in *Hansard.* It is there that we
must look for his portrait ; and it is evident that,
with all his fondness for rural pleasures, he carried his
political interests with him wherever he went. This
is strikingly illustrated by an anecdote to be found
in Lord Malmesbury's Diary, which must be well
known to most of my readers. When the late Lord
Derby was staying at Heron Court, and absorbed in
the delights of wild-fowl shooting, his countenance
was observed to fall when he heard that Disraeli
was expected, and he exclaimed in a tone of annoy-
ance, " Ah ! now we shall be obliged to talk politics."
Lord Beaconsfield, indeed, was unaffectedly fond of
the country, and birds, trees, and flowers retained
their charm for him to the last. He was sincerely
grieved when a wintry gale blew down a favourite ash ;
and once, when a half-witted peasant who was allowed
to wander about the park showed him a dead bird which
he had picked up, he said, "Take it away, I cannot
bear the sight of it." He was not without domestic
pets either, for he had a dog to which he was warmly attached ; and one can fancy him well with a grave Persian

cat, such as he describes in Baptist Hatton's chambers, sitting at his elbow or climbing on to his shoulders. His peacocks, which were a present from Sir Philip Rose, were after his death taken charge of by the Queen. But for all that his heart was in the House of Commons; and I suspect that his love of the country was rather love of her external beauty than the deeper sympathy of Wordsworth or Scott, who found the charm which enthralled them rather in the heart than in the face of nature.

He was a very good-natured and a very kind-hearted man, fond of children, and always ready to assist struggling merit. He was proud of his connection with literature, and was a good friend to many working brothers of the Press. In his own neighbourhood he was extremely popular with the peasantry and the farmers. He was most anxious to make the cottagers on his small estate comfortable; and was quite able to enjoy a chat with the mothers and grandmothers of the hamlet over their afternoon tea. He contrived, when at Hughenden, to get all his official business completed by four o'clock in the afternoon, so as to leave himself time for his walk or drive before dinner. He was never tired of the Chiltern Hills, or of talking of the interesting historical events of which they were the cradle.

Of his life in London in his younger days we might construct a picture to ourselves out of his letters to his sister. But of his personal appearance, his coats and his trousers, his cuffs and his cravats, his ringlets and his jewellery, the world, I think, has heard enough. It would not differ materially from the life of any other young man about town when the present century was young. Quite recently an addition has been made to the history of his social peculiarities by the Duke of Coburg

14

who says that he used to go out to dinner with his arm in a sling, though there was nothing the matter with him, to make himself look interesting. The story we think, may be consigned to the same limbo as the story of the black satin shirt and the green velvet trousers. We are all more interested in knowing how he lived and talked and amused himself during the last thirty years of his life, when he was before the public and a leading actor on the stage.

But of such information there is but little to be had. He was no sportsman; he was no farmer. He was neither the head of a family, nor the lord of a large estate, interested in the fortunes of sons and daughters, or busied with large schemes of local improvement. He was no leader of religious or philanthropical societies; he seems to have cared little for travelling, and of mere social excitement he had probably drunk his fill in early youth. He was a good classical scholar, his favourite ancient authors being Sophocles and Horace, but in his intervals of leisure he seems to have found employment rather in composition than in study. I should think it is doubtful whether he even read much contemporary literature.

It was a pleasure to see him in his library, and to hear him discourse of books. If circumstance had at any time diverted his attention from politics, he would probably have drunk deep of " those pellucid streams " to which he referred with unaffected enthusiasm in a speech at the Literary Fund banquet,* and have rivalled as an author the fame which awaited him as a statesman. But his choice was made in youth, and he never for one single instant appears to have regretted it.

---

* 1868.

At Hughenden Lady Beaconsfield during her lifetime was the brightest of hostesses ; and to walk with her in the surrounding woods, and hear her discourse about her husband—it is needless to say, her favourite topic—was a treat not soon to be forgotten. She was particularly fond of telling how, after a capital division in the House of Commons in 1867, he refused an invitation to supper at the Carlton, that he might carry the good news to Grosvenor Gate without delay. " Dizzy came home to me," she used to say, with a triumphant air.

His domestic life, there is every reason to suppose, was one of unclouded happiness, and, due in great part to Lady Beaconsfield's exertions, of general cheerfulness. His wife was devoted to him, and he returned her affection with sincerity. This aspect of Lord Beaconsfield's life was touched upon in feeling tones by Mr. Gladstone in the speech from which I have already quoted :—

There was also another feeling, Sir, lying nearer to the very centre of his existence, which, though a domestic feeling, may now be referred to without indelicacy. I mean his profound, devoted, tender, and grateful affection for his wife which, if, as may be the case, it deprived him of the honour of public obsequies, has nevertheless left for him a more permanent title as one who knew, amid the calls and temptations of political life, what was due to the sanctity and strength of the domestic affections, and made him in that respect an example to the country in which he lived.

Lady John Manners has given us an interesting account of his private life after the death of Lady Beaconsfield, interesting, however, not so much from what she tells, as from the character which they serve to illustrate. He had long ceased to care for society on a large scale, even if he ever did, but enjoyed very much the company of a few chosen friends, " not more than the Muses nor less than the Graces," with whom he would converse freely and without any apparent reserve, about his own literary and political career. But except on such occasions he was rather a silent host, and liked others to talk. I have heard, however, that he was no foe to merriment, and, like his own Marquis of Monmouth, rather liked "boisterous gaiety," in which he was not called upon to take a part.

The world has no doubt a good deal more to learn of Lord Beaconsfield behind the scenes. Both of his public and his private life the recesses have still to be explored. Of his early political trials after he entered the House of Commons little is known that is authentic; while of his private affairs, and the pecuniary troubles with which for years he was condemned to struggle, most people are entirely ignorant. When the whole drama of his life shall be displayed to view; when his relations with his colleagues and his opponents, with the Crown and the aristocracy, with friends and enemies, shall stand fully revealed to us; when all the difficulties and all the jealousies which impeded him on the threshold of his career shall be clearly understood: then, indeed, we think that the life of Benjamin Disraeli will be recognised as one of the most "wondrous tales" which sober truth has ever told.

THE END.

APPENDIX.

Franchise Clauses 3 to 7 of Reform Bill of 1867, as originally introduced to the House of Commons.

3. Every Man shall be entitled to be registered as a Voter, and, when registered, to vote for a Member or Members to serve in Parliament for a Borough, who is qualified as follows; that is to say:

    1. Is of full age, and not subject to any legal Incapacity; and

    2. Is on the *last Day of July* in any Year and has during the whole of the preceding *Two* Years been an Inhabitant Occupier, as Owner or Tenant, of any Dwelling House within the Borough; and

    3. Has during the Time of such Occupation been rated in respect of the Premises so occupied by him within the Borough to all Rates (if any) made for the Relief of the Poor in respect of such Premises; and

    4. Has before the *Twentieth Day of July* in the same Year paid all Poor Rates that have become payable by him in respect of the said Premises up to the preceding *Fifth Day of January.*

4. Every Man shall be entitled to be registered as a Voter, and, when registered, to vote for a Member or Members to serve in Parliament for a County, who is qualified as follows; that is to say:

    1. Is of full Age, and not subject to any legal Incapacity; and

    2. Is on the *last Day of July* in any Year and has during the *Twelve Months* immediately preceding been the Occupier, as Owner or Tenant, of Pre-

mises of any Tenure within the County of the rateable Value of *Fifteen Pounds* or upwards; and

3. Has during the Time of such Occupation been rated in respect to the Premises so occupied by him to all Rates (if any) made for the Relief of the Poor in respect of the said Premises; and

4. Has before the *Twentieth Day of July* in the same Year paid all Poor Rates that have become payable by him in respect of the said Premises up to the preceding *Fifth Day of January.*

5. Every Man shall be entitled to be registered, and, when registered, to vote at the Election of a Member or Members to serve in Parliament for a County or Borough, who is of full Age, and not subject to any legal Incapacity, and is on the *last Day of July* in any Year and has during the Year immediately preceding been resident in such County or Borough, and is possessed of any One or more of the Qualifications following; that is to say:

1. Is, and has been during the Period of such Residence, a Graduate or Associate in Arts of any University of the United Kingdom; or a Male Person who has passed at any Senior Middle Class Examination of any University of the United Kingdom:

2. Is, and has been during the Period aforesaid, an ordained Priest or Deacon of the Church of England; or

3. Is, and has been during the Period aforesaid, a Minister of any other Religious Denomination appointed either alone or with not more than One Colleague to the Charge of any registered Chapel or Place of Worship, and is, and has been during such Period, officiating as the Minister thereof; or

4. Is, and has been during the Period aforesaid, a Serjeant-at-Law or Barrister-at-Law in any of the Inns of Court in England, or a Certificated Pleader or Certificated Conveyancer; or

5. Is, and has been during the Period aforesaid, a Certificated Attorney or Solicitor or Proctor in England or Wales; or

6. **Is,** and has been during the Period aforesaid, a duly qualified Medical Practitioner registered under the Medical Act, 1858; or

7. **Is,** and has been during the Period aforesaid, a Schoolmaster holding a Certificate from the Committee of Her Majesty's Council on Education:

Provided that no Person shall be entitled to be registered as a Voter or to vote in respect of any of the Qualifications mentioned in this Section in more than one Place.

6. Every Man shall be entitled to be registered, and, when registered, to vote at the Election of a Member or Members to serve in Parliament for a County or Borough, who is of full Age, and not subject to any legal Incapacity, and is on the *First Day of July* in any Year and has during the *Two Years* immediately preceding been resident in such County or Borough, and is possessed of any One or more of the Qualifications following; that is to say:

1. Has on the *First Day of July* in any Year, and has had during the *Two Years* immediately preceding, a Balance of not less than *Fifty Pounds* deposited in some Savings Bank in his own sole Name, and for his own Use; or

2. Holds on the *First Day of July* in any Year, and has held during the *Two Years* immediately preceding, in the Books of the Governor and Company of the Bank of England or Ireland in his own sole Name and for his own Use any Parliamentary Stocks or Funds of the United Kingdom to the Amount of not less than *Fifty Pounds*; or

3. Has during the *Twelve Months* immediately preceding the Fifth Day of April in any Year been charged with a Sum of not less than *Twenty Shillings* in the whole of the Year for Assessed Taxes and Income Tax, or either of such Taxes, and has before the *Twentieth Day of July* in that Year paid all such Taxes due from him up to the preceding *Fifth Day of January*:

Provided, first, that every Person entitled to vote in respect of any of the Qualifications mentioned in this Section shall on or before the Twentieth Day of July in each Year claim to be registered as a Voter; secondly, that no Person shall be entitled to be registered as a Voter or to vote in respect of any of the Qualifications mentioned in this Section for more than One Place.

7. A Person registered as a Voter for a Borough by reason of his having been charged with and paid the requisite Amount of Assessed Taxes and Income Tax, or either of such Taxes, shall not by reason of being so registered lose any right to which he may be entitled (if otherwise duly qualified) to be registered as a Voter for the same Borough in respect of any Franchise involving Occupation of Premises and Payment of Rates, and when so registered in respect of such double Qualification he shall be entitled to give Two Votes for the Member, or (if there be more than One) for each Member to be returned to serve in Parliament for the said Borough.

INDEX.

A.

Aberdeen, Lord, becomes Premier, 84 ; resigns, 90.
Abyssinian war, the, 117.
" Adullam, the Cave of," 109.
Affghan war, 150–152.
Agricultural distress, speeches on, 61, 62, 71–73.
Agricultural Holdings Act, 132.
Alarcos, 198.
Alroy, Wondrous Tale of, 188, 190.

B.

Bath Letter, the, 125, note.
Beaconsfield, Lord. *See* Disraeli, Benjamin.
Beaconsfield, Lady. *See* Disraeli, Mary Ann.
Bedchamber Plot, 25.
Bentinck, Lord George, 69, 70 ; *Life of*, 63, 67, 75–77, 202.
Berlin Memorandum, 138 ; Congress of, 143–149.
Buckinghamshire, Disraeli returned for, 69.
Budgets. *See inf.* Disraeli.
Bulgarian atrocities, 139.
Bulwer, Lytton, 7, 8.

C.

Carnarvon, Lord, 110, 111, 129, 142.
Chartists, the, 25, 53, 73.
Church, position of the, 46, 56, 103–108, 130, 134, 173–175.
Church and Queen, 103.
Cobden, Richard, 31, 94.
Coningsby, 22, 33, 37 ; plot of, 40 –46, 192–93 ; doctrines of, 41– 46 ; characters in, 48, 194–95.
Conservatism, 22, 35, 44, 163– 172.
Contarini Fleming, 5, 189.
Cranborne, Lord. *See* Salisbury.
Crimean war, 88–91.
Crisis Examined, the, 11, 200.
Croker, J. W., 48, 75.
Cyprus, acquisition of, 150.

D.

Derby, Earl of, and Disraeli, 70 ; declines office, 73 ; first ministry, 78–84 ; again declines office, 91 ; second ministry, 95– 101 ; third ministry, 110–114.
Derby, Earl of (son of above), 95, 109, 110, 129, 142.
Disraeli, Benjamin, birth-place of, 1 ; education, 2 ; first appear-

15

www.ingramcontent.com/pod-product-compliance
Lightning Source LLC
Chambersburg PA
CBHW030821020726
47499CB00006B/2018